A Prairie Mourning

Patricia H. Walsh

Copyright © 2016 by Patricia H. Walsh
Second edition cover art, cover design and cover text by Cassandra J. Valdez. Author photo by Cassandra J. Valdez and Laura Robertson

Walsh, Patricia H.
A Prairie Mourning
1.   Mystery. 2. Wildlife. 3. Prairie dogs.
4. Native American History. 5. Sand Creek Massacre.
6. Silas Soule. 7. Colorado

Little Horse Mesa Press
P.O. Box 843
Raton, NM 87740

Dedicated to all my relations
of the prairie

July 13, 1865
Tremont House
Denver, Colorado Territory

Cavalry Lieutenant James Cannon struggled up off the sweat-drenched bedclothes and stumbled to the enameled wash basin, gagging. He barely reached the pan before his gut seized and he retched over and over until only drool came from his mouth.

Trembling, he wiped his mouth with the back of his hand and staggered to the open window. Clutching his abdomen, he tried to focus on the dark street below, still muddy from yesterday's storm. Across the way he could see lights in the saloon where only a few hours ago he'd been on a winning streak of faro. The piano player was still at it. Beyond the saloon the jail stood dark where that murderer Squier sat awaiting his fate, thanks largely to Cannon.

Gut pain sucked the stifling July air from his lungs and he bent over, clutching at the sill. The urge drove him to the chamber pot, where his bowels let loose in a putrid stream. He made a vague attempt to clean himself before crawling across the wood floor toward the bed. He reached the ladder-back chair and tried to pull himself up, only to knock the chair over, dumping the dark blue uniform jacket with the lieutenant's insignia onto the floor next to him. He felt sweat dripping onto the cloth as he pulled himself to the bed and climbed up. What in God's name was happening to him?

The seizures began again. His head slammed against the headstand, thumping the flimsy wall behind. Colors flared and men shouted. His buckskin mare leaped sideways as two Indian youngsters burst from the buffalo skin lodge. They held hands as they ran barefoot over the cold ground towards the Big Sandy Creek.

"Oh no you don't," yelled the soldier to Cannon's left. The soldier spurred his big sorrel gelding after the pair. When the horse was almost on top of them, the two knelt down and embraced. The soldier fired and blood splattered. Then he jumped off his horse and began slashing with his saber.

Cannon groaned, twisted onto his side and retched onto the sheets. Slowly he pulled himself nearly upright. Was it bad food? Bad whiskey? He groped for the flask on the nightstand. Hair of the dog. He brought the whiskey to his lips and managed to take in a few drops before his gut lit on fire and he choked. Seizures took him again. Thump. Thump. Thump. Clots of dirt falling on the casket while the captain's young widow Hersa stood a few paces away. And Silas there in his box, tucked away with a hole in his head. Silas and his self-righteous morals.

"Look," Cannon muttered into the damp pillow, his teeth chattering. "Look where. They've got. You now. And me." Thump. Thump. And then the thumping stopped.

1

John Fox awoke with a start. His heart pounded and his fists were clenched. He felt resistance on the covers and he kicked violently, sending three startled cats off the bed. The German shepherd stayed put, unfazed by her human's occasional nightmares. Now she raised her head and looked at him with a steady, intelligent gaze.

"Shit. Sorry guys," he called to the now invisible cats as he rose up on one elbow and rubbed sleep from his eyes. On the floor next to the bed he saw the copy of the 1865 Denver Post article he'd been reading the night before. The page must have slid off the bed during his antics. The newspaper piece described how James Cannon had been found dead on July 14, 1865 in his Denver hotel room, just days after he caught the man who assassinated Silas Soule. Fox realized that in only a few weeks, July 14, 2005 would mark 140 years since Cannon was found. The autopsy—or what passed for an autopsy back then—had talked about liquid on the brain. But the symptoms described in the news report on the death made John Fox think of poison, often a woman's weapon of choice.

Suddenly he was back in his nightmare, bound to a hard chair as a woman in a long skirt forced a cup to his lips. In the dream he tried to twist his head away and struggled violently against the ropes holding him. Now he realized that since he'd been studying the Sand Creek Massacre of 1864 in southern Colorado, this was his first nightmare as one of the white guys from the story instead of one of the Cheyenne or Arapaho kids running for their lives. Odd that it would have been Cannon instead of Silas Soule. Cannon, who apparently followed orders to take part in the massacre, while Silas Soule quietly led his troops away from the blood bath. Sometimes in his dreams, the screams of Sand Creek morphed into the cries of soldiers bleeding onto the floor of his chopper in 'Nam. But when his hand moved on the stick, the machine hovered in place, refusing to rise out of the firefight...

Fox sighed and reached out for Abby, stroking the black fur on her face. Women came and went, but Dog stayed. He smiled and crawled out of bed to try to make amends to the felines in the family before he went to work.

By the time he showered, dressed and stood before the bathroom mirror to adjust the name tag on his clean uniform shirt, he'd been forgiven. The cats competed to rub against his pristine blue jeans while Fox fastened his badge above the other shirt pocket. Cops—even critter cops—have to keep up appearances. He grabbed the electric razor and did a quick shave job over the sink. Fox blamed his fast-growing, salt-and-pepper stubble on the white man's blood swimming alongside the Lakota Sioux's in his veins. Fox had required special permission to keep the long braid down his back, which he now gave a quick check for neatness.

Fox fed the cats and scrambled some eggs for himself. He double-checked the knobs on the stove before heading to his tiny home office in the town of Keyhole. On the way, he passed a stack of unread newspapers and noticed the pile had begun leaning to the left. His own personal Tower of Pisa. In the second bedroom-cum-office, Fox turned on his computer for any new emails and inspected his phone answering machine. The only new call had come in while he was in the shower this morning. Some woman sure she was seeing a mountain lion behind her house. On Colorado's Front Range, the booming two-legged population never ceased to find ways to run into strange situations with four-leggeds, two-wingeds and creepy crawlers. Game wardens in suburban areas don't have to wait for big game season for entertainment.

Picking up his notebook with a running list of people to contact, he whistled for Abby, a pointless gesture that ignored the fact that she always beat him to the front door. At the side table he strapped on his duty belt. His hand on the doorknob, he stopped. Fox walked back to the kitchen to make sure he'd turned off the stove.

"So early this morning you saw the lion where?"

Fox watched the thirty-something, stay-at-home blonde run a hand through her goldilocks. Preening? Flirting? It was one thing to be old and another to be a fool, but Fox despised the idea of an old fool. He'd gotten better about keeping a certain something in his pants. A man in his fifties had earned a right to a simple life if he wanted one. And sex was never simple.

"I could see it from here." She waved her hand toward the sliding glass doors that separated the dining room from the deck. The deck of a new house situated on unincorporated land in Green Mountain County. The subdivision sat about halfway between the towns of Keyhole and Green Mountain proper. Beyond the raised deck and the manicured lawn with a plastic swing set, Fox could see a prairie dog town that stretched to a line of cottonwood trees flanking a creek. The dirt burrows fashioned by little paws stood like mini-volcanoes in the barren stretch, broken by patches of dark green bindweed.

"What was the lion doing?" Fox asked.

"It looked like it was eating something," the woman said, burying her hand in the ruff of a black chow that looked up at her expectantly. "I was about to let Chow Mein"—she used her head to gesture down at the dog—"outside when I got up and saw the mountain lion."

Fox knew young cougars without an established territory often followed creeks out onto what used to be the plains, and now served as suburbia. And calling them mountain lions just confused people. Before the whites showed up, cougars ranged from coast to coast, from the Florida Everglades to Western forests. Hunters had nearly wiped them out by the turn of the 20th Century, but they had begun to make a comeback–to the delight of some and the dread of others. So the woman may have indeed spotted a big cat.

"Chad—my husband—is out of town and I was terrified

the lion might jump our fence and come after my little girl," the woman said, breaking into his thoughts. "So I called the police and they connected me with you folks."

Fox again scanned the land visible beyond the wooden privacy fence. His eye caught on something tan and lumpy on the ground. Definitely not a lion. Maybe a lion kill, a mulie. Mule deer love the burbs–all that nicely watered grass. On the other hand, many a concerned citizen had mistaken coyotes, foxes and even domestic cats for lions. And the lump could be somebody's trash that blew away.

"Okay. Thanks. I'll go take a look out there."

"If you want, come back after and I'll get you something to drink. It's already getting hot."

And a little too hot in here, Fox thought as he slid out her front door.

Fox parked his official Dodge Ram truck on the dirt road that ran west past the subdivision in unincorporated Green Mountain County. A white van sat parked a couple hundred yards up ahead. "Abby, stay." The dog yawned. Getting out of his vehicle, Fox expected to see prairie dogs and hear their birdlike chirps–that sophisticated communication alerting their neighbors about something new and possibly dangerous in town. Instead, the scene came off unnaturally still. Passing by a burrow, Fox saw wadded newspaper in the entrance. "Poison man been and gone," Fox muttered. This section of land was slated for more McMansions, and developers were legally allowed to remove prairie dogs however they saw fit–except for shooting within city limits.

They weren't required to let the Division of Wildlife know their plans, unless they wanted to take the path less traveled and more expensive by actually relocating the animals. For that they needed a permit–and hardest of all, a receiving site for the critters. Some opted to have the prairie dogs trapped and taken away for ferret food, under the black-footed ferret recovery program. This at least sounded more politically correct than killing them in their burrows or paving over top of them.

Looking across the prairie dog town toward the mound he'd spotted from the house, Fox saw what looked to be a plastic animal carrier. His intuition began flashing red as the shape on the ground began to take on human form. A woman on her side, her back toward him, khaki pants, white T-shirt. The shiny black ponytail seemed familiar.

Fox started to jog. He stopped abruptly.

"Breathe."

One slow in, one slow out. Smoking the mental cigarette of an emergency responder.

He reached for the radio extension on his shoulder and pressed the call button.

"Green Mountain dispatch, Wildlife 6-2."

"Go ahead, Wildlife 6-2."

"I have a person unconscious in a field behind 982 Prairie View Lane. I need an ambulance. I'll be at the scene."

Fox signed off after promising to relay more information soon. He walked directly up to the woman's back, resisting the urge to go around tracking his size 12 boot prints over a possible crime scene. Fox stepped over what looked like coyote tracks, and avoided a Nalgene water bottle lying on the ground, its lid unscrewed but still attached by a plastic strap. Then he caught the smell of shit, and saw that her pants were soiled.

"Hey, are you okay?" He put his hand on the woman's upper arm and shook. The arm felt hard and stiff. Knowing it was probably pointless, Fox bent over the woman and placed his fingers on her carotid artery to feel for a pulse. Only then did he see the blood at her mouth. And the vomit on the ground near her.

Prairie dog activist Trish O'Neill was dead. Big time.

2

Faith O'Neill looked at her phone and shook her head. She hit the speed dial number and waited for her sister's recorded voice to end.

"Hey," she said into the phone. "I'm used to you standing me up, but usually you're nice enough to give me a heads up. I was really looking forward to beignets at Lucille's. And since when do you not answer your cell? Talk to me."

Faith set the phone aside and took a sip of coffee. There were advantages to pulling the late shift at the library, like sitting on her front porch swing and enjoying the morning. Sonar, her Russian gray soul-mate, sat on the wood railing nearby and purred under Faith's hand. Faith had stretched financially to buy her miniature 1890 Victorian in old town Keyhole. But enchanted by the pale yellow frame house with green and purple trim, she had scraped by and now the place felt like a sanctuary. Her street sported the signs of early summer. The leaves on the tulip poplars in her front yard rustled a deeper green and the snowball bush boasted big clusters of white flowers.

Faith sighed and opened the laptop computer. She had learned the hard way that she could waste a lot of time waiting on her sister. She might as well work on the book that she couldn't seem to finish. A historical fiction novella. She would not give up, even if she winced at the cliché of a librarian hoping to become a published author. She owed it to Silas to keep trying.

***

"Unsung Hero"
By Faith O'Neill
Chapter One

Summer 1864
Coberly Ranch, Colorado Territory

The rooster let loose in the darkness of pre-dawn. Hersa moaned and pulled the down pillow over her head.

"Blast you, Ulysses."

"It's your turn," came the muffled voice of her sister. Hersa yawned and elbowed the girl next to her. "Stop flapping. I know my duty, your highness. And you better know yours."

Hersa slid her hand over the warm fur of the cat curled at her belly. "Breakfast time, Missy." She found the box of matches near the bed and lit the lamp, carefully placing the glass chimney over the low flame. Although she knew perfectly well where she left her day dress and rough shoes, she had no intention of playing with scorpions or snakes that might have found their way inside overnight.

In the kitchen she made for the pot-bellied stove and

struck a match to the kindling she'd left ready. Setting a pot on the stove and satisfied her father would have hot water to pour over the sock filled with ground coffee, she grabbed a cold biscuit and started for the barn in the cool darkness. Even on the hottest day of summer, by dawn the prairie cooled down, a slight nip in the air. The lantern lit a circle before her and Missy darted back and forth, rubbing against her skirts and mewing pathetically.

"Silly kitty," Hersa said as she finished the biscuit. "What makes you think I would give you anything?"

Inside the barn door, Hersa took the clean bucket off the nail and headed for the stall. Marzipan lowed, anticipating relief. Hersa hung her lantern on the nail at the stall and grabbed her three-legged stool. She rubbed her hands together briskly, a habit her father had engrained no matter the season. Her hands began working the teats and milk hissed into the metal bucket. Missy yowled.

"You greedy thing. Well, sit then."

Hersa turned her face sideways toward the black cat that now sat with its front feet in the air. Hersa cocked one teat and shot a stream of milk directly into the cat's mouth.

"Well I'll be a son of a–" A man's voice.

Hersa shrieked and fell over backwards.

"Damnation!" Hersa sucked in her breath as she realized what she'd said, but her anger carried her on. Her shriek had startled the cow, who in turn kicked the milk bucket over. Hersa sat sprawled in the straw and muck of Marzipan's stall, moisture from the overturned bucket seeping into her skirt. "Who on God's green earth are you?"

The man approached her with his hand outstretched, but Hersa put her palm up to stop him. In the light from the lantern she could see he wore the blue pants of the cavalry, held up by suspenders over his red long-john undershirt. No matter. Uniform or no, handsome or no, there were plenty of misbehaving soldiers to go around out West. Yes, quite handsome...

"My apologies, ma'am. My name is Silas Soule, captain in the First Colorado Cavalry, D Company."

Hersa could see Soule's dark eyes twinkling as he struggled to hide a grin that kept sneaking up under his ginger mustache. Well, she must be making quite the pretty sight. The smell of cow dung reached her. She struggled to her feet, fighting with her long skirt. She slapped at the dirty straw clinging to her. Hersa glanced to the side, finding the handle of the pitchfork sticking above the wood of the stall alongside. For the first time she noticed a striking gray horse looking back at her.

"And tell me why you are here. Quick now, before I start screaming for my father and his shotgun." His hair was brown, with copper glints...

"I'm traveling from Fort Lyon bound for Denver. I wanted an early start today but my mare pulled up lame. I had heard the Coberly Ranch was friendly to passing soldiers–" Soule paused, again fighting off a smirk. "I didn't want to disturb your slumber so I put Delilah in the empty stall there and I put myself down in the hay for a nap before sunrise. I fully intend to compensate your family."

Hersa looked him up and down, deciding.

"You look like you could use some breakfast. Sit yourself down—I have milking to finish."

Soule did as he was told.

13

"You can have the loan of one of my horses."

Sundown dimmed the ranch house where James Coberly sat at the kitchen table, wiping the body of the fiddle with a piece of blue flannel. "As long as you'll be bringing it back."

Soule glanced at Hersa, who smiled. She had taken great care with her dark wavy hair, pinning her locks neatly in place. Her green plaid dress set off her twinkling eyes and an ample bosom that Silas pretended not to notice.

"Of course, sir. Besides, I have to come back for my fine horse Delilah, once she is mended."

"And now you must pay the fiddler by dancing with these fine women of mine." Coberly drew the bow across the strings and jumped into a fast Irish air.

Soule was no fool. He walked straight up to matriarch Sarah Coberly to ask her for the first dance. Sarah blushed and touched her graying blonde hair as if she were 13 instead of 43. Then they were moving across the wooden floor, avoiding the table and chairs pushed to the side where the audience members sat clapping and hooting. Hersa's brother Bill bowed extravagantly before the younger sister Mattie, who extended her hand as if she were Marie Antoinette. The two couples whirled around each other, nearly colliding at one point and prompting giggles from Hersa and her other brother Joe.

With two quick strokes, James Coberly finished the tune and held up his bow with a flourish. Before the clapping stopped, Silas put himself in front of Hersa.

"Milady?"

"Pray let me check my dance card, kind sir." Hersa waved an invisible card before her. "Why, look at that. I have an empty spot right here."

Her father had already begun the next tune. Silas held her firmly as they whisked across the planks.

"It was very kind of you to show me around the ranch today."

"I hope the delay won't cause you difficulty."

"I was ahead of schedule. I thought I might have time to buy myself a winter coat."

"Isn't it a bit early for that?"

"There are hard things about being in the military, but if there's one I can't abide it's being cold. I never know when I'll be near a city, so I try to plan ahead."

"A wise man. So you don't know when you'll be making another trip."

"No, but I will stop by here on my way back from Denver. To pick up my horse and return your father's to him."

"Ah. Well, if I haven't gone to Paris for the season, you may have the opportunity to see me again."

"I hear Paris is rather muggy this time of year."

"That is true. And of course, my personal maid just resigned and I must find a new one before I leave. So I may well be here on your return."

Silas leaned his head toward her. "I certainly hope that will be the case. Perhaps I could assist the milk maid on my next visit."

"Only if you bring your own bucket."

"Gladly."

3

"Weird."

With that pronouncement, Green Mountain County Sheriff's Detective Pierce Wilson moved his chaw to the other cheek before a discrete spit into his empty Coke can. "Whaddya think happened?"

Fox watched the crime scene photographer adjust her digital camera for another shot. Fox had interacted with Trish a few times. He remembered the charming smile and quick wit that veiled her steely determination. He remembered wondering if he could trust her. Now she was dead.

"Medical examiner coming out?" he asked.

"Yeah. Said he was delayed."

The men stood silently. Only 9 a.m. and already the sun was blazing hot in a Colorado blue sky. Hot days until the monsoon rains began.

"You didn't answer me," Wilson said. "Blood, shit and vomit. Maybe some kind of disease?"

Fox had gone through police academy like all law officers in Colorado, but the human animal wasn't his turf.

His detective work involved things like headless bucks lying in the woods and trying to track down the SOB who would kill a handsome animal just for a trophy rack and the money it would bring. Still, Wilson was just a friend asking for a friendly opinion.

"Well, I got an idea."

"What are you waiting for, a drum roll?" Wilson leaned against the hood of the Green Mountain County Sheriff's Department SUV.

"There are wads of newspaper in most of the prairie dog holes." Fox held up his hand to ward off Wilson's question. "That's what the poison crews do to keep the gas inside the burrows. Knowing Trish, I'm thinking maybe she dug out the burrow to fish for sick prairie dogs and got a mouthful of gas. But don't quote me."

"What makes you think that?"

"The poison makes prairie dogs bleed out," Fox said. "I've heard of a couple cases where like some kid is digging in dirt and inhales gas and gets sick. Guess it depends on how strong the gas is, how much moisture's in the soil."

"Do you know when the poison people were here? There are lots of partial footprints around."

"Nope."

Wilson spit into his Coke can. "Well, she might have been lying here since last night, since she's pretty stiff. And you saw coyote tracks?"

"Just sniffing around, is all. The gal who said she saw a cougar probably doesn't wanna admit she needs glasses." Fox looked up. Two dark shapes circled lazily overhead. "Wonder if they're hoping for a breakfast buffet."

Wilson turned toward him, squinting. "Huh?"

"Turkey vultures."

Wilson peered at the dark shapes wobbling against the backdrop of the Rocky Mountain foothills, revealing the black and gray T-pattern on their undersides. Wilson scowled. "Gross."

"Vultures are cool," Fox said. "Most birds have no sense of smell, but these guys can sniff dead stuff a long way off. The cleanup crew."

"You should sign up for Animal Planet. I..." Wilson stopped and both men turned back toward the road, toward the sound of a woman's voice.

"Just tell me what's going on! I told you, that's my sister's van. I can't find her. I've been trying to call her all morning and I've been driving around forever and I find her car and you won't tell me what's going on?"

The sheriff's deputy held her ground. "Sorry ma'am, you can't go in there just yet. I'll try to get someone to help you."

Fox exchanged a look with Wilson. "This is your gig, man. But I can come along for moral support, since I knew Trish." Wilson nodded.

Fox studied the woman as they approached and realized he also knew her from somewhere. He wouldn't have guessed she was related to Trish. This woman had short dark hair and a taller, gawkier build, compared to Trish's smaller, more full-figured frame. And whereas Trish seemed to make a fashion statement even in field khakis and sunhat, this woman in her T-shirt and jeans seemed, well, a bit sloppy. Like she didn't spend much time in front of mirrors. Probably gay, Fox thought. Lots of lesbians in Green Mountain County.

The woman aimed her blazing green eyes at the approaching men. "I'm looking for my sister, Trish O'Neill. Is she—" She stopped speaking, apparently reading something in their faces.

"Miss…?"

"Faith O'Neill. Tell me what's happening."

Wilson inhaled. "I'm so sorry. We found your sister this morning."

The woman stared at him. "What do you mean, you found her? Is she okay? Where is she?"

"I'm sorry," Wilson said again. "Your sister is dead."

"No."

Faith O'Neill's face paled beneath her freckles. She seemed to be having trouble breathing. The woman turned to Fox, as if hoping for a different story. He gave a brief nod of confirmation. "I—" Her face crumpled and her legs gave way.

Fox and Wilson grabbed her arms and led her to the SUV. Wilson opened the back door and Faith sat on the vehicle's back seat, her hands twisting the bottom of her T-shirt.

"How? Where is she?" She looked to Wilson, then Fox.

"She was found out there in the prairie dog town," Wilson said. "And we're not sure how she died."

"This is crazy. She's only 46."

Fox glanced at Wilson, who gave him a brief nod.

"I found her out by a burrow. She had a pet carrier nearby."

"I want to see her."

"You will," Wilson assured her. "But right now we're taking photos."

"Photos?"

"We're still investigating."

"What happened to her? Tell me."

"We don't know," Wilson said. "Can you think why she might be out here, digging in prairie dog holes? Maybe inhaled some poison gas?"

Faith O'Neill shook her head. "No way. Trish knows what she's doing when she…"

"When she what?"

"I guess it doesn't matter now." Faith O'Neill sighed and looked out over the prairie dog town. "When she tries to dig up poisoned dogs. She looks for dogs that are still alive and takes them to a vet."

"Dogs?" Pierce Wilson looked confused.

"Prairie dogs," the woman said.

Fox glanced at the detective. "It's illegal for someone to dig up prairie dogs after they've been poisoned. Prairie dog re-locators have to get permits from us at the Division to move prairie dogs. Getting arrested for digging them up might mean no relocation permits. That's probably why she was out here after dark."

John Fox looked toward Trish's sister for confirmation, but she was gazing out toward the field.

"When's the last time you talked to your sister?" Wilson asked.

The woman seemed not to hear him and instead turned to Fox.

"I know you. You're the bleach guy."

Fox caught Wilson's glance, gave him a tiny shrug. Belatedly he remembered a face behind the library counter. This woman's face.

"All those books on Sand Creek. They came back smelling like bleach." Now she turned to Pierce Wilson. "And the last time I talked to my sister was last night. We made plans for breakfast. I wanted beignets…"

And with that, her voice choked on the tears finally making their appearance.

4

Faith pulled down the narrow blinds and crawled into bed, curling in a fetal position. Within seconds, Sonar jumped up and settled in the crook of Faith's right arm. She reached to the night stand for a box of tissues ahead of the next round of weeping. She had called the library and briefly explained. There was no way Faith could face the public in the shape she was in. Her boss told her to take tomorrow as well.

Now, the stage set for a complete breakdown, it didn't come. Instead when she closed her eyes she saw Trish's gray face and bloody mouth framed by the black body bag, her eyelids half closed over those baby blues. The guys from the medical examiner's office had stopped the gurney at Wilson's request, giving Faith a chance to identify her dead sister.

Dead.

She ought to be used to it by now—two parents killed by lung cancer. Trish the only close relative left, doubling as her best friend. A vast empty void stretched before Faith. How would she cope without the woman who shielded her, allowed her to retreat to a safe world of books? Trish,

22

always the brave one, always willing to speak up and fight the naysayers. Faith contentedly served as the sounding board when Trish had a problem, giving advice that her sister sometimes heeded but more often ignored.

"You're the strong one," Trish insisted one evening as they sipped red wine on Faith's front porch. "You're the thinker. I leap before I look."

But wasn't there a patronizing shadow behind those words? Faith, the little mouse who hid at the sound of big footsteps while her lion-hearted sister took on the world…

Faith sat up in bed, frustrated at her inability to slide into mindless sleep. Desperate for distraction, she stumbled into her living room and grabbed her laptop, opening the file for her novella.

***

"Unsung Hero"
By Faith O'Neill
Chapter Two

Midday, August 1864
Coberly Ranch, Colorado Territory

"I swear, that man. Never met a horse he didn't like. Ignores my dinner bell like it never happened. And him in a hurry to get to Franktown this afternoon. Hersa, go fetch him in here would you?"

"I'll tell him you pulled out a fresh jar of apple butter from the cellar. That should do the trick, don't you think?"

"Worth trying." Sarah Coberly turned back to the

stove to stir the potatoes and onions in the skillet. She wiped the sweat off her forehead with the corner of her apron. It might be August and hot as blazes outside, but she was fond of saying folks needed a hot midday meal to run proper.

Hersa walked outside and squinted against the glaring sun. Missy ran up and rubbed against her ankles, practically tripping her as she made her way to the corral.

"Hey now, hey now, quiet down now." Her father stood in the center of the wooden structure, hand on the rope connecting him to a horse dancing sideways.

"She sure is a looker." Hersa held her hand up to her forehead to shield her eyes. The pinto mare danced backwards, pulling against the rope. Beyond the horse a thunderhead in the shape of an anvil was building low in the western sky. Rain or no rain, the clouds could provide welcome cooling from the broiling sun. Hersa ran a finger under the hair sticking to the back of her neck.

"And stubborn. Just like my oldest daughter." James Coberly threw a grin at her before aiming his tobacco spit into the dust.

"Mama says come to dinner." Hersa gestured at the pinto. "Do you think I could ride her sometime?"

"Dunno. We'll see. She needs some work still."

"And how is Silas's—I mean, how is Captain Soule's mare?"

"Eager for a return visit, are you?" James Coberly grinned.

Hersa felt herself blushing. "We better go in. Mama's just opened a new jar of apple butter."

"Did she now? Well, then, I best finish up." Coberly shortened the rope, pulling the mare toward him. "I'll be there shortly. I want to check on that bay I'm taking over to Franktown. And a good price I'm getting." He grinned at his daughter.

"Best hurry. Mama's got that look to her."

"Oh, the tyranny of a woman with food to be praised."

Hersa smiled and shook her head slightly. She turned back toward the house. She was almost to the porch when she stopped.

"Missy?" The cat usually made sure to sit by the front door during the midday meal, the better to catch the odd scraps that somehow made their way there.

"Where's Missy?" Hersa removed her bonnet and hung it on a peg inside the door.

"You and that cat," her sister Mattie said from the stove. "I like dogs better."

"Hmmph. But you're not the only one who misses Franklin," Hersa said. "I heard they've got puppies at the Rafferty place."

Mattie pulled a tray of biscuits from the oven with a towel-wrapped hand. "My turn to pick. Franklin was always too puny. This time I'll pick a big barker, not a pitiful runt. Where's Joe at?"

"Franklin was not a runt!" Hersa glared at her sister. "He was just particular."

"Joe's in the outhouse. We need to get two dogs this time, anyways," said Bill, reaching for one of the biscuits only to be slapped away with the towel. "That way they can protect each other from the coyotes."

"Who cares if they protect each other? It's us they need to be protecting," Mattie said. She uncapped the jar of apple butter and stuck a knife into the mix. "We need Hersa to write back to that nice captain of hers. Too bad he hasn't been by to pick up his horse. Be nice if he got a few more of those soldier boys coming around."

Hersa felt her face heat up again.

"Mind your own business, and I'll mind mine."

"Well, if you aren't interested, maybe I'll write him a letter of my own. You're too old for him anyway. An old maid."

"I'm only nineteen!" Hersa protested.

"Who's too old for who?" Joe walked in adjusting his belt.

"Matilda Coberly, stop your jawing and help me get this pork roast out of the oven."

Hersa smiled at her mother and headed for the silverware box. Sarah Coberly had argued with her husband, insisting on bringing her own mother's silverware when they headed west in the crowded wagon almost six years earlier. "If it doesn't come along, I don't come along," she'd said.

"Smells like heaven on earth!" Jimmy Coberly stood in the doorway licking his lips.

The light was fading as Sarah Coberly sat in her favorite chair mending a pair of Joe's pants and squinting as her silver needle moved in and out of the fabric.

"Mama, why haven't you lit the lamps?" Hersa asked, reaching for the matches. "You'll hurt your eyes."

"Didn't think of it," her mother replied. But Hersa suspected her mother was refusing to acknowledge the hour, since they had expected Jimmy Coberly home by now. He had left before noon on the 18-mile trip, promising to do his business quickly and be back by 7 at the latest. Even though it was only 8 p.m., she had watched her mother walk to the porch three times in the last half hour. Jimmy Coberly prided himself on his punctuality. A blustery thunderstorm had blown through during the afternoon, with many cracks of lightning and pounding rain. Hersa imagined her father struggling with the horse he was riding plus the bay he was leading. She knew her father's horse Moses was steady as a rock, but the bay was young and skittish. Could her father have been thrown and be lying hurt somewhere?

Footsteps sounded on the porch and Bill swung open the cabin door.

"Mama, there's a wagon coming."

Sarah's hands dropped to her lap as she appeared to consider her son's words.

"Who is it?" she asked.

Hersa decided her mother was showing restraint, but she headed for the porch to see for herself.

"I don't recognize the rig," Bill said.

Hersa and Bill went out onto the porch, with their mother behind them. Joe came out of the barn and Mattie closed the door of the henhouse. All of them stood side by side on the porch, watching the wagon approach in the evening gloom.

Unable to stand the wait, Hersa ran down the porch steps and held up her skirts so she could rush toward the wagon. The driver reined in the horse and her heart lurched when she recognized him as John Black—the rancher from near Franktown who was buying Jimmy Coberly's bay.

The man gave her a sad look and tipped his wide-brimmed straw hat.

"I'm so sorry, Miss Hersa, but..."

By this time, Hersa had reached the low side of the

buckboard, where on the bed of the wagon a body lay under a blue and yellow quilt stained with blood. Black must have gotten down from the wagon, because she could hear him speaking at her shoulder, but she did not hear his words. She had pulled back the quilt and now stared at the unblemished face of her father. Were it not for the blood and the wagon, he might be sleeping.

"Jimmy!" her mother screamed.

Her mother lifted her skirts and scrambled into the back of the wagon. She ripped the quilt from his body and cradled his head. His shirt front was red and splotched with dirt. Pink spittle had dried near his mouth.

"No. No. Old man, don't you dare leave me." Sarah rocked her husband close to her chest. "No. No."

Hersa went to the back of the wagon, desperate to touch her father. She grabbed one of his booted feet and clutched it to her. She was barely aware of Mattie, Bill and Joe coming up and surrounding her.

John Black stood nearby, twisting his hat in his hands, his brown hair plastered to his skull. "Injuns got him just outside my place. Stole the horses, left him beside the road. I'm so sorry. So sorry. He had already passed when I found him there."

Her mother's words had transformed into a low keening. Joe climbed in and put his arm around her. "Let's get Papa inside," Joe said. Then they were all lifting Jimmy Coberly, working as one to take him into the cabin.

To bring him home.

5

"Isn't there anyone you could contact?"

John Fox nursed his Americano coffee and waited for Faith O'Neill to respond. He'd been surprised when she called him, but figured he could spare an hour. Now she sat huddled over an iced chai, but hadn't taken a sip. The skinny guy at the next table tapped frantically on his laptop.

"Our folks are dead." Faith played with a plastic swizzle stick, bending it in two, then straightening the plastic. "Trish doesn't have—didn't—doesn't have kids. She's separated from her husband. I gave his name to the detective, but I don't want to talk to him right now. My brother-in-law, I mean."

"Mmm." Fox looked out the plate glass onto Keyhole's main street, where cars idled at the intersection with heat waves shimmering over their hoods. Abby was inside her carrier in the back of the truck, so she'd be okay. Inside the coffee shop, the air conditioning made the idea of drinking something hot seem like a good idea. The red brick walls sported paintings by local artists, while cushy sofas invited patrons to stick around and beat the heat.

"Thanks for—this." Faith looked up briefly with puffy-lidded eyes. "I couldn't go to work, couldn't be at home."

"No problem."

Fox stole a look at his wristwatch beneath the small round table. He still had several calls to deal with, and handholding wasn't listed in his job description. But part of him was flattered she had called. And she might know something that would shed light on Trish's death. People cast surreptitious looks their way, reminding him how hard it was to go low profile when you're six-foot-three, wearing a uniform and a gun. And the long braid down his back didn't help. Watching this woman struggle for composure, he wished he were a little less conspicuous.

"I've seen death before, but I still don't get it," Faith said. "How you can talk and be with someone one minute and then—" Her voice choked to a stop. She cupped the chai with both hands and took a sip. "Did you know her?"

Fox hesitated. Had he? Giving up on the philosophical question, he nodded.

"I only transferred to this district last year, but I worked with her on a couple of relocation permits." Fox paused again. "She sure cared about what she was doing."

Fox remembered how his predecessor had put it during the brief, "I'm retiring, here's the gist" speech. "You need to watch out for Trish O'Neill and her damned prairie rats," he'd said. "She'll dance all around the truth to get what she wants." Obviously, the guy had ignored the memo. The Division of Wildlife was singing a new tune about the controversial critters, even going so far as to pay ranchers subsidies to keep prairie dogs on their land. The outgoing game warden was retiring to Colorado's Western Slope, where real men didn't have to deal with all the "hippies and granola freaks and do-gooders" cluttering the Front Range.

Fox drank some coffee. Faith snapped the swizzle stick on the table.

"You are the one, aren't you? With all the bleachy books? Tracy—she works behind the counter sometimes—she's allergic to bleach and she asked me to deal with your returns."

It was Fox's turn to stare down at the table. "Yeah, that's me."

"Why?"

He paused. "It's a long story."

Faith waited for him to continue, but Fox kept his peace. Finally she said, "I probably wouldn't have noticed except some of the books you checked out are on the massacre."

"Are you into Sand Creek?"

"Yeah. I'm…"

"You're what?" Fox asked.

"I don't talk about it much. Especially at the library. Every second librarian is a writer wannabe."

"So you're writing about Sand Creek?"

"Yeah," Faith said. "Sort of. Trying to. Was trying to."

Glad for the opportunity to steer the conversation away from dead sisters and bleached books, Fox looked at her over his coffee.

"It's one of my hobbies, I guess, learning about the massacre," Fox said. "I remember being in school, trying to tell the teacher there was stuff missing in our history book about the whites settling the West. She didn't seem real grateful. You know, I'd like to read what you've written. I mean, if you're okay with that."

"I—it may not be very good."

"Sorry, I didn't mean to put you on the spot." Fox took another sip. "I just like to read everything I can about it. It still gets me how Wounded Knee is so well known, but hardly anyone's heard of Sand Creek—even though that's what kicked the Indian wars into high gear. When I think about those women and kids trying to hide in that river bank, little boys using bows and arrows against rifles—"

Faith O'Neill covered her face with her hand.

"I'm sorry. I'm not very good at this," Fox said.

"I need Kleenex before the snot runs down my hand," she said, her voice muffled by her fingers.

Fox made a beeline for the napkin dispenser.

Faith blew her nose.

"I don't buy it," she announced as she balled up the used napkin in her fist.

"Buy what?"

"I don't believe it was an accident. I think someone killed Trish."

6

John Fox didn't get home until after 8 p.m. After he'd left Faith, Fox had removed a pregnant raccoon from a ledge in a chimney and moved her to a stretch of protected open space along the St. Vrain River. Then he'd spent an hour trying to persuade an elderly couple to put a radio under their front porch and turn up a hard rock station overnight. They wanted him to kill the skunk hiding there, instead of using loud music to push the animal toward quieter digs.

In between tasks, he found himself thinking of Trish, and Faith—who was so convinced her sister could not have died by accident.

"Okay, okay, hold your horses," Fox told the horde of four-leggeds milling around him in his old-fashioned kitchen. The food bowl went down for Abby first, with the cats getting their chow afterward.

Fox plopped into his beat-up easy chair, where kitty claws had left their mark on the upholstery while shunning the over-priced scratching post in the corner. He positioned Faith's manuscript on the arm of the chair and unwrapped the chop sticks for his Chinese takeout. Digging into his

General Tso's chicken, Fox turned to the pages. He had warned himself against high expectations, but by the time he reached Chapter Three, he was hooked.

***

"Unsung Hero"
By Faith O'Neill
Chapter Three

September 4, 1864
Fort Lyon, Colorado Territory

Soule selected two cards from his miserable hand and slid them face down. Smoothly he replaced them with two from the deck on the scarred wooden table. Oak. Someone had hauled the heavy thing from back East. Two aces. His fortunes were improving and the heat be damned. Soule wiped his forehead, pushing back a lock of red brown hair.

"So there I am," Soule said, returning to his narrative embellished with a thick Irish brogue. "Sixteen years of age heading West with my family on the steamboat David Tatum, bound and determined to keep Kansas a free state. We were thirteen days from St. Louis to Kansas City."

He paused to study the men around him in the lantern light. His friend Joe Cramer had a winning hand for sure—never could hide a thing on that sweaty honest face of his. Major Ned Wynkoop, now, was another kettle of fish. Maybe having been a sheriff taught a man to keep a straight face and always look cool as a cucumber.

"And this woman goes ahead and has her baby right

there on the boat," Soule continued. "So I start calling the tyke David Tatum. Even registered his birth that way in the boat's Bible."

A sip of whiskey. God. What Soule would give for a glass of the good stuff instead of the rotgut the army provided. Lieutenant James Cannon to his right didn't seem to care. You'd think the stuff had come straight off the boat from Scotland.

"Pretty soon, don't you know, everyone on the boat is calling the boy David Tatum. So the mother surrendered and named him David Tatum Wentworth."

The men rewarded him with a satisfying guffaw.

"Captain Soule, you're talking like the Irishman you're not–a sure sign of trouble. I'm out." Ned threw down his cards.

Joseph Cramer scratched his nose with his own cards. "But Major, he's always–"

"A comedian. Yes, Joe, I know," Ned said. "And trouble's always right behind."

Heeding Ned's words, everyone but Soule threw in their cards. Silas grinned and began raking in his coins.

"Speaking of trouble, you hear the news about the Coberlys?" James Cannon spoke around a cigar as he dealt.

Soule stopped stacking his pennies and turned toward the man. "What happened?"

"Indian raid. Killed old Jimmy."

Soule groaned. He pulled out his tobacco pouch. "And the girls?" he asked, tapping out a pinch of the crushed brown leaves onto the wrapping paper. He did not raise his eyes.

"Word is it happened away from the ranch," Cannon said, moving the cigar to the other corner of his mouth.

"Heard it from an old trapper who passed through today. He said there are different stories going 'round. But you can bet the family will be packing up and headin' to town."

"Poor Sarah Coberly." Ned shook his head. "They've always been kind to our troops. I'll have to send them our condolences. It won't be the same not seeing the Coberlys on the way to Denver."

A rap on the door was immediately followed by the appearance of a private who looked like he belonged in grammar school. Another disappointed gold miner turned to soldiering to keep himself in grub. A story Soule knew all too well.

"Beg pardon sir," the boy said, panting and adjusting the strap of his rifle on his shoulder. "There's some Injuns at the gate, sir. Say they want to parley."

"How many?" Ned rose and reached for his officer's blouse. Heat or no, a commanding officer had to look proper before the enemy. A lowdown enemy. Soule thought of Jimmy Coberly playing his fiddle, and the feel of Hersa in his arms when he'd returned for his horse. Silas had written her, and mentioned that as a teen he had helped slaves escape through Kansas. He had not heard back, and had wondered if his work on the Underground Railroad troubled her.

"Three sir. Two bucks and a squaw."

"All right. Go round up John."

Soule took a last puff off his cigarette before crushing it under his boot. He buttoned his own blouse and tried to keep pace with Ned's long legs. Silas patted the Colt in its holster. Better prepared than sorry.

But in the light of a lantern held by the young soldier who had announced their arrival, the three scrawny

Indians at the gate looked too malnourished to put up any kind of a fight. Silas watched Ned take their measure and address them in rudimentary Cheyenne. One of the men stepped forward and extended one hand. At first Soule thought he wanted to shake, a custom Indians usually avoided for fear of a trick. Then he saw the envelope in the man's weathered brown hand.

"Bring the lantern closer," Ned ordered.

Three young soldiers kept their rifles at the ready while Ned opened the letter. Soule saw Ned's eyes drop to the end.

"It looks like it was written by Bent's son."

William Bent was a trader who had done well before the cavalry had shown up in force, but the ornery coot had burned his trading post back in the 1850s rather than let the troops use it. He had a squaw and some half-breed sons. Ned read rapidly, with translator John Smith peering over his shoulder.

Ned handed the missive to Soule with arched eyebrows. "Here, see what you think of this."

The note introduced One-Eye, Min-im-mie, and One-Eye's squaw. The letter, in rough English, said the three Cheyenne had come as messengers for Cheyenne Chief Black Kettle, who wanted to meet with the whites for peace talks, and to discuss the return of some white prisoners held by various bands. Soule's eyes widened.

"Could be a trick, Ned. I haven't seen a reason yet to trust any of them since I got to Indian Country."

Ned stroked his mustache. "Could be. But I'd feel a right fool if it turned out there was a chance to get back some of our people, and I didn't take the risk. Let's put it to a discussion. Round up the other officers and we'll meet in my quarters."

"They could be setting us up for an ambush." Cannon's cigar had gone out, but he still chewed on the stump. "Lure us out a few miles and then wipe us out."

Ned rubbed his jaw. "I suppose. What do they get out of a deal like that though?"

"Could be Dog Soldiers itching for a fight, smart enough to use Black Kettle's name. I wouldn't put it past those renegade Indians." Soule perched his behind on Ned's desk.

"How do you think the men will respond?" Ned asked.

Cramer spoke first. "Well sir, they respect you. I do believe they will follow your lead, to a point anyways."

"Here's what I'm thinking." Ned looked down at his long clean fingers. "We bring the big guns with us and we stay primed and ready to fight. Any indication they're up to something and we hit hard."

The men around him nodded and followed him back to the gate where the Indians and soldiers still stood. The soldiers' rifles remained trained on the threesome.

Ned Wynkoop turned to John Smith. "Ask them if they can take us to Black Kettle."

The translator carried out the brief exchange. "They said Black Kettle's camp is about three day's ride and they can take us."

Ned fingered his mustache again.

"Tell them they will all go with us, and if there are any tricks, they will be killed immediately."

Soule watched as the grim message was translated, but the faces of the three Indians remained blank—at least to his eyes. For the first time he found himself wondering how the red man defined courage, and whether he was witnessing a bit of it.

Finally, One-Eye spoke. Ned seemed to understand some, but Soule had to wait for Smith's translation.

"I am Cheyenne. Cheyenne people keep their word. If my people did not keep their word, I would not want to live."

7

Danger lurked beneath the upside-down cardboard box that only a day or two before had been full of containers of Kellogg's Corn Flakes. John Fox approached the box slowly and quietly, trying to ignore the audience gathered outside the back door of the King Soopers store in Green Mountain. Beyond the back parking lot, young cottonwood trees rustled in the hot breeze, indicating a small stream meandered nearby. Heat waves shimmered off the asphalt.

"I'd advise you all to move back," Fox said quietly. The crowd responded immediately, but stayed within visual range. Too good a show to miss.

Fox positioned himself beside the box and took a deep breath. Careful. He tipped the box back with one steady motion. The animal did not move and the white and black striped tail stayed blessedly parallel to the ground. The head inside the strawberry Yoplait container swiveled in Fox's direction as the creature tried and failed to see the being hovering nearby. Taking another breath, Fox put one hand on the animal's neck and the other on the container and gently pulled. Back in the sighted world, the creature blinked and Fox took a giant step backwards, praying under his breath. The skunk took a quick look in Fox's direction before waddling off toward the stream. As it disappeared into the undergrowth, the crowd burst into applause.

Fox nodded his head briefly in response but wasn't in the mood for more drama. The skunk had done him a favor, forcing him to focus all his concentration on something other than the memory of Trish's body.

"Wow." The young clerk with green highlights and a lip ring shook his hand. "And I kept telling 'em not to call you guys, that there was some law or something that skunks have to be killed 'cause they might have rabies. Which really sucks, since it's not fair they should die because of jars they can get in but can't get out of."

Fox paused. "Well now, it wouldn't be safe for me to fire my weapon here, on the pavement and in city limits an' all."

"Thank the Goddess."

The kid–had to be a Milarepa University student–moved away and Fox headed back to his truck. Short guy with a high voice? Tall girl with a low? Did his-her hairdresser even know for sure? Fox occasionally served as a guest presenter on Native American studies at Milarepa, and he always got a kick out of the myriad of piercings, tattoos and rainbow haircuts arrayed before him. Their naïve sincerity and idealism left him shaking his head over what was sure to be future disillusion. Green Mountain might only be 16 miles southwest of Keyhole, but it was truly a world away. Except as more folks moved into Green Mountain County, many liberals unable to afford Green Mountain's pricy real estate had started infiltrating the one-time conservative agricultural community of Keyhole. Bumper stickers demanding "Don't Green Mountainize Keyhole" reflected the unhappiness of longtime Keyhole residents.

Fox let Abby out of her crate, leashed her and took her for a quick walk while he listened to voicemail on his cell. Twenty-four hours had passed since he found Trish's body. Now Faith O'Neill's voice was in his ear.

"The detective says in a case like this they'll send her blood off for toxicology tests and it could be weeks before they get the results back. They don't know much about this stuff, the poison used on prairie dogs. Maybe they've already asked you for more input, maybe I'm being a pest. But would you be willing to talk to that policeman and tell him what you know? I mean, if you're not too busy. I'm sorry. I'm babbling. I'm grasping at straws. Trish knew what she was doing, she'd done this before. There has to be something else that—damn, I'm sorry. I'll shut up. Thanks."

Fox steered Abby back to the car. He drove down the street until he found the coffee shop with WiFi. Fox parked, pushed back the driver's seat and turned on his laptop. He didn't need caffeine, just the wireless signal, and that could be had from the parking lot. He entered the word *Phostoxin*. Paused. Added *human fatality*.

He got a bunch of hits. The one called "Safety Data Sheet" looked promising. When the information came up on the screen, one of the first things Fox noticed was an orange box with a black skull and crossbones inside and the words "Very Toxic" across the bottom. The data sheet listed a manufacturer in the United Kingdom, and included a paragraph on symptoms:

"Mild exposure by inhalation causes malaise, ringing in the ears, fatigue, nausea, and chest pressure. Moderate poisoning causes weakness, vomiting, pains above the stomach and in the chest, diarrhea and difficulty breathing. In severe cases, coma, convulsions, pulmonary oedema and death occur."

Fox translated the British "oedema" to American "edema" and punched that in the search line. He scanned a couple sites, picking up phrases: *Fluid in the lungs. Coughing up blood.* Read about how phosphine gas was created when the product came in contact with moisture. Found out that garlic odor is added to the otherwise odorless gas—kind of like the smell added to the natural gas used in his stove. He paused over the "immediate lethal dose" for humans: 2800 mg/m3. Chemistry was definitely not his strong point. He'd have to find someone to translate. There followed a list of lethal doses for a variety of rats. The rats were followed by times. Male rat, four hours. Female rat, one hour.

Trish slinging traps into the back of her battered van. "You know it takes hours, even days to kill them," she had said. "If I come back as a prairie dog, I'd rather be shot."

Fox shook off the memory and plugged in prairie dogs, poison and humans to see what he'd get. There in front of him was a line from a 2001 EPA news release warning prairie dog rescuers. He pulled up the whole segment.

Denver – Well-meaning people who interfere with prairie dog poisoning by digging up and removing deadly pesticides place themselves and others at risk for sickness, even death, the U.S. Environmental Protection Agency warned today. A recent conflict in Green Mountain County over prairie dog control triggered the warning.

"We want people to know that the phosphine gas produced when aluminum phosphide (AlP) is used to kill rodents, can sicken or kill humans, too," said EPA enforcement specialist Tim Osag. He said the agency today sent a "cautionary message" to parties involved in the Green Mountain County conflict last month and posted the message on the Agency's website. "We will also send the message to other parts of our six-state Region where prairie dog control is an issue."

EPA is not taking a position on conflicts over prairie dog control. Typically, a prescribed amount of the pellets is placed in a rodent burrow and the hole is sealed. The pellets react with moisture in the air or soil to produce phosphine gas. The gas is highly toxic when inhaled by rodents or humans. Last August, a South Dakota girl died when AlP was applied near the family home.

AlP is a "restricted use pesticide." Only people certified by EPA or a State can apply it or supervise its use. It is a fumigant registered for control of insects in stored grain and burrowing rodents in agricultural areas. Improper use or disposal of any pesticide violates federal law. Symptoms of phosphine poisoning include headache, dizziness, and nausea, breathing difficulty, vomiting and diarrhea. Breathing the gas can produce pulmonary edema, a buildup of fluid in the lungs which can be fatal. Edema can occur hours after exposure. EPA urges immediate medical treatment if poisoning is suspected. In lesser amounts, the gas can harm the liver, kidneys, lungs, nervous and circulatory systems.

Fox decided he agreed with Trish.
He'd rather be shot.

John Fox had cut open his share of bodies. The most recent was a young mountain lion, probably not even a year old but grown out of his spots. Probably a starving orphan who wandered past a yard in the foothills desperate for a meal and spotted a cockapoo named Peewee—easy pickin's. The owner heard a ruckus and called the police, who then called the Division of Wildlife. John Fox was the lucky one who got to shoot the little lion standing over the carcass of the pooch. Hauled the lion's thin body down to the DOW office in Denver and cut him open to find what Fox already knew he would—pieces of Peewee on their way to digestion in the lion's tummy.

Still, the body before him this time was human, and a human he had known and talked to. Standing uneasily next to Trish O'Neill's naked body, he briefly noted the full breasts, the graying pubic hair that gave away the secret of the black head of hair lying on the stainless steel. He shifted his focus to the floor and silently apologized to Trish for violating her privacy.

"You sure you're okay?" Sheriff's Department Detective Pierce Wilson, the man who'd gotten Fox a ticket into this show, glanced over.

"Fine."

Medical Examiner Arnie MacIntosh pressed a lever with

his foot to turn on the recording microphone hanging over them and state the day and time.

"The subject is Patricia O'Neill, 46. Subject appears well-nourished."

MacIntosh picked up Trish's hand and flexed it, revealing a slice of his black skin above the purple latex glove. "Moderate rigor is present. Post mortem lividity is present in the left side of the body and shows a red-purple color. There is cyanosis of the lips and nails. There is blood at the mouth. No other apparent signs of trauma."

MacIntosh picked up the scalpel with long fingers and ran the blade from the base of the throat down the body. A nice clean cut, no blood to make things messy. In the progression from there, Fox noticed the little things, like how the small saw used to cut through the rib cage made a very annoying high-pitched whine. Like how the human heart seemed both bigger and smaller than it should be, especially lying in a metal tub.

As MacIntosh rattled on, Pierce quietly translated for Fox's benefit.

"The pooling of blood indicates she was lying like that at least a few hours after she died. Based on the last time we know someone saw her alive, that means she probably died between 8 p.m. and 2 a.m. on Monday night or Tuesday morning."

MacIntosh continued his monologue as he removed the lungs and weighed them, noting they were sunken and congested. He went on to describe her heart (healthy), her liver (slightly congested) kidneys (normal), stomach (empty), skeleton and muscles (no abnormalities.)

"Well, gentlemen, your guess is as good as mine until the

toxicology reports come back in. However, at this point, I'd say the theory that she knocked over her water bottle and inhaled a mouthful of phosphine gas is a good one for the moment. Problem is, if that's the case, we won't find phosphine in her lungs or blood because the stuff is so reactive and breaks down fast."

"In which case we're stuck with the circumstances." Pierce Wilson chewed on his mustache.

Fox rubbed the back of his neck.

"If it's so reactive, wouldn't it be hard for her to inhale enough to kill her out in the open air like that?"

"Depends, I guess." The medical examiner peeled off the purple examining gloves. "You told Pierce here you'd heard of kids being poisoned?"

Fox nodded.

"I have too," MacIntosh said. "Awhile back a colleague told me about a case of two kids playing on a pile of wheat somewhere in Europe. There were pesticide pellets in the wheat to kill mice, but it ended up killing the kids. Course, with little guys, they may have been rolling around in the stuff or digging into it. But they were outside and they got a fatal dose."

Fox pulled out his pocket notebook. "Remember when or where?"

"France? I'm not sure," MacIntosh said. "And it goes back awhile, maybe to the '80s. I don't know much about pesticides. But I'm pretty sure aluminum phosphide was involved."

"Thanks Mac." Pierce moved his eyes to signal Fox they should head out. In the hallway, the sheriff's detective paused by the doorway.

"I appreciate you letting me watch." Fox turned to look back at Trish's now sheet-covered remains beyond the glass window.

"No sweat."

"Anything you can tell me?" Fox asked. "The sister is a loner and I've been doing some hand-holding."

"Really? I didn't think she was your type. More like Trish in there."

"Nobody is my type these days. I've had enough 'types,' including two wives. I like my life just like it is, thank you very much."

"Yeah, well, funny how things like that can change."

Fox rolled his eyes.

"Okay, okay, you wanna be a monk, who am I to say different. We're gonna be out today chattin' up Trish's nearest and dearest, including her not-quite-ex, who—" A classical melody filled the air. Before Fox could make a wisecrack about Pierce being partial to Beethoven, the detective reached for the cell phone on his belt, read the text and groaned.

"Jesus. Looks like we got a really bad domestic, dead kids and all and we're short-staffed. I'll call when I can."

As Fox watched Pierce run for the nearest exit, he had a feeling that call might be awhile in coming.

8

They had put her on hold.

Apparently, things were crazy over at the Medical Examiner's Office, what with some mass murder Faith had heard about on the news. Some idiot had driven around Green Mountain County taking out family members, including his ex-wife, his four kids and his former in-laws before finally and belatedly turning the gun on himself. No, the woman on the phone did not know when Trish O'Neill's body would be released. No, her supervisor was not available. Yes, Faith O'Neill could wait on hold if she wanted, but it could be a long time before anyone could talk to her.

Holding her portable phone in lieu of the cell phone that needed charging, Faith paced a route around the perimeter of her small dining room and the adjoining—and even smaller—living room. She hadn't slept well the night before and a morning walk had done little to dissipate the nervous energy bubbling inside her.

Frustrated, she told herself to do something useful while she waited. Faith found her laptop and settled into her favorite chair, determined to keep editing her manuscript while the world put her on hold.

***

"Unsung Hero"
By Faith O'Neill
Chapter Four

Sept. 6, 1864
Northeast of Fort Lyon, Colorado Territory

Silas Soule pulled out his bandana and rested the knotted reins on the saddle horn. He pushed up his broad-brimmed cavalry hat and mopped the sweat off his forehead. Delilah plodded on, content to keep pace with the other horses in the troop. The big mare's sprain had not been serious and had healed nicely. Soule was glad– he had killed horses and mules in the past and it was not a pleasant memory. He shuddered at the thought of Glorieta Pass in New Mexico territory, the bayonet and all that blood. No cavalry man should be ordered to do what they had, necessary though it was. They had tried to run off most of the Confederate supply train mules and horses, but the stragglers had been slaughtered one by one as the supply wagons were torched nearby. He still woke up from dreams, holding the bridle of that first mule, already rolling its eyes and snorting in terror amid the flames and the smell of the blood of his mates falling nearby. But destroying the supply train and killing those mules had helped win the battle for them against the Southerners. The South and its slave trade had to be stopped. Glorieta Pass was a solid victory for Chivington and the men who fought with him. Soule thought of how he had revered the big bearded man at the time. It might have been better if he had not gone on to work as Chivington's adjutant and seen the colder side of the man's ambition.

Soule shook off his memories of Glorieta. The sun of early September blazed down as the troops headed upstream, stopping occasionally amid the big cottonwoods and smaller willows along the bank. Thanks to the monsoon rains of August, a trickle of water flowed in the creek. A coyote ran out of the shrubs to their right. A soldier that Soule knew to be a failed farmer pulled his pistol and let off a shot. The horses flinched but mostly stayed steady—they had been trained to handle the sound of gunfire. Meanwhile the coyote disappeared and the troops hooted at the apparent miss.

"How about we save that shot for the Cheyenne? We may need it," Soule said over the jingle of horse bridles and creaky saddles.

"Yessir," the young man grumbled.

Soule watched Ned Wynkoop conferring with interpreter John Smith and their Indian escorts. Last night at the fire they had said through Smith that the troops likely would reach Black Kettle's band today in the Smoky Hill country of Kansas. The free state of Kansas, Silas amended to himself.

In the meanwhile, the traditional cavalry cadence of walking, trotting, loping, then dismounting to lead their horses through the prairie grass had a hypnotic quality. At the moment they were riding at a walk and Soule's thoughts wandered to Hersa at the Coberly Ranch. He had written a short letter of condolence but it was too early to expect a reply, if one were to come. Although her mother seemed hardy, families that lost their men on the prairie tended to head for the nearest city or return to familiar ground back east. His own mother in Maine was proof of that. When Silas' father died four years ago, Sophia Soule wiped the Kansas dust off her shoes and boarded a train. Indeed, he was past owing his mother a letter. The maple trees would be just now thinking of changing their colors. God, for some fresh maple syrup on hotcakes. He could almost taste it…

"Major!"

The sergeant riding next to Ned Wynkoop pointed off to a slight rise in the distance where an Indian could just be seen astride a pony. Then another, and another joined together on the rise. The number rose until there were at least 500 braves on the hill. The Indians yelped and shook their rifles, the sun glinting off gun metal.

Wynkoop held up his gloved hand and the troops reined in. Altogether they were 127 men, and greatly outnumbered. Even with the two howitzers Wynkoop had ordered brought along.

Wynkoop looked over and caught Silas Soule's eye.

"Guess we're committed now, eh Captain?"

"Guess so, Major."

"Well then. Let's see what they have in mind."

***

"IF YOU WANT TO MAKE A CALL, PLEASE HANG UP AND…"

The recorded voice on the open telephone line finally penetrated Faith's slumber. Groggily she sat up and pushed aside the computer. How long had she been out? Her

52

stomach rumbled and she realized she hadn't eaten since breakfast the day before. Shortly before she found out about Trish. What time was it now? Probably close to lunch time. She thought again about how she and Trish were so different. Trish would simply forget to eat meals, while Faith always lived for the next one. Despite this, Trish was heavier than Faith and often complained about the unfairness of life.

"Oh!" Faith jerked out of the chair, grabbing the lap top and her car keys.

She wasn't the only one who needed to eat.

Polly woke up from her post-lunch nap in the crook of Faith's elbow, stretched her prairie dog limbs and settled on top of the legal pad in front of Faith. Her tummy now full of oats, Polly used her tiny paws to pull Faith's right thumb away from the pen and began to suck—a remnant of her pre-weaning days. Faith sighed.

"Okay. I surrender." Faith stroked the soft tan fur with her free hand. "Man, what suction you have. Leave me some thumb, okay? I know you miss her. I do too."

Hoping rodent teeth wouldn't do much of a number on her flesh, Faith let her head fall back against the chair and looked out Trish's double doors leading to the redwood deck and the ponderosa pine forest beyond. Trish and her husband had invested his money in a few high-country acres some fifteen minutes west of the city of Green Mountain. The city sat with its back to the mountains and its face toward the plains. One local Front Range joke was that an environmentalist was someone who already had their home in the mountains. True, homes were creeping further and further into forested areas, making things challenging for born-again foresters who wanted to see the woods burn every few years to thin them out. But there was no denying the appeal of the susurration of ponderosa pines in the breeze and chattering birds compared to traffic jams on I-25 through Denver and endless bland suburbs colonizing the short grass prairie.

Here, someone like Trish could set up a way station in her big storage shed for prairie dogs in the process of relocation. Usually, the animals only stayed in hay-stuffed kennels for days or, at most, a few weeks before going out to their new site. But one time, the county had stalled in providing a relocation site, leaving Trish stuck with dozens of animals for months. Faith had gone up to Trish's place a few times to help with the massive chore of cleaning dirty hay out of kennels, working around frightened prairie dogs. So she was standing next to Trish when her sister made a dramatic discovery.

"Oh God," Trish had said.

Faith looked over and saw that Trish cupped two tiny prairie dog pups in her hands. Eyes still closed, they were pink and hairless.

"The mother's dead," Trish moaned. "She must have just gotten pregnant before I caught her, but I can't believe she didn't abort the fetuses. That she actually gave birth in the kennel."

Trish handed the pups to Faith while she searched the hay to make sure there were no other offspring.

"What will you do?" Faith asked, looking down at the

tiny beings.

"Fuck. If they don't die first, I guess I'll have to try to feed them."

Trish took back one of the pups. "This one isn't looking too good."

The pup in Faith's hand, however, began to wriggle around on her palm.

"I think this one wants to live," Faith announced.

And so it was that Trish ended up playing mom to a prairie dog she named Polly, feeding her round-the-clock with minute amounts of food from an eye dropper. Polly, of course, grew up thinking she was a human. "I can't release her," Trish said. "She's totally imprinted on humans. She wouldn't last two days in the wild."

Now, a year later, Trish was the one dead while Polly lived on.

"Ow!" Faith jerked her thumb out of Polly's mouth. "Look, you are never going to get milk out of that thumb no matter how hard you try."

Polly returned to the crook of Faith's arm and curled up.

Faith looked back at the legal pad where she had written a list of names, and wondered if she was wasting her time. Could Trish actually inhale enough gas to kill her, out there in the open? But then, Trish did have asthma. Maybe Faith was crazy and Trish really did die of stupidity. And if not, well, the sheriff's detective seemed competent. He probably had the same list in front of him. After all, anyone could find people who didn't like Trish. Hell, Faith could put herself on the list for a Chinese menu full of reasons. Maybe she was on the detective's list herself. Love, hate, they got mixed up in the same brew.

Trish provoked extremes in people. Like the first person on Faith's list, Trish's estranged husband Tom Baker. Faith felt a twinge, remembering Tom's arms around her on that first date. Then Tom met Trish, and it was all over but the shouting. Tom, the calm, logical lawyer who went daffy over the passionate animal rights activist. And how far could Trish have gotten in her quest without his money? That is, until he wearied of competing with animals for her attention and walked out.

Faith heard a faint sound and looked down at the sleeping prairie dog. Did prairie dogs snore?

The next person on Faith's list, Green Mountain-based developer Frank Borsich, came across like a modern Buddy Epsen who wandered out of that old show "The Beverly Hillbillies." But he reigned over an empire of chain box stores in the West, and one of the early Borsmarts had landed in Keyhole almost 30 years ago. Aiming to profit from recent population growth, the company proposed a new mega version on the west side of town three years ago. Protests rained down on city officials over competition with local merchants, low worker pay, and because the store would demolish a prairie dog town. Trish led repeated protests before the Keyhole City Council, but in the end the prairie dogs were poisoned and the store went forward. Now the company was back, pushing for a third store on the east side of town on the site of yet another prairie dog town— one of the last within city limits and on land still zoned agricultural. Fighting the rezoning proposal, Trish lost her cool at a recent city meeting and called Borsich a Nazi for poisoning instead of relocating prairie dogs. Faith, sitting in the back row of the meeting, had cringed at her sister's words. Of course, the local reporter present made the comment the lead of his story.

Then there was Keyhole Mayor Violet "Vi" Brady—aka the Wicked Witch of the West as dubbed by Trish. When word got out that Brady supported Borsich's rezoning proposal, Trish swore the mayor wanted a big box store on every corner and would personally bulldoze any prairie dogs in her path.

Faith sighed. It was almost easier to list the handful of people Trish hadn't managed to alienate. Shawn Colvin crooned "Sunny Came Home" from Trish's stereo and Faith felt a tear of self-pity slide down her left cheek. Who was she without her sister for contrast? Trish was the one who needed to look into her own death. Faith barely had the strength to brush her teeth in the morning even before Trish died. Faith lacked imagination. Hadn't Trish said so a hundred times? Trish was the trail-blazer, the one who tried one thing and if that didn't work, went right on to the next.

Trish. Who would never again piss her off by being an hour and a half late for Faith's birthday dinner ("Sorry Sweetie. We were flushing and the pump on the tank broke and it was too hot to keep the dogs in the van so I had to take 'em over to...") She would never again argue with Trish that she was putting prairie dogs in front of everything and everyone else in her life. And she would never again try to irritate Trish by eating mouth-watering fried chicken in front of her—the staunch vegan who still missed the taste of greasy crispy meat in her mouth.

Faith shuddered, remembering the day Trish made her announcement. "I'm a vegan now," she had proclaimed when their mother tried to pass a plate of juicy roast beef her way. Trish had been fifteen, Faith nine, and Faith idolized her. "Can I be a vegan? What's a vegan?" Faith asked.

"What idiotic thing are you up to now?" Chris O'Neill had aimed his laser eyes at his elder daughter and Faith cringed. "Chris, honey—" Their mother shifted in her chair, still holding the roast beef platter.

"Don't 'Chris honey' me," he snarled before turning his attention back to Trish. "Young lady, I asked you a question."

Trish raised her chin in the way of 15-year-olds across the planet. "I don't eat meat or wear any products made from animals who suffer at the hands of mankind."

"You'll damn well eat this meat. I worked hard enough to get the money to pay for it and you'll damn well eat it. Or I can tell you who'll be suffering at the hands of mankind."

"Chris—" their mother said, staring helplessly as her husband grabbed the platter and began shoveling slices of roast beef onto Trish's plate. By this time Faith had hidden her shaking hands under the table.

"Eat it."

"No."

"Eat it."

"NO. You wouldn't have made your precious dead son Elliot eat it. Why should I?"

Chris O'Neill's face bloomed purple.

"If you'd been watching him like you were supposed to, that car wouldn't have run him over and he'd be eating roast beef at this table!" he roared.

Tears appeared in Trish's eyes but Chris O'Neill did not wait for her to respond. He picked up a piece of meat, stepped behind Trish's chair, pinched the girl's nose shut with his free hand and used his thick arms to pin her while she flailed at him. The second her mouth opened he shoved the meat in and clamped his hand over Trish's mouth, ignoring the screams of his wife and the wails of his youngest child. Trish began to retch and buck in the chair. At that point Winnie O'Neill tried to pull his arm away. Chris O'Neill swung a fist at Winnie. Trish had pulled free, knocking her chair over and fleeing from the house...

Faith shook her head and took a breath. Trips down that part of memory lane she could do without, thank you very much.

"Ouch!" Somehow Faith's thumb had found its way back into Polly's mouth. Faith rubbed at the spot where Polly's teeth had gotten too enthusiastic. "You're supposed to be an herbivore, remember?" Polly slid across the notepad and snuggled closer to her chest as Faith wondered yet again what she would do with Trish's illegal four-legged child.

Weary of confronting life as it had become, she reached down beside the chair for her laptop and her chosen escape route to the past of her devising.

***

"Unsung Hero"
By Faith O'Neill
Chapter Five

September 6, 1864
Northeast of Fort Lyon, Colorado Territory

Wynkoop ordered the supply wagons into a circle and

his men into cavalry formation. As the troops and their cannons moved toward the Indians, the ponies of the braves danced in anticipation. The Indians whooped and gestured. Soule felt trickles of sweat at his back and armpits.

When only a couple hundred yards separated the two groups, Wynkoop raised his arm to halt his men and turned to Smith, who he had kept at his side along with the messenger One-Eye.

"Send him up."

Smith muttered some words to the Cheyenne on the pinto horse. Immediately the pinto leaped forward and made a dash to the noisy warriors facing them. The soldiers worked to rein in their horses, who snorted and threw their heads.

"We'll know soon enough," Wynkoop muttered to Soule, who felt an uncomfortable urge to take a piss.

"Sooner than later I hope. I need to take a leak."

"Me too." The two men shared a quick grin.

When One-Eye's horse reached the other group, warriors clustered near him. Soule decided there might be more than 500 Indians, and thought again how he really ought to write that last letter for his ma in Maine. Of course, he'd thought that about a dozen times in the last couple years and never seemed to do it.

"Shee-yit, why don't they make up their stupid injun minds!" The voice erupted a few feet to the left of Soule.

"'Cause they don't have minds, you idiot."

"Easy, gentlemen," Cramer said.

Soule glanced a thank you at Cramer and worked on settling his own nerves. At that moment, One-Eye broke out of the crowd across from them, loping back on the pony. To Soule's eye it seemed the braves facing them were a bit quieter.

One-Eye spoke with Smith.

"They don't understand. If we want peace, why'd we bring all our guns and cannons? They want us to pull back a few miles and set up camp, and then Black Kettle will come for a council."

"Tell them we were ready to fight if this was a trick," Wynkoop said. "Tell them if they pull back, we'll set up camp nearby and wait for Black Kettle."

One-Eye did another back and forth. Wynkoop waited to see the Indians begin to withdraw, then he signaled for his men to turn.

Soule pulled out his bandana. It went back into his pocket soaking wet.

Two hours later, the horses were tied to lines under the leafy cottonwood trees and eating the grain put down for them. The men looked through their gear for chaws of tobacco or loose tobacco to roll their own. The cook had coffee going and soldiers lined up with their tin cups for a jolt. Others were down at the nearby stream, refilling canteens. Soule thought it looked downright peaceful. Except that when someone stepped on a dry twig, all heads whipped in that direction and hands sought out pistols in their holsters. Lookouts had been posted around the perimeter of their camp, but everyone was jumpy just the same.

Cramer stood near Soule, trying to get his pipe to draw.

"There's easier ways to get at tobacco, Joe."

"Not as elegant, though, Cap'n."

"Granted."

"You think they'll come?"

"Are you hoping they will? Or that they won't?"

"The men are nervous."

Soule glanced around. "We're used to fighting. This is different. No way to know what to expect."

Cramer grunted. Soule took it as a sign of the mood in the camp—Joe could talk your ear off and would at every opportunity. Except this one.

"Rider coming!"

A horse with one of the lookouts galloped up to the crowd of men.

"Where's the Major?" the soldier on horseback demanded. Men crowded around the horse. Voices tumbled over one another: "Are they coming?" "How many?" "Any whites with 'em?"

Ned moved through the crowd, parting the waters.

"Report."

"Looks like about 50 injuns sir, headin' our way."

Wynkoop paused, waiting for the voices stirring around him to stop.

"All right. Company commanders, make sure your men are ready but not in battle formation. We will treat these people as our guests unless they give us cause to do otherwise."

"Hope they give us cause," one soldier muttered.

Ned shot him an icy stare and the man looked down at his boots.

9

"Okay, you are not my favorite hemorrhoid right now."

Rajul ignored the back-handed compliment and continued walking across Fox's Wednesday morning paper. The cat plopped down in the middle of the newsprint, folded himself over like Jabba the Hut and began licking his anus. Fox was beginning to rethink his loyalty to the printed page and his resistance to the digital era.

"Lovely. So inspiring at breakfast."

John Fox grabbed his bowl of Grapenuts to save it from the long, caramel-colored tail fur flicking that way. Digging his spoon in the crunchy goo, Fox elbowed Rajul just enough to see the article. A paw at the end of a long, long, long cat leg reached for his arm and snagged him with sharp claws.

"Damn it!" Fox sat down his bowl, pushed the beast off the table and rescued his newspaper. How did a guy with obsessive-compulsive issues end up with three cats anyway? The lead article was a sketchy report about a late-breaking discovery of several bodies at a home just outside the Green Mountain city limits. The story cited an unnamed source in

63

the Sheriff's Department as saying some of the dead were children.

Fox figured Pierce Wilson was currently up to his eyeballs in the hunt for the murderer, believed to be an ex-husband enraged that his former wife had launched a new relationship. Fox's eye caught the name "Chivington" in another front-page headline and began reading.

City officials are scheduled to study the possibility of changing the name of Chivington Way in Keyhole, because Col. John Chivington is generally considered responsible for the 1864 Sand Creek massacre of Cheyenne and Arapaho Indians in southern Colorado.

Mayor Violet Brady, asked about a campaign by local residents and Native American groups to change the street name, said the city council would wait for a decision from the planning and zoning department.

"The street has been called Chivington Way since the road was built 31 years ago," she said. "While I can understand the sensitivity about this, we have to be practical. Changing street names means changing the address of everyone living on that street, and changing city maps. The cost would be significant."

Col. Chivington was a Methodist minister who led the troops involved in the Sand Creek Massacre in southeastern Colorado in November 1864. As many as about 160 Cheyenne and Arapahos died, mostly women, children and elderly tribal members.

Leaders of the non-profit Native American Relief (NAR), based in Green Mountain, told the council that their group was prepared to launch street protests if

Chivington's name is not removed.

"No one would allow a 'Hitler Avenue' in Keyhole," said NAR director Henry Grayfeather. "Chivington and his men slaughtered women, kids and old people who had already surrendered to the whites. They cut off body parts for souvenirs. Does Keyhole want a street named for this man?"

Keyhole resident Manning Roberts, author of a new book that contends the massacre was actually a battle fought between soldiers and armed Indians, said he opposes changing the street name.

"The Indians were using their usual strategy of making 'peace' during the winter, while preparing to resume warfare in the summer," Roberts said. "Chivington's leadership saved the lives of many frontier citizens..."

Fox snorted and turned to the next page of the paper. There at the top was an article about Trish. He wondered if her death got bumped inside because of the late-breaking domestic murder case.

Animal Activist Found Dead Within
Recently Poisoned Prairie Dog Colony

Authorities found animal rights activist Trish O'Neill, 46, dead Tuesday in a prairie dog town outside Keyhole where the rodents had been poisoned the previous day.

"The cause of death has not been determined and is under investigation," said spokeswoman Jenny Fairchild of the Green Mountain County Sheriff's Department. "One possibility is Ms. O'Neill accidentally inhaled some of the toxic gas when she tried to remove prairie dogs from poisoned burrows."

Fairchild added no one should try to dig out a poisoned prairie dog hole because inhaling the fumes can cause illness or even death.

O'Neill was a frequent speaker at Keyhole City Council meetings regarding the fate of prairie dog colonies slated for development in the area. O'Neill was the director of Prairie Promise, a non-profit organization focused on relocating prairie dogs from development sites to protected areas on public open space.

The body of the Green Mountain resident was found near the Prairie View subdivision by a Colorado district wildlife manager, who was investigating a report of a possible cougar sighting, Fairchild said. She did not release the name of the game warden involved, but did say there was no indication a mountain lion had been near the scene.

The property where O'Neill's body was found is slated for construction of a new housing subdivision...

In his mind's eye, Fox saw Trish sprawled in the dirt near the kennel, the nearly empty water bottle tipped on its side near the burrow. In Green Mountain County nearly everyone had their own water bottle, usually a Nalgene. Famous for its breathtaking views of the Colorado Front Range mountains, Green Mountain County experienced a dry climate with maybe 18 or 19 inches of rain a year. Staying hydrated was important at an elevation of 5,400 feet. Local folks held onto their trusty re-usable water bottles, the better to keep plastic out of landfills. Fox's personal Nalgene bottle was pretty old, a scratched translucent white with a blue mountain lion graphic. So it was entirely possible that Trish had taken a slug from her bottle and unthinkingly set it down near the burrow where she was working. How much water would it take to spill into the burrow, interact with leftover dry poison and create a fatal gas?

Fox pushed the paper away. Technically today was his day off. He tried to force himself to take Wednesdays off, despite the Division's unwritten code that game wardens worked 24-7. Game wardens tend to be the busiest on Saturday and Sunday, when most folks grab their fishing poles or hunting rifles. Still, he always checked phone messages on Wednesday, the better to ward off emergencies. In the small room he used as an office, he found seven messages on his DOW voicemail. Oh well.

"Hello, Mr. Fox. I really hope you can help me." The woman sounded eighty if she was a day. "I have a family of raccoons living under my porch and they scare me to death. What if they have rabies? My Chihuahua Pickle loves that porch. But I don't really want to poison them. My daughter says I should..." Fox sighed and waited for the woman to give her number. She ended by saying "Please call me as soon as you can," without leaving her name or number. Fox pushed nine for delete.

The man in the second message identified himself as Frank Borsich. Fox felt his eyebrows rising. Borsich's company was taking heat for preparing to build another store in Keyhole, this time on the east side. The local merchants were arguing enough was enough, that the new store would take away even more of their critical business. Meanwhile, some city residents opposed the store on moral grounds—products made in China, construction on one of the last remaining prairie dog towns, etc.

This was déjà vu all over again. There had been a fierce battle over the second Borsmart built in Keyhole, as protesters led by Trish packed zoning meetings and city commission sessions. Despite the protests, the City Council rubberstamped the recommendation of the city planning and zoning committee in favor of the development. Only one councilman held out—retired teacher Tim Fraser. Most recently, Trish and her supporters had vowed that if the rezoning went through for the third store, they would picket the site non-stop.

Fox found it hard to believe Keyhole needed three of the box stores. But the town was growing and at near 100,000 people, Borsich must figure the community could support a third location. Fox didn't talk about his shopping habits, but he avoided the place. Except the one day he couldn't find a cheap orange hunting vest anywhere but there. He had gritted his teeth, marching in and out with that one four-dollar purchase.

Borsich's message was ending. He had said little, only asking Fox to call him back. Fox wondered what Borsich thought of Trish's death. He began punching in the numbers Borsich had left for him.

Faith paused at the front door of the downtown Green Mountain townhouse and stood listening to the strains of the cello. The sad, haunting notes seemed out of kilter on this row of posh new homes standing side by side in the golden sunshine, the Flatrocks providing their signature backdrop in the distance. It still surprised her a little that Tom had moved to such a modern location in a town where owning a vintage, updated Victorian was considered the epitome of Green Mountain status. A woman jogger pushing a big-wheeled baby stroller trotted by. The music stopped and Faith pushed the doorbell.

The door opened and her brother-in-law faced her, his eyes widening in surprise. Some other emotion—fear?—slid across his face too quickly for Faith to register. Then the lawyer's training reasserted itself and he gave her a sad smile.

"Faith." Tom hugged her, then gestured inside. "Come in, come in."

Faith walked past her brother-in-law into a high-ceilinged room flooded with light from huge plate glass windows and skylights. A textured cement floor painted blood red accented the stainless steel kitchen appliances at the far end of the open-concept room. Toward the front windows, the cello rested on its stand. Tom still held the bow in his right hand.

"Please, sit, sit. Can I get you some herbal tea or something?"

The British had their Ceylon; Green Mountainites had Heavenly Seasonings. Of course, a few years back the local tea company outraged the community and triggered a boycott by poisoning prairie dogs on its property. The firm made amends, creating a "private ecological park" for the critters and forking out $50,000 to local environmental groups.

"Yeah, sure, anything." Faith sat in a fat beige leather chair and sank low.

Tom bustled around the kitchen.

"When the police came last night and told me I didn't believe them," Tom said, filling a black and white, Holstein motif tea kettle with water from a big ceramic jug perched on a wooden stand. "I mean, Trish can't be dead. Someone like Trish doesn't just die like that. How are you holding up?"

"I don't know. I just feel numb, mostly."

"I know it's been three months since we split, but I kept thinking we'd work it out, you know?" Tom pulled two glass coffee mugs from a cupboard and set them on the granite countertop. He pulled two tea bags out of a box—it looked like Lemon Pinger from where Faith sat—and dropped one in each cup. "Honey?"

Faith paused, hesitating over the word.

"No thanks. Straight is fine."

Another cupboard was opened and closed. Tom placed a plastic bear of honey on the counter. He pulled open a drawer and took out a spoon. Then he turned back to the stove, as if he could make the kettle whistle a little sooner by staring.

"How have you been?"

Hadn't he just asked her that? Faith struggled out of the plush chair and stood looking out the front window at the small but manicured yard full of politically correct xeriscape plants that need little water. The prairie coneflowers and Mexican Hats bloomed in gaudy yellows and garnet reds, contrasting with the white flower clusters on the taller yarrow. She mused about the size of Tom's mortgage payment. Even on a lawyer's salary, he might be stretched paying for this place and the mountain house. Home prices in and near Green Mountain were obscene. She guessed he had paid at least $500,000 for this townhouse. And according to Trish, he had reluctantly agreed to keep paying on the mountain house while they figured out whether they had a future as a couple.

"Tom, had you talked to her lately?"

The kettle finally began to whistle—a faint note growing shrill then fading away.

"The last time I called, like a few days ago, she hung up on me." She heard him bustling again behind her. "Here you go."

She turned as he placed one mug on the glass-topped table next to the chair where she had been sitting. He stood with his own tea, apparently waiting for her to return to the chair before he settled on a place. Faith sat on the squishy edge of the leather chair and took the mug in both hands. Odd that the warmth should feel so good in the middle of summer. The smell of citrus curled into her nostrils and for a moment she felt at peace.

Faith sighed. "We have to decide, I mean, what to do about—"

"Tommy, have you seen my—"

The young woman—the very young woman—stood at the top of the open staircase. The oversized T-shirt barely reached the tops of her bare legs. Faith jumped to her feet, spilling her tea and burning the tops of her own legs.

"Uh, hello?" the girl-woman said.

Tom Baker looked at Faith, who now realized why her

71

brother-in-law hadn't been thrilled to see her at his front door.

"This, um, this is Melissa." Switching his gaze to the woman with spiky blonde hair looking down at them, Tom added, "Mel, this is my sister-in-law, Faith."

Faith's face prickled with heat as she studied the young woman. Had she fallen into a vintage snapshot from her childhood? Aside from the hair and the diamond in her nose, this woman-girl looking down at her was nearly a carbon copy of Trish 25 years ago. She felt sick.

With shaking hands, Faith put down the full mug of tea she had yet to taste.

"I have to go," she said.

10

The juvenile bald eagle flew from one of the elderly cottonwood trees right after Fox pulled his state truck onto the field where a large sign proclaimed "Future Home of Borsmart Mega Store!" Looking out his window, John noted the blotchy black and white pattern on the underside of the bird. Young balds didn't look anything like bald eagles for the first several years of their lives. They went through various patterns of dark and light until finishing with their trademark white head and white tail at about four or five years old. One time he'd met an Indian named "Spotted Eagle Boy" and theorized he was named after a young bald. Prairie dogs yipped at his truck from the tops of their mounds across the 50-acre lot. They were hard to see, their tan bodies blending in with the dirt of the burrow entrances. Abby looked out the window at them with only mild interest. Fox figured there hadn't been much traffic on the site yet, otherwise the prairie dogs would be more acclimated to humans and their vehicles. Fox wondered what other critters the store would displace. Prairie dog burrows also provided shelter for numerous animals including rabbits, thirteen-lined ground squirrels, snakes and the burrowing owl—which was on the state's list of threatened species. And decades ago, the burrows may have sheltered black-footed ferrets, but these fierce tiny predators needed vast colonies of prairie dogs to survive, and vast colonies were hard to come by these days. No black-footed ferrets had been documented on the Front Range in recent times. Still, it pleased Fox that within Keyhole city limits a person could still see prairie wildlife, including the country's national symbol.

As the eagle cruised with a slow graceful flap toward the east, a shiny yellow Volkswagen Beetle zipped into the lot and stopped alongside Fox's Dodge. Fox could see the man inside had white hair pulled into a ponytail. Some lost soul needing directions probably.

The man got out and walked toward Fox's truck. At that point Fox realized that this Jed Clampett look-alike was none other than Frank Borsich in the flesh. Fox watched his own stereotypes duke it out inside his head. He'd been looking for something like a black Hummer and a guy in a $1,000 suit. Instead, this man sported a gray ponytail, a white short-sleeved shirt, blue jeans and running shoes. Ah hah, he thought, recognizing the brand. Very expensive running shoes.

"Thanks for coming." Borsich stretched out his hand to Fox who had just climbed out of his truck. Fox shook his hand. In the cab of the truck, Abby growled softly. Fox gave her the evil eye and she laid down and pretended not to care.

"I was hoping you could give me some advice. Once the land is rezoned, I'd like to get rolling on this project." Borsich waved his hand in a broad stroke. "What would it take to move these critters somewhere else?"

Fox paused, noting Borsich's complete confidence that the rezoning would happen.

"You're talking prairie dog relocation?"

"Sure, whatever they call it."

An interesting turnabout. Was Borsich worried that Trish's death would spike controversy if he poisoned again?

"You'd need a place to take them." Fox turned to watch prairie dogs chasing each other. "I'd have to evaluate the receiving site, to see how many animals it could handle. You'd need someone to do the actual relocation. And you'd have to work up the paperwork for a Division permit."

Borsich fingered the gold loop in his left ear. What was the old saying for guys who wanted to wear ear bling without confusion about their orientation? Right is wrong, or some such.

"I heard we could also trap 'em and give 'em to the black-footed ferret people. For ferret food. Probably be cheaper."

"You could. Might still have protesters though."

"Yeah." Borsich paused. "You know our company has launched a new campaign—the Green Team thing?" Borsich glanced at Fox, who rewarded him with a brief nod. "Anyway, I was thinking that we might be able to smooth things over now that—well, under the current climate. Maybe move these critters somewhere else."

Borsich's face had turned pink.

"I guess Trish O'Neill's dying has changed things some," Fox said. "Probably not good for business if protesters fight the store in her name and make her a martyr."

Pink went to red.

"That woman was flat nuts." Borsich's eyes narrowed and his mouth twisted into a scowl. "Called me a goddamned Nazi in public, no less. A Nazi! My mother's family died in Auschwitz and that woman had the fucking nerve to call me a Nazi? Pardon my French. I swear that woman was one of those crazies who can't have children and turns animals into her kids. She had the balls to compare prairie dogs to people? Flat nuts."

Fox waited. Borsich took a breath. Then another.

"Sorry. Still working on those anger issues. My new wife has even got me going to yoga. And a shrink. Said it was her way or the highway. You married?"

"Was."

When Fox failed to elaborate, Borsich took the hint.

"Guess I got off the subject. Anyway, I'll have one of my people get a hold of you and start working out the details."

One of the prairie dogs slowly came out of a burrow about 50 feet away and sat up straight, eyeballing the men and their cars.

"What is it about those buggers that gets people so riled up, anyway?" Borsich shook his head. "I mean, people kill mice in their house. Why can't I kill rodents on my own property?"

"You can."

"Sure, if I don't mind protest signs and candlelight vigils by the road. Don't these people want jobs? Sales tax money?"

"I guess different people have different priorities."

"I guess you're right." Borsich turned to shake Fox's hand. "Anyway, I really appreciate your help on this. I'm a man who likes to show his gratitude."

Fox hesitated. Was that what this meeting was about? A bribe from the big man? "Just part of my job." He shook the man's hand briefly.

Borsich climbed back in his lemony Volkswagen, made a circle in the dirt and drove out. The prairie dog standing on its burrow did the famous prairie dog jump-yip, looking for all the world like a miniature cheerleader.

All clear, in prairie-dog speak.

"So what can you tell me about him?

Fox waited for the response to his question, the cell phone at his ear. Outside his truck many of the prairie dogs had emerged and were grazing on the slim pickings of the future Borsmart site. He dug his fingers into the fur on Abby's neck and scratched slowly. The dog's eyelids drooped in pleasure. Still no comment from the man on the other end of the phone. Sam Gary reminded Fox of Gary Cooper in High Noon. Slow. Deliberate. Unshakeable in his integrity.

"Sam? You still there?"

"I only dealt with him a couple times, indirectly," Sam Gary said finally. "Mostly through his gofers."

Fox pictured Sam turning slowly in his wheelchair, taking in the limited view outside the window of his assistant director's office in the sprawling DOW Denver headquarters. There was no hiding the fact that the complex had once been a warehouse. Many offices had no windows at all. The thought made Fox shiver. God forbid he ever had

77

to choose between a windowless cubicle and being out of work.

"Actually he's not so bad, as they go," Sam Gary added, *they* being the developers that were intent on turning every last square inch of the Colorado Front Range into a shopping mall or a subdivision.

"Borsich was stubborn at first," Gary continued. "Didn't see why he should bother with wildlife. But lately he got himself a young trophy wife who is big into saving the whales and such. Maybe that made a difference, I'm not sure. But after that, his folks seemed a little more willing to consider wildlife issues. Emphasis on 'a little.' They agreed not to make a concrete ditch out of a creek at one of their subdivisions. They put a bike path in next to the stream and then put out a lot of PR about how the neighborhood included 'shimmering streams and open space.'"

Fox considered Gary's words. "So he's willing to play along as long as he gets something out of it?"

"Pretty typical of his type, if you ask me. At least he's willing to make some concessions. That's more than I can say about a lot of them."

"Mmm. Okay. Well, for a minute I thought he was trying to buy me off. You ever hear anything along those lines?"

"Nah."

"He also blew a fuse when I brought up Trish O'Neill," Fox said. "Kinda made me wonder if O'Neill might have had more enemies than is good for a person."

"Huh. I heard it was an accident. That O'Neill sucked in poison trying to dig out some prairie dogs."

"Yeah, that's the theory."

"You think otherwise?"

Fox watched some immature prairie dogs chase each other.

"I don't know. Trish's sister sure isn't buying it. Thinks Trish was too smart for something like that. You know me, I just don't like loose ends."

"Speaking of loose ends," Sam Gary said, "I'm hearing rumors you're thinking of getting out when you get to 20."

"If I were a short-timer, would I be picking your brain like this?"

"Fox, you've always been a hard man to read."

John Fox chuckled as he cut the connection. His stomach rumbled, complaining about the postponed lunch. He started the truck and headed toward Noodles for some carbs. He had brought Faith's manuscript along, and figured he'd get through a few more pages while chowing down on some mushroom stroganoff.

***

"Unsung Hero"
By Faith O'Neill
Chapter Six

9:30 a.m. Sept. 10, 1864
Smoky Hill Country, Kansas

Soule took the long wooden pipe in his hands, glancing at the feathers that dangled in ornamentation—maybe hawk, maybe eagle, he wasn't sure. He looked at the end of the pipe. He wasn't keen on putting his mouth there, right after the chief to his left—was it Bull Bear?

His eyes slid over to Wynkoop. Ned jerked his chin slightly in Silas' direction. Silas put the warm moist pipe end in his mouth and drew the acrid smoke into his lungs. A far cry from the gentle tobacco back east, but he struggled to let the taste flow in and out of him. He guessed even Indians didn't appreciate rudeness, and he had heard they considered burning tobacco some kind of sacred link with their sky god or some such.

Silas passed the pipe to Cramer on his right and then tried to surreptitiously study the chiefs seated cross-legged in the circle of about a dozen men. There were mostly Cheyenne chiefs, but Wynkoop had pointed out a couple Arapaho when the Indians rode up. Silas's sit-bones ground into the dirt and he shifted. Ned had insisted they all sit on the ground, same as the Indians. A warm breeze ruffled the leaves of the big cottonwoods nearby, and the low murmur of the creek made Silas wish he'd remembered to bring his canteen. Sunlight danced on the heart-shaped leaves of the trees—large, but no match for the giant oaks and maples he remembered from Maine—and for some odd reason Hersa's face popped into his mind as she sat angry and disgusted in the cow manure.

"...so upon receiving the letter brought to us by One-Eye..." Ned paused, waiting for Smith to translate, "...I believed you were acting in good faith, so I brought my men to speak with you."

The Indian next to Silas began speaking in a gruff tone.

"He says, if you wanted peace talk, why did you bring so many guns?"

Ned looked in the direction of Bull Bear, but not

straight into his eyes. "It's a sign of disrespect, to look 'em straight in the eyes," he'd told Silas one night over cards. "But that don't make sense," Cramer had popped up. "Why, that's the best way to know a man's not lyin' to ya." "That's just their way," Ned had said.

"There are good Indians and bad Indians," Ned was saying. "I brought enough troops to fight you if I had to. But we don't want trouble. We want to take the white prisoners home. We want to listen to what you have to tell us. But I am not a big enough chief to make a treaty with you. I do not have information about the Indian prisoners you spoke of in your letter. But if you give up the white prisoners, I will take you to Denver to speak with the Great Father. I believe peace can be made. I pledge on my life I will return you safely to your tribes, and my officers pledge the same."

Ned turned to Silas. "Do you endorse what I have just said and the pledge I have made?"

"Yes sir." One by one the officers and translator John Smith pledged themselves. Silas studied the expressionless red faces. He felt like he was at a poker table, trying to read the emotions of his opponents. But these people didn't twitch or blink or tap their fingers or blow their noses or scratch their ears. Silas wished he'd known what their trick was when he'd been sitting in that Maine schoolhouse and Miss Brownwell rapped his knuckles with her ruler to stop him fidgeting in his seat.

Bull Bear began rumbling next to Silas once more.

"I have tried to live well with the whites," Smith translated. There followed a long involved story about Bull Bear's brother being killed by some soldiers, and some Indian horses supposedly stolen by the whites.

"You whites are the ones to blame for the trouble, not

us. White people are foxes. The only way to deal with them is to fight."

Silas felt his gut tighten. Cramer caught his eye and he lifted his eyebrows in return. His hand slid down to where his sidearm should be–but wasn't. No one sitting in this council had a weapon.

"Major! I need to speak to you sir!" Lt. Hardin rushed up to Ned, who stood. "Sir, the Indians are crowding in on us. One of them sat on a cannon and began putting grapeshot down the barrel. We cannot keep them back, sir!"

Ned's face stiffened and Silas imagined he was biting back a reply. Instead, Ned turned toward Joe.

"Lieutenant Cramer, please assist Lieutenant Hardin."

Silas watched the two men leave as Smith apparently translated some of the situation to the chiefs. Muttering braves began crowding around the council. Silas felt a hand slip in and out of his jacket pocket. He went to slap the hand away and realized his tobacco pouch was missing. Saucy bastards. Silas felt the blood rush to his face. He clenched his fists. If this was the end, he'd be damned if he'd roll over without a fight. The white officers began to stand, preparing to go at it barehanded if necessary. Ned's jaw tightened and he looked straight at Black Kettle. "Smith, tell him he must tell his braves to leave the camp." Silas had heard that tone before, and he was always grateful when it was directed at someone other than himself.

Smith translated, but before he could finish, One-Eye stood up stock straight, looked out at the braves and began speaking.

"I walked into the Fort Lyon with the letter written by our chiefs and risked my life." The braves crowding the council fell silent. Silas found himself drawn to the face of One-Eye, letting Smith's translation overlay the voice of the Indian. Ned motioned for the officers to sit again and they did so, if reluctantly. "I was willing to risk dying if we might reach peace with the whites. I believed the chiefs spoke the truth and would do as they agreed. I believe the Cheyenne people do not lie, so I told the tall chief I would die if the Cheyenne broke their word. I am ashamed to hear the words of Bull Bear in council. I feel bad to hear chiefs speak of a few horses during this council. I will hand over my best horses if no more will be said about that here. Do we not mean what we say? If we are not going to keep our word, I will go fight with the whites. I will take my people with me."

Silas felt his eyebrows rising. He had never heard of Indians disagreeing among themselves this way.

Bull Bear spoke briefly, and Smith said he had accepted One-Eye's offer of horses. The Indians who had crowded up to the council slowly ebbed away and left the camp. Silas let out the breath he'd been holding.

Another Indian was speaking.

"I am Black Kettle of the Cheyenne. I asked for the letter to be written and asked One-Eye and Min-im-mie to bring it to the tall chief at Fort Lyon. I am glad that the Cheyenne are true to their word. If the tall chief is true to his word, we will bring the prisoners and go to Denver."

Silas felt a surge of triumph and saw its reflection in Ned's eyes. He had trouble following Black Kettle after that. Something about the whites starting the trouble at Smoky Hill because they had stolen stock from the

Indians. Then some Indians found some horses or cattle and tried to leave them at a ranch but since no one was there, took the animals with them. Soldiers showed up, fighting broke out, several Indians were killed. Then something about another time when Arapaho Chief Left Hand got shot at when he approached Fort Larned with a white flag to help the whites recover some stock the Kiowas had taken. Left Hand and his tribe took off, but some of the young Arapahos were angry and decided to go on the war path and Left Hand couldn't stop them....

What was Hersa doing at this hour? Was she still on the ranch or mourning in some house in Denver City? Either way, there was a chance he could see her if they took these Indians up to meet with the governor.

A gust of wind ruffled the leaves overhead and Silas heard Ned speaking again.

"Yes, I can give you three or four days to gather the prisoners and buy some of them from the Sioux. I understand you cannot force the Sioux to turn over their prisoners, but I expect you to bring all the prisoners you can. Then we will travel to Denver together."

The Indians began speaking rapidly to each other and Smith could not keep up with the translation, only saying "They are disagreeing over whether they can trust you. They want you to promise peace."

"Tell them again I don't have the power to make that decision."

The Indians again began speaking among themselves.

"Black Kettle says they must speak of this more. He wants to know if you will wait for a decision. He says it would be better for you to march back a half-day's march toward Fort Lyon, so he can keep the young braves away

84

from you."

"Tell him we'll march back toward Fort Lyon and wait for three days," Ned said.

After Smith translated, the Indians stood up and the whites followed suit, shaking their legs to bring life back into them.

About this time, Cramer returned and came up to Ned and Silas. His face was pale and his eyes were blazing.

"I'm so angry I could spit. Far as I could make out, them young bucks were just putting on a show, sitting on the cannon. But Hardin, the damn drunk fool, started putting the men in formation and meanwhile the braves were grabbing up their bows and arrows."

"Jesus, Mary and Joseph and all the saints," Silas swore.

"What happened Joe?" Ned's voice was steady.

"I dismissed the men, sir. Told 'em to gather in small groups near the wagons in case they needed to defend themselves. Meanwhile an Indian came up from the direction of the council and spoke to the braves and then they got on their horses and left."

Joe rubbed the back of his neck. "I'll tell you sir, I was afraid they were going to gobble us up."

"Good work, Lieutenant. Outstanding judgment. Black Kettle agreed to send the braves away after you left the council." Ned turned and headed toward the rest of the troops to organize the march back toward the fort.

Silas and Cramer, in unspoken agreement, walked toward the small creek nearby.

"That was a wee bit too close for comfort," Silas said, slipping into his false brogue.

Cramer ran his fingers roughly through his hair. "Did we just wager our lives to protect them? I mean, if they actually bring some prisoners and we go to Denver and all."

"Reckon we did." Silas looked up into the branches of a tall cottonwood. Somewhere across the tiny creek he heard a meadowlark call. "I reckon we did."

11

"Thanks for coming in."

The female deputy in front of Faith looked like she should still be in high school. Either that or Faith was getting older faster than she thought. She had stopped in at the Sheriff's Department on her way home from Trish's mountain house, leaving Polly huddled in a small kennel out in the car with the windows rolled down. Faith needed to get home and set up Polly's wire cage with its elaborate fabric ramps and plastic tube tunnels. Then watch to see how her cat took to the new arrangement. She sucked in a breath and studied the items on the table before her. Faith reached for Trish's planner.

"Please don't touch it. All of it has to stay as evidence for now. What we need you to do is take a look and see if you see anything unusual."

Faith pulled her hand back. Aside from the black leather planner, a jumble of items cluttered the long wooden table in the Green Mountain County Sheriff's Office, including Trish's beat up purple backpack. Trish shunned women's purses and used the backpack as her carryall. Water bottle.

Sun block—the kind that specified no animal testing, of course. Crumpled wrapper from a fast food burrito joint. Pack of spearmint chewing gum. Pale blue rain jacket. Small first aid kit, still in its wrapper from the drugstore. A small Leatherman in its case. The one she had given Trish several Christmases ago. Trish loved the multi-purpose tool and used to joke that no woman needed a man as long as she had a Leatherman, duct tape and WD-40.

"She always wore the Leatherman on her belt. Was it in her backpack?"

"My understanding is that some stuff here was found with her or in her vehicle," said the young deputy. She probably didn't even top five feet tall.

Faith noticed a business card inside a plastic Ziploc bag with an official looking number written on it. She leaned over the desk. The card offered the services of something called "Prairie Solutions" and included the names of Carl and Becca Whiteman.

"Can I look at that?"

"Sure, just leave it in the bag."

Faith picked up the bag and looked at the back. There was only one word, in Trish's handwriting: "Borsich?"

"Does it mean anything to you?" The deputy had a pen and a little notebook in her hand. Ready for action.

"Not much." Faith put the card back on the table. "Borsich is probably Frank Borsich, a developer. The business card is from a company that catches prairie dogs to feed to black-footed ferrets."

The deputy clicked away the point of her pen and put the pen in her pocket. Faith got the sense the woman felt annoyed by the false alarm. Duty had to be calling somewhere, but it didn't seem to be here.

"What do you think the chain is for?" The deputy gestured toward a six-inch-long piece of chain, each link about a half-inch long. There was a clip at one end.

"For her traps." Faith looked up and saw the question in the young woman's eyes. "She uses—used short chains like that to lock open prairie dog traps overnight."

The deputy's eyebrows went up.

"To keep from catching other animals, you know, that might get hurt or die before she found them."

The young woman shrugged.

Another large Ziploc bag appeared to have cereal inside. Faith smiled.

"What is that?"

"Sweet Feed. It's like oats and molasses and stuff, that they feed horses. She used it to bait the traps. Sometimes she'd stick a bag in her backpack in case she ran out of bait at a site."

Faith swept her eyes over the odd jumble of items with its clues to an unusual life. Something tugged at the back of her mind, but she couldn't dredge it up. She shook her head.

"I guess I don't see anything unusual."

"Okay. Thanks."

The deputy showed her to the door. Faith nearly walked into Detective Pierce Wilson.

"Oops, sorry. I heard you were here and I wanted to catch you." Wilson's eyes were bloodshot, the skin puffy beneath. Faith wondered when he had last gotten any sleep. "Did you look over your sister's things?"

Faith nodded. "I didn't notice anything unusual, though."

"Thanks for coming in," Detective Wilson said, "I'll let

the deputy know you can go ahead and take your sister's belongings. By the way, we did manage to get the autopsy in before all hell broke loose—you heard?"

"About the mass murder? Yeah."

"Anyway, I'm releasing Trish's body for burial. You can go ahead with your arrangements."

"What did you find out?"

"Very little. We'll be doing various tests, but it can take days or weeks to get back results. At this point, the medical examiner didn't find anything to suggest foul play."

Pierce ran his thumb and forefinger over his sandy mustache. "I'm sorry I haven't been able to stay in touch more."

"Are you writing her off?"

"Your sister? No, but there isn't much I can do unless I get something solid that indicates someone was involved in her death. I'm sorry, that's just how things are. How are you holding up?"

Faith watched as Pierce sneaked a glance at his wristwatch. She decided to cut the conversation short. "Fine," she said. Fucked up. Insecure. Neurotic. Emotional. Leftover support group slang. "I'm just fine."

Polly, however, did not seem fine. Once Faith had her wire castle reconstructed in a corner of the dining area, the prairie dog had tucked herself in one of her tunnels and refused to come out. Meanwhile, Sonar prowled around the perimeter of the structure, sniffing out the new resident.

"Don't even think about it," Faith warned her feline.

Actually, she wasn't too concerned. Sonar was a small cat and Polly was porky as prairie dogs went. Still, she would be keeping an eye on things for awhile. Faith plopped into her favorite chair with what she had begun to call her suspect list. She grabbed a pen and circled Tom's name twice. Faith burned again at the thought of the imitation Trish in his condo. If Trish could have proven that Tom was messing around before their separation, it might have given her a financial edge in a future divorce. Could Tom have figured out some way to murder Trish so he could secure all their assets? But how? And was he really that cold blooded? She had meant to ask him where he was the night Trish died, but the sight of his young lover had blindsided her, left her only wanting to escape. Faith would have to find a way to ask him, even though the idea of confronting him scared her. If he had killed Trish, what would he do to Faith if she carelessly revealed her suspicions? She glanced up and her eyes slid to the photo on her mantel where she and Trish stood smiling arm in arm. Her fear morphed into anger. She couldn't count on the police. They were distracted, and Trish's death was easy to write off. Faith noticed her laptop on the side table and considered her hero, Silas Soule. Surely he had felt fear, but he took a stand anyway. Couldn't she take a stand for Trish?

***

"Unsung Hero"
By Faith O'Neill
Chapter Seven

7 p.m., Sept. 10, 1864
Half-day's march from Smoky Hill meeting site

Silas jabbed his fork into the beans, making sure the biscuit stayed put on the side of the metal plate.

"Nothing like the army to make a man appreciate his mother's cooking," he grumbled.

"My sister Katie made the best cherry pie in the county." Cramer shoved a broken piece of biscuit into his mouth.

Silas groaned. "God, I think I'd sell my very soul for a piece of pie right now."

The men ate quickly, obeying the unspoken rule of the military: eat fast, as you may be interrupted.

Today proved the rule.

"Captain Soule! Sir! There's a right fight brewing among the men, sir."

Soule and Cramer jumped to their feet, wiping their fingers on their pants. Ned, who uncharacteristically had been eating far from the group, strode past them.

As the three made their way through camp, they began to hear voices raised. They came to a cluster of men pushing and shoving.

"I tell you he has led us here to be slaughtered," one man yelled, his face red. "He's a full idiot to believe them heathens. They are just setting us up to be murdered in our cots!"

"Sammy's right," another man yelled. "We have a right to protect ourselves. We should just pack up and leave now. Let him have the injuns all to himself."

"Major Wynkoop is a smart man—we should give him a chance."

"At the price of our lives?"

"Silence!"

At the sound of Ned's roar, the men stopped cold.

"What is going on here, Sergeant Wilkins?" Ned addressed the highest ranking man in the crowd, who also happened to be the one inciting mutiny.

The red-haired, red-faced man turned to the major, breathing hard. Silas could see the struggle in the man's face. Tell the truth and face the consequences, or try to mumble his way out of it.

"Major," he began. "Major, the men are afraid. They think the injuns are just setting us up for ambush. They're wonderin' why you trust them, the injuns I mean."

Silas tried to hide a slight smile. The man had chosen a careful path, leaving himself unnamed among the mutinous.

Ned stood staring at the man until the sergeant's gaze fell to the ground. Then Wynkoop moved his eyes over the men assembled. His stance, always tall and strong, somehow became more so.

"I understand how some men might be concerned. This is not what we are used to, is it." Ned stroked his chin. "But then many of you do not know directly what was said in the council. Black Kettle and the others have pledged themselves to peace, with turning over their white captives as the proof. Black Kettle and the chiefs are talking over whether to ride up to Denver, to talk peace with Governor Evans. Black Kettle said there were bad Indians and bad whites, but I think he is a good Indian and means to keep his word. If this is so, we could be putting an end to much of the fighting. My heart tells me Black Kettle is a man of his word. Neither I nor he want to see more of our men hurt. I am willing to give him a chance, but I also want us to keep our guard up, in case it is a trick. Will you stand with me?"

Silas watched as the red-haired man Wilkins exchanged looks with the men around him, many of them young and new to the military. Some message passed among them unspoken.

"Thank you sir. We'll stand with you sir," Wilkins said.

Ned's shoulders eased a fraction.

"Excellent. I plan on all of us getting home safe and sound."

12

For a person good at making enemies, Trish somehow managed to draw a fair-sized crowd for her memorial service. Or maybe they had just come to gloat.

Trish never bothered to make plans for her death; she was too busy saving the world for that. Faith had avoided talking to Tom about "the arrangements," although he had offered to help. Faith knew Trish—already reduced to a container of ashes—would roll in her non-existent grave if she knew her ex and his new cutie had been in on the plans. At least Faith had a basic idea of what Trish wanted, after hearing her rant about not wanting to be an environmentalist who ended up embalmed and pumped full of toxic chemicals after death. And she had often waxed poetic about the Buttes out at Pawnee National Grasslands in eastern Colorado, saying it would be a good place to scatter her ashes and let prairie dogs till them into the soil. Faith planned to make the two-hour drive as soon as the service was over. The last three days had been consumed by making the arrangements. She hoped the drive would give her a chance to think, to plan the next step in her amateur quest for the truth.

"Trish lived her passion, a true gift," the woman pastor said, standing in front of the metal picnic tables. Behind her, perhaps 50 yards away, a prairie dog did a jump-yip. Soft laughter bubbled out of Faith. She was joined in the tension-breaking chuckle by some of the folks who had worked with Trish on prairie dog relocation. Surely Trish was grinning too, wherever she was.

On the picnic table near the pastor, Faith had placed a photograph of Trish, barehanded, holding a prairie dog she had just flushed from a burrow. Suds covered the animal's face. Trish, a lock of dark hair falling over her forehead, was just about to slip the "dog" into a hay-filled kennel propped up on its end. Trish had attended the pastor's Unitarian church sporadically, but preferred to call herself a "born-again pagan" who mostly prayed to the gods of nature. So Faith couldn't bring herself to have this gathering at the church. She knew Trish would want to be remembered outside, near the animals she fought for. Now they huddled in the relatively cooler shade of a group shelter on Green Mountain County Open Space. In the distance above Rabbit Mountain with its prickly pear and mountain mahogany, Faith spotted a golden eagle cruising that blue, blue sky, considering which prairie dog to have for lunch in the valley below. The warming air stirred a breeze, ruffling both the native blue grama grass as well as the invasive cheat grass trying to choke out the grama.

Faith realized she had just heard her name. In the silence she looked at the pastor, who said, "Faith? Did you want to say something?"

She almost shook her head, then remembered this was

her idea. After all, didn't TV detectives always scope out everyone at the victim's funeral? Numb and half dazed, Faith now found the idea ridiculous, morbid and futile. Still, when one of Trish's volunteers nudged her shoulder, she stood.

"Thanks for coming." Faith looked out over 30, maybe 40 faces. Tom was there, minus the girlfriend, thank the gods. And the director of Keyhole's Open Space Department—what was his name? Trish had been working with him on a project to move prairie dogs from the local airport onto nearby open space.

"Awhile back, I was helping Trish flush dogs—prairie dogs—from a burrow over at the airport." Stan. Stan something. "I'm holding the hose and the foam is starting to bubble up from the hole. There was this big honking spider floating on, you know, trapped in the bubbles."

She gave up on Stan's last name, having noticed that John Fox had accepted her invitation and now smiled at her encouragingly.

"Trish reached out and rescued the spider with her bare hands." Geez, there was that old rancher, the one who rescued tigers. She thought his name was Simms. And was that Frank Borsich, Trish's "Nazi" developer? Was Borsich trying to show what a good sport he was? Or prove he had nothing to hide?

"Trish put the spider on the ground off to the side," Faith continued. "She said something like, 'Sorry little guy.' And then she kept going. That was Trish. She was on the side of every outcast animal–prairie dogs, spiders, snakes, you name it. She said they were misunderstood."

An older man in the group nodded. Faith recognized Tim

Fraser, the one city councilman who had voted against the latest Borsmart. Her throat tightened. Another breath.

"I think sometimes Trish was misunderstood. She just cared so much, and she couldn't hide it." Faith stopped, tears now choking her words. She dug a tissue from her pocket. She took a step back toward her seat, stopped, then returned to the front of the group.

"Maybe the world needs people who care like Trish. Maybe she carried some of our caring for us." Faith paused, watching the golden eagle circle once more before soaring off toward the horizon. "Well, now she's gone and we have to do it ourselves. That's all."

Fox stood aside as people gathered in gossipy clumps or wandered off toward the SUVs and pickup trucks waiting in the dirt lot. How did so-called environmentalists end up with vehicles that got, what, 12 or 15 miles per gallon? Of course, his government pickup got lousy mileage, but at least he actually went off road. The furthest these commuters went off pavement was a nice hard-packed parking lot like this one.

Local landowner Bob Simms broke away from one of the clumps, white cowboy hat in his hands.

"John, good to see you." He pumped Fox's hand.

"Same here Bob. How're things?"

"Can't complain—too much. Still waitin' on the city to make up its mind on the rezoning. Don't know how long my buyer's willing to sit around waiting."

Fox nodded. Simms stood to make out pretty good if his

land could transform into the town's third Borsmart.

"You ask me, she got what she deserved."

Fox blinked.

"You know." Simms pointed with his chin toward the photo of Trish back on the picnic table. "She was always pushing, pushing. Serves her right, going on private land, getting herself into that poison. Not like the world was created just for prairie dogs, for Chrissakes."

After debating various responses, including *"Not like the world was created just for people,"* Fox remembered he was in uniform and settled for a grunt.

"She pigeonholed me at one of those zoning meetings, asking about the prairie rats that had moved onto my site and would I move 'em. Course, I'd have to pay for the privilege. I showed her the door, so to speak. I got more important mouths to feed."

"So you came here because…?"

Simms looked down at his boots. He looked back up.

"I didn't like her. But she was tough as a tiger. Life's gonna be more boring without her."

"Speaking of which, how is Tigger these days?"

Simms smiled, apparently happy to change the subject.

"Bengals are amazing. That poor cat, you remember, just skin and bones. Skin and bones. I could horsewhip the numb-nuts who bought him off the circus and let him rot in a basement. And now–whoooee! He's the most gorgeous cat I've got. I don't know why that woman"—Simms gestured with his head toward the photo of Trish—"couldn't see that money from that land will help animals way more at risk than her damned prairie dogs."

John Fox shrugged, allowing Simms to take it as a

gesture of sympathy.

"Hey," Simms said. "By the way, can you come out for that damned inspection next week? I'm up for renewal."

Fox suggested a date to go to Simm's exotic cat sanctuary and make sure the facility still met requirements for a state license. He and Simms shook hands and Fox turned to find Faith O'Neill standing in front of him, along with another woman covered in white from head to toe– white baseball cap with a Foreign Legion-style cloth covering her neck, white long-sleeved shirt, white gloves, long white pants and white tennis shoes.

"Thanks for coming." Faith was looking at Fox, but Simms spoke first.

"Felt I should pay my respects." Simms dipped his cowboy hat and slid away into the sunshine waiting beyond the roof of the group shelter.

"I'm glad you're here," Faith said, reaching her hand out to Fox. "I figured you'd be too busy."

"Seemed like the right thing to do." Fox held her hand a beat longer than necessary and was startled at the sound of a new voice behind him.

"Faith, I'm so sorry for your loss." The man put out his hand toward her. "I'm Stan Rodgers, director of Keyhole Open Space. I worked with Trish on relocation stuff."

Faith nodded and shook his hand.

"Look, I know this may not be the best time, but Trish had mentioned you'd done some relocation work with her now and then."

"A bit. Here and there. When she was short-handed."

The mysterious woman in white stirred. "But Faith—" she said in a whispery tone. Fox saw Faith O'Neill cut a quick sideways glance at the tall woman, who went silent.

Stan Rodgers didn't seem to notice, saying "Well, we contracted Trish to move the prairie dogs at the airport. Now we're in a bind. Some pilots are talking lawsuits and we're under the gun here. I thought, well, I wondered if you might be able to help us out? We'd pay you the same as Trish."

In the silence, Fox heard a ripple of yippy alarm calls go through the prairie dog colony nearby. Looking up he saw a red-tailed hawk circling, the sun flashing off its orange tail feathers. Red-tails weren't as good at catching prairie dogs as golden eagles, but prairie dogs survived by considering everything a potential threat. One researcher had proven that prairie dogs employed an extensive catalogue of calls, distinguishing coyotes from people, and people with guns versus people without.

"I already have a full-time job," said Faith.

Rodgers fingered the one-page sheet with Trish's photo on it and an outline of the day's memorial service.

"Even if you could work on it part time, that would help. And I know Trish had some volunteers working with her. If I can't get them relocated, the airport board may press me to take other measures. Look, don't decide right now. Just think about it."

Rodgers fished a card from his wallet and wandered off toward the vehicles.

"Why didn't you tell him?" The woman in white said to Faith. "Besides, you're on leave from the library anyway."

"Tell him what?" Fox asked the tall woman. "Oh, sorry, I should have introduced myself. I'm John Fox, game warden." The woman barely touched his outstretched hand. Fox hated wishy-washy handshakes.

"I'm Hope Packard," came the whispery voice. God, Fox thought. All they needed now was for Shirley MacLaine to bounce up as Charity and they'd have enough names to embroider an inspirational pillow.

"I worked with Trish on the prairie dogs," the woman said softly. "And Trish told me she learned most of this stuff from Faith."

Puzzled, Fox turned to look at Faith O'Neill, who actually blushed. "What haven't you told me?"

"I was a wildlife biologist in another life. My ex-husband and I researched prairie dogs, which included killing them when necessary. I tried to justify what we did but finally I called it quits—with him, with the work."

"So why didn't you want Stan Rodgers to know?"

Faith looked off at the rocky hills. "I don't want to do that work anymore. He'd just pile on the pressure if he knew."

Fox studied her. "Aren't you just full of surprises."

Hope Packard put a large hand on Faith's shoulder. "I'll help you. We could do it. Look, I've got to run. Let me know what you decide."

As Packard walked away, Fox noticed her athletic stride and realized he had underestimated her because of the odd getup and baby girl voice.

"She's allergic to the sun," Faith said. "Everyone's always curious but no one asks her and she likes to stay mysterious. But really it's dead serious."

Faith paused. "Can you imagine? Loving nature and being outdoors and then finding out you're allergic to the sun?"

Fox shuddered at the thought. Bad enough the idea of

dying in some hospital or nursing home with stale air and fluorescent light bulbs. His secret wish was death by mountain lion, but knew the cougar would be caught and killed. He wondered if there were a way to disguise a lion kill as something else–the reverse plot of Nevada Barr's *Track of the Cat*. His mind went back to Hope Packard and her strange malady. To be allergic to his favorite star? The giver of life? And Fox realized that he too would walk around like an escapee from the mummy's tomb if that's what it took to be outside, on the land.

Faith leaned her head against the passenger window of Fox's truck, letting the rural landscape slide by. After the memorial service, Fox had offered to drive her and Trish's ashes out to the Buttes. She'd said no at first, but Fox's persuasion and her own exhaustion won out. They had driven from Keyhole to I-25 and headed north briefly before turning east on State Highway 14. His personal truck was a black Toyota extended cab, and Faith suspected his dog Abby was a little miffed at being relegated to the small backseat. The box with Trish's ashes sat on the bench seat between her and Fox. Faith had peeked—the remains were sealed in a plastic bag within the box, avoiding an oh-so-awkward spill on the truck upholstery. Now there was an interesting etiquette question—I spilled my sister on a guy's truck upholstery; should I vacuum her up? And what's an appropriate apology? Faith giggled and covered her mouth as John Fox looked over. She shrugged an explanation and he smiled before returning his focus to the road. They were both old enough to understand that grief manifests in many ways. Faith was just grateful he had offered to drive her and Trish's ashes out to the Buttes after the memorial service.

She gazed at the flat landscape, the big sky, thinking about how different it would seem on horseback in Silas's time.

***

"Unsung Hero"
By Faith O'Neill
Chapter Eight

Sept. 11, 1864
Indian Country

Soule recognized the Indian on the gray pony as the Arapaho chief, Left Hand. The girl sitting the little bay next to him was white. Brown hair coming undone, blue calico dress hiked up so she could ride. Left Hand, the girl and two other Indians rode into the camp as soldiers stood speechless, taking in the spectacle.

Left Hand rode up to Ned and stopped. Ned reached up and pulled the girl off the horse.

"My dear girl, I am Major Ned Wynkoop, at your service. How are you?"

The girl's lips quivered and tears slid down her cheeks.

"I'm— I'm— "

Ned caught the eye of a nearby private.

"Bring us some coffee and food."

He turned back to the girl and led her to his camp

chair. "Please sit here, Miss…?"

"I'm Laura. Roper."

"Very pleased to meet you, Miss Laura."

Laura Roper's hand strayed to her wild hair and Silas marveled at Ned's ability to bring comfort and normality to the most abnormal situation. When the coffee and a plate of beans and bacon appeared, Ned excused himself and headed back to Left Hand who still stood by his pony. Silas followed three steps behind.

Ned called to another soldier to get the translator, but Left Hand interrupted.

"I can speak with you directly, Major."

Silas felt his eyebrows rising even as Ned's eyes opened wide.

"You speak English beautifully, Chief Left Hand."

"My sister married a white trapper. He taught me English when I was a boy."

With a flash of understanding, Silas realized that Left Hand had been the Indians' ace in the hole during the negotiations a few days earlier, able to understand the whites directly and monitor the translations.

"Thank you for bringing us the girl."

"I told her I'd bring her back if we reached an agreement with you."

Ned paused. Silas studied this Indian who spoke better English than some whites he knew.

"Our agreement was for all the whites being held," Ned said. "Where are the rest?"

"I have word that Black Kettle will be here tomorrow with more of the whites. Black Kettle is a man who keeps his promises."

Silas wondered if Left Hand was making a veiled reference to the many treaties broken by the whites.

"You and the others must stay here until Black Kettle arrives," Ned said. He turned to another soldier. "Take these men to the far side of the camp under guard, but make sure they have food and water."

Left Hand nodded to Ned and then turned to join the braves with him.

Silas leaned toward Ned.

"I do believe he's older than I first thought."

Ned turned back toward the girl who was wolfing down food in a most unladylike fashion.

"And I do believe she's younger," he said.

"Mr. and Mrs. Eubanks was walking me home along the Blue River. She was toting the baby and he was minding Belle. When we got inside the woods, we heard these awful yells and we knowed it was the Indians."

Laura Roper twisted Ned's handkerchief in her hands. Silas had a hunch Ned wouldn't be getting it back. They were sitting in camp chairs under a huge cottonwood, apart from the rest of the soldiers. The tiny creek flowed quietly a few feet away.

"We was hidin' behind some bur oaks and Belle started a cryin' and Mr. Eubanks tried and tried to hush her but she was so scared the poor thing, she couldn't stop. We was terrified. Finally he put his handkerchief in her mouth to make her quiet up. We hid in the bushes 'til the Indians rode by and we waited a long time. Finally we thought we was safe so Mr. Eubanks took the handkerchief out but Belle took to wailing again and the Indians were coming back and they heard her. They rode in like the devil, screaming and whooping and they shot Mr. Eubanks right in front of us. They—they scalped him. There was so much blood and Mrs. Eubanks was screaming and screaming. They tied my hands behind my back and shoved me up on a horse and—"

The girl's voice broke. She put her face in her hands.

"Why couldn't she stop?" she said. "Why couldn't she stop crying?"

Ned cut a sideways look at Silas.

Kneeling next to her chair, Ned patted the girl's shoulder.

"There there. It's all over now. It's all over."

As the girl's sobs slowed, Ned cleared his throat.

"Did the Indians..." Ned started over. "I mean, were you treated like a lady?"

Laura Roper looked up, her pale blue eyes rimmed with red.

"It's the strangest thing, you know? A couple days later the horse I was ridin' stumbled and I fell off and broke my nose. And they took care of me. Kindly even. I was with 'em a few weeks, I think, then they traded me to the Indians of Left Hand. What day is today?"

"September 11," Silas said.

"They took us on August 8, so I've been gone a whole month..." The girl's lips began to quiver again. "There were other white women in camp. One of them run off and they chased her and got her back. That night, she— she hung herself in a lodge. With strips of her own calico dress." She put her face in her hands.

"I think you should rest," Ned said, rising up and offering his arm to the girl. "You can sleep in my tent. There will be a guard outside. You'll be completely safe."

The girl looked out at the creek. "I keep havin' the

same nightmare. The Indians are coming and Belle's screamin' and I'm trying to get my apron off to put it in her mouth but the knot's so tight I can't get the thing untied and the harder I try, the tighter it gets."

Laura Roper got out of the chair and let Ned lead her toward the tents.

"We would a' been okay," Silas heard her say as they walked off. "We would a' been okay if she'd just stopped crying."

***

Faith kept trying to catch up to Trish.

"Slow down! You're going too fast."

Trish ignored her and charged ahead. Her dark ponytail hung below her helmet and she kept a tight grip on the Uzi slung over her shoulder.

"Wait for me!" Faith yelled. The figure up ahead stopped and turned. Faith looked down at the prairie dog as it swung the Uzi in her direction, the animal's eyes blazing with fury. Suddenly she found herself face to face with the animal. "Hey, I'm on your side!" Faith yelled, putting her hands in front of her face. "You think you're so smart," the prairie dog said. "It's time for you to wake up. Wake up. WAKE UP FAITH."

Faith leaped upwards only to be restrained by the seatbelt. She panted. In front of the car the two-lane highway stretched east through farm and ranch land. Fox gave her a concerned look.

"Are you okay?"

Faith rubbed her eyes.

"Bad dream."

"Yeah, seemed that way."

Faith yawned and looked out the side window. Sunlight glinted off a silver grain silo. Storm clouds were building to the southwest.

"Thanks for driving. I didn't realize how tired I was."

"No problem. I've been wanting to get back out to the Buttes for a long time."

Faith wondered if this were true or if he was being polite.

"Do you think it's legal?" she asked. "To spread the ashes on a National Grassland?"

"Who knows. This is probably one of those cases where you're better off asking forgiveness instead of permission," Fox said.

They cruised through a town with a silver grain silo on one side of the highway and a convenience store on the other and not much else in sight except for a few run-down homes.

"I wonder what it's like to live in a place like this." Faith watched an older blue pickup turn a corner with an Australian shepherd standing in the truck bed, its front paws on the utility box. Faith reached back over the seat to pet Abby. "Bet you'd never throw her in the back of a pickup loose like that."

"Nah. I have a crate in the back of my work truck. But usually she rides up front with me. It's a long tradition, you know, game wardens driving around with their dogs. Gets kinda lonely otherwise."

"She's so beautiful. Look! She's smiling!"

Fox grinned. "Didn't you know German shepherds could do that? Weird, huh. When I come home she smiles and kinda snaps her jaws. But when she's in attack mode, it's a whole different story."

"Don't let him talk about you that way, girlfriend." Faith rubbed Abby's ears.

"You have any pets?"

"Just a cat, and—" Faith stopped. Her eyes slid towards Fox, then she turned to look out the side window.

"And?" Fox asked.

"And, uh, that's enough for me."

"Mm."

Faith looked at a field of alfalfa being watered with a center sprinkler pipe on wheels, the kind that sucks water out of the Ogallala Aquifer and never gives it back. For that matter, it was so hot that probably most the water was evaporating before the drops hit the ground, much less being able to flow into the nearest stream.

"Have you ever been to Sand Creek?" she asked.

"Nope. Wanted to, but it was private land and then the National Park Service started negotiating to buy the place. Down the road I'm sure they'll open it up to the public, although I kinda worry about tourists on sacred ground. However…"

"However?

"Back in the late nineties they started this run, a healing run, from Sand Creek to Denver and out to Silas's grave out in Riverside Cemetery. They do 180 miles in three days, people taking turns running and walking. I want to do it, but they stage it in November on the anniversary of the massacre, and I've always got too much work to do, deer hunts and stuff."

There was a pause, each of them lost in their own

thoughts.

"I've heard they've pretty much figured out the exact site of the massacre," Faith said. "Maybe from bullet casings and stuff? Sometimes I think the only way I'll really be able to picture it is by going down there. To see how wide the creek is, how shallow the banks are."

Fox nodded. "I read about a soldier who said the few braves in the camp dug into the shallow banks and fought the troops all day, giving the women and kids time to get away. Of course, the 'braves' were probably just kids themselves. Anyway, the soldier seemed impressed despite himself."

The flat farmlands were starting to give way to gently rolling prairie.

"You know," Faith said. "There are hints in the testimony that Silas used his troops to shield some of the women and kids as they ran."

Fox nodded again. "But he didn't say so in his letters, so I guess we'll never know. Hey, I think we're getting close."

The truck slowed and turned north.

13

Pawnee National Grasslands stretched to the horizon below them, every angle apparent under the short, overgrazed vegetation. Faith clutched the box to her chest and gazed out at the prairie kingdom spread before her. From their perch atop the 300-foot-tall butte that was part of the public land, she looked east at a herd of Angus cattle. The black storm clouds in the southwest had begun joining forces to build a dark anvil shape that spelled trouble with a capital T. The wind was picking up. Soon the clouds would swallow the sun that for the moment still blazed down on their heads.

"You hear about the hoo-hah in Keyhole over the Chivington Street name?" Fox asked.

"No. I haven't been reading newspapers lately."

"Well, you'd think the Indian wars were still being fought, the way they're going at it."

Faith looked down at the box with Trish's remains. "Life is so short. I don't understand people like Chivington. Why do you think he did it?"

"Same old. Power, fame, money." Fox used his head to gesture toward the storm. "We don't want to be here when that gets going. And Abby really doesn't want to be here."

The big dog was plastered to Fox's side.

"She hates thunder."

Faith nodded. "So I just keep remembering the scene from *The Big Lebowski*, where the two dopey guys try to scatter their friend's ashes off a cliff overlooking the sea and the wind blows the ashes back in their faces. Isn't that a stupid thing to be thinking about?"

"You don't have to scatter them over the edge. Maybe just kneel down and spread them on the ground. After all, you have to admit Trish will have a helluva view from on top here."

Faith smiled, then her chin began to quiver.

"You okay?"

Faith nodded and drew a deep breath. She crouched down next to a clump of blue grama grass, with its seed heads shaped like eyelashes swaying in the wind. She removed the lid of the box, looked inside and bowed her head. Fox took off his cowboy hat and held it in front of him. Faith removed the bag and shook out the ashes around the blue grama. Tears slid down her cheeks and dropped into the ash, forming tiny craters. Faith put the lid back on the box and turned away from Fox.

"My nose is running. Got a tissue?"

Fox placed a Kleenex in her hand without looking at her face. Suddenly the light dimmed and shadows vanished. Thunder rumbled in the distance.

"I hate to rush you, but I think we need to get off this butte."

Faith nodded and got up. She stood looking down at the pile of gray ash.

"I'm going to finish Trish's job at the airport."

"Do you think you're up to that?"

"I don't know, but I have to try." Faith looked out at the approaching clouds—huge, magnificent, terrifying. "Do you believe in God?"

Fox rubbed the back of his neck. "I believe in Dog."

"Right, right. Do you?"

The game warden sighed. "I pray the old way, the way I was taught by an Elder. But really, I believe in energy."

Faith looked at him, eyebrows raised.

"Energy. Cycles. Systems theory. Everything connected. You know, the butterfly flapping its wings in Michigan and a hurricane starts off the coast of Africa. In the end we're just atoms, molecules, little particles overlapping."

"Do you think my sister died accidentally?"

"Maybe. Probably."

"I just keep thinking about it. That she'd done it before, dug out dogs. That she was too smart to breathe in that much gas. That someone wanted to hurt her."

A gust of wind rocked them.

"Okay, take that as a sign and let's get going," Fox said.

They hiked down the butte, whipped by the gale. Jagged lightning struck against the horizon, then again closer. Thunder boomed. Rain began to pelt them, stinging their faces. Staying dry wasn't an option, so they kept moving.

They were nearly at the car when Faith grabbed Fox's arm.

"Look!"

She pointed back to the top of the butte where they'd

been standing. A thick black cloud nearly grazed the surface. And as they watched, lightning struck the top of the butte. The thunder was immediate and deafening. A very wet Abby cowered at her master's feet.

Faith looked at Fox.

"Was that a good omen or a bad one?" she yelled over the wind.

"Take your pick," he yelled back. He opened the car door and hustled her and Abby inside.

Faith walked in her front door, relieved to be alone with her grief. She went to the kitchen, determined to eat something, but found herself staring numbly at the contents of her refrigerator. The relief she had felt at being alone transformed into emptiness and despair. She shut the fridge and headed for her laptop, determined to escape into another world and time.

***

"Unsung Hero"
By Faith O'Neill
Chapter Nine

12:30 p.m. Sept. 12, 1864
Indian Country

"Ned, he's coming and he's got white children with him."

Soule stood next to the major, who was shaving while looking into a small round mirror hung from a tree branch. Wynkoop stopped in mid-stroke, holding the leather strap of the razor.

"You're sure? Black Kettle's bringing more children?"

"That old trapper Sikes just rode into camp all aflutter with the news."

"Amazing. First Left Hand brings back Laura Roper, and now this. What an incredible opportunity. Just wait 'til the governor hears. I don't know of any other officers who've made so much progress toward peace."

"Don't let it go to your head, sir. It's plenty big already."

"Careful there, if you're looking for a promotion from the likes of me." Wynkoop grabbed a small towel and wiped the soap off his face.

"And with half and half whiskers," Soule added.

"Remind me, why was it I asked for you in my command? I have clean forgotten." Ned put on his uniform jacket and dusted off a sleeve.

"Entertainment, sir. Pure entertainment."

"Ah yes. How could I have forgotten. Let's ride out to meet the chief, hmm?"

"I wouldn't miss it for the world."

Wynkoop, Soule, Cramer, Chief Left Hand and a handful of soldiers mounted up and headed out of camp at a trot. The sky overhead was a brilliant blue decorated with puffy white clouds. Soule noticed the prairie grasses were beginning to shift colors to soft mauves and purples. A far cry from the brilliant copper and orange hues of autumn maples back in Maine. Then again, Soule thought the more subtle seasonal change was moving in its own fashion.

About two miles out of the camp, Soule spotted ten

ponies and riders coming toward them through the grass. As the group got closer, Silas could see that three of the Indians had a child with them.

Black Kettle himself was in the group and sitting in front of him on a thin-looking paint was a small girl, maybe three or four. Sunburn had reddened the child's face and arms, and dirt smudged her green gingham dress. Ned rode up to Black Kettle's horse and the child immediately opened her arms. Ned reached over and swung the girl onto his own horse. The child wrapped her arms around Ned's neck.

"What's your name little one?"

The child had buried her face in Ned's jacket and did not answer. Soule caught Ned's eyes and shrugged. Silas turned toward another Indian with a red-headed boy.

"Hello, son. We've come to take you back to your family. My name is Silas. Who are you?"

The boy's dull brown eyes locked on Silas. "I'm Danny. Danny Marble, sir."

"Pleased to make your acquaintance, Danny."

Tears began rolling down the child's face.

"My mama is gonna whip me something fierce. She told me not to go down by the river alone and I did it anyway."

Silas fished in his pocket for a handkerchief that wasn't beyond using and handed it to the boy. "Somehow I don't think your mama is gonna be whipping you for a very long time, son. She's going to be so happy to have you home she'll forget all about a whupping."

"You think?"

"Darn tootin."

Ned broke in. "Let's get these children back to the camp."

They began escorting the Indians and the children back and Joe Cramer sidled his horse up to Silas.

"Guess what that one told me," he said in a low voice muffled by the jingle of the horse bridles.

Silas turned his head to get a look at the other boy in the group. Lots of thick black hair and freckles.

"Says his name is Ambrose Archer."

Soule waited. There had to be more to it than that.

"Says he'd just as lief stay with the Indians as not."

Silas looked at Joe. He couldn't think of anything to say so he said nothing. For his part, Cramer kept his thoughts to himself for the rest of the ride back to camp.

"So what do you think?" Ned peered at Silas over the top of the letter.

"Read me the part about the council with Black Kettle again, where you say you told the Indians you weren't authorized to talk peace," Soule said.

Ned cleared his throat.

"'I told them I was not authorized to conclude terms of peace with them, but if they acceded to my proposition I would take what chiefs they might choose to select to the Governor of Colorado Territory, state the circumstances to him, and that I believed it would result in what it was their desire to accomplish, 'peace with their white brothers.'"

"Impressive. Don't see how the governor can avoid giving you a medal."

"Then it's done." Wynkoop picked up the last page of the letter to his Excellency John Evans, governor of

Colorado Territory, and signed it with a flourish. He blew on his signature to dry the ink.

"Now all that's left is to get this group up to Denver. You know, I don't recall any of the chiefs referring to the governor's offer, do you?" Ned said, folding his letter.

"Left Hand mentioned it to me last night. He said when the tribes heard the governor's directive for peaceful Indians to report in last summer, he and Black Kettle decided this was the moment to sue for peace."

"How are the children?"

"Laura is looking after the little ones. I think that's a good thing for all four of them. Despite what Laura said about the little Eubanks girl, she greeted her with open arms and not a speck of accusation."

"Good. That should help on the trip. Did the horehound candy suffice?"

"Ambrose damn near made himself sick on it."

Ned smiled.

Silas picked up the letter to the governor. "Just think of it. We ride into town with four rescued children and several Indian chiefs. Should be quite the spectacle."

"Agreed. But my mind is more on the trip up there. I worry about some of the men."

Silas put the letter down and stared at his friend.

"Ned, you are the best officer I have ever served under. I do believe the men would follow you to hell and back."

Wynkoop sighed and stroked his mustache.

"Let's hope that won't be necessary."

14

Sunlight glinted off the light plane on its descent, making Faith squint and turn back toward Open Space Director Stan Rodgers.

"What did you say your deadline was?"

"City Council gave us until mid-August. Any animals left will be poisoned," Rodgers said.

Faith did the math. "That's less than six weeks."

"That's why I offered to meet with you on a Saturday," Rodgers countered.

She had called Rodgers Friday afternoon on her return from the Buttes and was surprised when he asked if she'd meet him the next day, Saturday, at the airport. Now Rodgers and airport manager Herbert Manson walked along the runway with Faith to give her a chance to scout the prairie dog town.

"Trish planned on flushing first, then trapping the holdouts," Rodgers said. "She said the flushing would go fast."

That method might have gone fast for Trish, but not for me, Faith thought, but kept her mouth shut. Faith had accompanied Trish on a flush or two, but she was no expert. Trish, for her part, could run a flushing operation single-handedly—and sometimes preferred doing so over working with a newbie. Faith had visited her a couple times when Trish was running solo. Trish used one hand to kink a garden hose so that soapy froth flowed down into a burrow. Meanwhile, Trish kept the other hand and forearm flat and still in the entrance of the burrow, waiting for a dog to surface. Faith knew if you didn't kink the hose properly, you could flood the burrow with water and drown the prairie dogs. But you had to let out enough water pressure to get good soap suds shooting down the hole. Eventually the bubbles would begin to surface and cover your arm. The trick was to wait until the prairie dog walked onto your hand with its four tiny feet–"Fairy feet" Trish called them. If there was a lot of foam, you couldn't even see the animal–only feel it. If you tried to grab too soon, the critter would back abruptly into the burrow. Faith had lost a couple that way, although Trish got them later. Trish always managed to wait for the perfect moment, then scoop the animal up by its belly and plop the dog in its own hay-filled kennel sitting on end next to her.

Trapping was another matter, slower and less dramatic. It called for more endurance than flair, and Faith was good at that. The airport site was bigger than any she'd done before. She figured she'd be running at least a hundred traps at once. The key was to get the traps in position soon, lock their doors open and put down bait for at least a week or two. That way, by the time the traps were set, the dogs were used to going in and out of them.

Walking along the runway with Rodgers, Faith tried to

get a sense of population density. Ahead of them a prairie dog was crouched atop its burrow, yipping repeatedly to warn its coterie mates of the approaching humans. With each warning call, the dog's black-tipped tail jerked forward, like a wind-up toy. Although the call sounded a bit like a regular dog's yip, prairie dogs bore no relation to canines. They got their name from the French term "*petit chien*" or little dog, because early explorers thought their calls sounded like barking. Actually, prairie dogs were rodents and cousins of squirrels. Trish had often joked that if she could just teach them to climb trees, everyone's troubles would be solved. And Trish's troubles? Faith watched the yipping dog. Perhaps the more she could step into Trish's life, the better the chances Faith could understand her death. Suddenly the animal disappeared into the hole, leaving silence behind. A section of taller grass behind the burrow marked the territorial boundary line for this coterie; neighboring prairie dogs would see this as a no-trespassing sign.

"How many acres?" Faith asked.

"The critical areas are right along and between the runways," said airport manager Manson. "We figure about thirty to forty acres."

"And how much are you setting aside in the back? For the relocation site?"

Stan Rodgers responded, "About eighteen."

Not good. That meant they'd be trying to squeeze dogs into about half the space they had now. But better than nothing.

"Let's head to the office and get something to drink." Herbert Manson waved his hand toward the small airport building to the north and the three of them moved in that direction. They passed a couple rows of parked Cessnas and Pipers, some small and older, others newer and practically shouting money.

"Howdy, madam mayor."

A figure clad in navy blue overalls turned at the open door of a shiny white plane.

"Hey there, Herb."

Faith recognized Violet Brady, Keyhole mayor and apparently aviator as well. The woman wiped her hands on a faded red rag as she approached the group.

"You must be Trish's sister. Sorry for your loss." Violet Brady stuck out her hand.

Faith nodded and tried not to wince at the woman's grip.

"Glad to have you aboard." The mayor swiped at a strand of salt and pepper hair on her forehead. "We've got some pilots hot to trot to get those prairie dogs off the runway. Lots of near accidents 'cause folks don't wanna squash the cute little devils. People are talking about taking their business to another airport. When do you plan to start?"

Violet Brady's flinty gray eyes locked onto Faith's.

"As soon as I can."

"Good. Glad to hear it. Well, I have a flight to make."

Brady turned her back on the group and strode away, a woman with more important things to do.

John Fox spread the plans out over the layer of papers on his desk in his little home office. Hissyfit immediately jumped on top of the neat blue lines. Damn. That meant he'd have to pull out the bleach. Then he wondered if the lines would bleed. Why did cats feel the need to plant their butts on top of whatever you were reading?

"Off." He pushed the black feline onto the floor. She walked off, flicking the tip of her tail. "Right. Take it to kitty court."

Borsich's planned development spread out in front of him. Another mega store taking the place of a prairie dog town nestled beneath hundred-year-old cottonwoods. The battle over the new store was still going strong, with citizens lined up to speak at city meetings dragging long into the night. Fox had witnessed some of it by accident. He'd shown up in uniform one night to see what the city council would do with a proposed wildlife management plan for the city's open space. Fox had taken part in some advisory meetings for the plan, while aware that such "stakeholder" meetings were mainly for show. Stan Rodgers already knew what he wanted, but it was politically correct to invite stakeholders in for cheap cookies and hours of nearly meaningless roundtable talks. At the council meeting, Fox picked a seat near the back door for a quick escape. Instead he became fascinated by the Borsmart drama. Even though the issue was technically before the city's planning and zoning committee, opponents of the development brought their beef to the city council. Their impassioned comments lasted so long that the wildlife plan got bumped to another day.

Fox thought about the prairie dogs that Borsmart had poisoned at the earlier store site, and the ones in jeopardy at the new proposed location. It actually wasn't so strange that prairie dogs lived on both sites. In fact, Fox had learned of the "ring effect" that explained why prairie dogs seemed to occupy almost every vacant lot up for development along the Front Range. For about a hundred years, farmers and ranchers waged war against what they saw as pests—usually with poison pellets down prairie dog burrows. But on the outskirts of Denver, Keyhole and other Front Range cities, farmers stopped farming and instead waited for land prices to rise. In the interim, prairie dogs spread the word—look at all that disturbed land just begging to be colonized! Or perhaps, re-colonized. So the prairie dog population boomed on former "ag" land slated for development.

Fox tried to focus on the blueprints again, and instead remembered Trish's bloody mouth. God. It had to have been an accident.

He shook off the memory and wandered to the kitchen for the bleach. He pulled on yellow rubber gloves, poured a capful into a plastic bowl and added an equal amount of water. He found a clean rag, dipped the cloth in the fifty-fifty solution and squeezed it out. How would a blueprint react to this?

Back in his home office he lightly dabbed the blueprint where Hissyfit had landed. The lines began to smear and Fox stopped. As he studied the damage, he caught something he should have noticed from the start. The footprint of this store required removing the mature cottonwoods he'd seen on his visit with Borsich. Fox thought of the spotted eagle that had flown over him. Wasn't that area a winter roosting site for balds? The eagles were no longer on the endangered species list, but didn't the town's proposed wildlife management plan require the city to protect sites like this?

Fox pushed the power button on his computer to look up

the plan. In the meantime, he decided to take a break. He needed to get outside, to move. Minutes later, he jogged down the tree-lined streets in his gym shorts and T-shirt, a bandana around his head.

"Spirit of the East, South, West and North," he prayed as he ran. "Thank you for this day…"

15

"...winter roosting habitat for bald eagles should be preserved to the extent possible, in cooperation between the developer and the City of Keyhole..."

Fox sighed and absentmindedly petted Bodhi, who cuddled on his lap while he sat before his computer and read through the draft wildlife management plan. This was truly one of the bennies of his job, occasionally working from home amid his critters. He knew his cats by the feel of their fur. Poor Abby, the lone dog in a house with three cats.

The plan was just that, words on a page without official approval. Even if the Keyhole City Council signed off on the plan, compliance would be essentially voluntary, up to the goodwill and PR sensitivity of the developer. Despite the good intentions of the Endangered Species Act, the law only protected the species itself, not the habitat. Sure, we'll protect those bald eagles but not the trees they need to rest in, or the prairie dog towns where they feed during the winter. Typical old world culture, thinking you can chop things up into small pieces instead of seeing the whole

127

picture.

Still, the words in the plan provided some ammunition, a little bit of leverage for those who wanted to use it. Trish would have been one of those people, looking for any toehold to stop the development through public pressure, or force Borsich to pay for prairie dog relocation. Of course, that also meant finding a relocation site to take the prairie dogs, not an easy task these days.

Fox picked up the phone and dialed Borsich's cell number.

"Borsich."

Fox could barely hear the man's voice over the roar of big engines. "Yes sir, this is John Fox, from DOW," Fox said loudly. "We met a few days ago at your Keyhole site, on Wednesday."

"Of course. What can I do for you?"

"Well, sir…" Fox held the phone away from his ear as the engines revved even louder.

"Sorry about the noise. I'm at one of my construction sites. I'm getting into my car. There." A car door slammed and the noise level dropped a few decibels.

Fox took a breath. "Did Trish O'Neill ever talk to you directly about prairie dog relocation?"

"Actually I asked her to give me an estimate. Ridiculous. The price was something like two hundred dollars per prairie dog. She must have thought I was an idiot."

Fox paused. He knew Trish wasn't cheap. He also knew that the relocation process was extremely labor intensive and involved. A local builder had shown him one of Trish's invoices from a relocation job. She rented a water trailer to pump soap suds into burrows. She paid someone to use a

Bobcat, a tiny backhoe, to dig artificial burrows, and someone else to construct wooden boxes that served as temporary underground dens for the animals. The black polyethylene pipe that led from the boxes up to ground level wasn't cheap either. Still, he was more interested in the fact that Borsich hadn't mentioned this conversation the first time they had spoken.

"So what did you tell her?"

"I blew her off. That's when she started her smear campaign."

"What do you mean?"

"The flyers were up all over town. I can't believe you never saw them."

Fox thought. "You mean the 'Save a prairie dog—shoot a Borsmart developer' thing? How do you know that was Trish?"

"Who else?"

"She wasn't the only one out there on the issue."

"Well, she sure was the nuttiest," Borsich responded. "I was starting to think I'd need to hire a bodyguard or something."

"Why didn't you tell me about this before?"

"Didn't think it was important now that she's dead."

"You sound like you're happy about that."

"That she's dead? Damn right I am. People like that stand in the way of progress and our way of life. I'm trying to serve my customers, people who can't afford to pay the markups of other stores and appreciate the fact that I provide them with the basics for less cost."

"So what changed your mind about perhaps doing a relocation at the Keyhole site?"

Borsich laughed.

"Capitalism and competition, my boy, it's a wonderful thing," Borsich said. "Somebody else jumped into O'Neill's ring and does the job a helluva lot cheaper."

That was news to Fox.

"Who would that be?"

"Some outfit called Prairie Answers or something. Oh yeah, Prairie Solutions. Actually run by wildlife biologists. They really seem to know what they're doing."

"What's the name of the people in charge?"

"Let me think. Whittman? No, Whiteman. Some guy and his wife."

Fox groaned.

"What did you say?"

"Nothing. Thanks for your time, Mr. Borsich."

Lunch beckoned. Fox picked up Faith's manuscript to read while he ate a sandwich.

***

"Unsung Hero"
By Faith O'Neill
Chapter 10

Midday, Sept. 19, 1864
En route to Denver City

"My butt is sore just watching them," Silas Soule said, shifting in his saddle. He reined in Delilah and glanced over at the jouncing buckboard in which the Indian chiefs sat on the wooden floor, presumably feeling every rock and rut in the crude road that would eventually bring them more than 150 miles to Denver City. Soule questioned the decision to stick the chiefs in a wagon like bags of flour, but he acknowledged the citizens of Denver might get startled if the Indians rode proudly into town on their ponies. They were one day into the journey. The September sky stretched over their heads, a deeper blue than he'd ever seen in Maine—or even Kansas, for that matter. The temperature was almost balmy.

"They deserve every ache and pain," Joe Cramer responded. "Remember the Coberlys?"

"No one knows which Indians did that."

"Maybe this is all a trick. Keep us busy talking peace while their young braves are out raising hell."

"Could be, I suppose." Silas took off his hat and ran a hand over his head. "Still, if you're correct, these chiefs are pretty foolish, putting themselves completely at our mercy. I mean, would you do the same thing if you were in their shoes?"

Cramer cocked an eyebrow and nodded an acknowledgment that such a thing would be damned unlikely. Many of the men in fact seemed at a loss regarding what to make of their strange traveling companions, but the talk had changed from possible mutiny to hopes of glory once they reached Denver City. After all, there were ladies to be wooed and toasts to be made before they had to ride back to Fort Lyon. Surely they would be the talk of the town, the brave men who brought in the major chiefs for peace talks.

All the main chiefs, that is, except for Left Hand. The other chiefs said he was too ill to make the trip.

"Have you heard anything from Hersa?"

Silas replaced his hat. "Not a word. Well, I barely

131

knew her, now did I."

They rode in silent companionship for a few minutes until Cramer asked, "So do you think we'll be in for a promotion when this is done?"

"It's Ned that deserves the promotion for seizing the opportunity," Silas said. "I don't know that I would have done the same."

"True, but our necks were on the line as much as his."

"Granted."

Ahead of them Wynkoop gave a signal for the caravan to stop for the midday break.

"So the major is likely to be a lieutenant colonel soon, you reckon?"

"Seems likely. Have you heard of any other army officer achieving a similar accomplishment?"

Soule and Cramer went over to where Wynkoop sat in a camp chair, part of a circle of such seats. The chiefs occupied some of the chairs, along with the rest of the cavalry officers.

"I know Ned wants to treat them like guests, but don't you think everyone would be happier if they ate by themselves?" Joe whispered to Silas.

Silas hushed him with a look. The camp cooks were handing out metal plates of hardtack crackers and salt pork, and pouring coffee. Although Silas and Joe had these same items in their pack, they were following Ned's orders to eat with the Indians and be served at the same time.

"You think this hardtack won't have worm castles?" Joe whispered again to Silas, who couldn't help but grin.

"Cross your fingers," he whispered back.

Ned took a small canvas bag of sugar from one of the

cooks and a small silver spoon. Carefully he scooped a spoonful into his cup. Silas noticed the chiefs watching this procedure closely. It was no secret that Indians loved sugar almost as much as whiskey. He wondered why Ned had not given the sugar to the Indians first like a proper host, then he decided Ned had opted to give them a small etiquette lesson on using silverware. When he was done, Wynkoop handed the sugar and the spoon to Black Kettle, who imitated Ned to a T. Black Kettle then passed the items to the next chief.

Maybe the chiefs didn't need a lesson, Silas thought. In the past few years, some Indians had traveled to Washington D.C. to meet the "Great White Father." Indeed, some had crossed the ocean to England where their visits were quite celebrated, going all the way back to Pocahontas.

"Coffee captain?"

Soule reached down for his mug and nearly touched a scorpion by his chair. He jerked back and his arm bumped the cook.

"Aaaagh!" Hot coffee soaked his shirt sleeve and his arm. "Jesus Christ on a crutch!" Silas leapt up, clutching his arm. He might as well have stuck his limb in the camp fire.

People gathered around him, all asking him if he were all right. He wanted to scream at them—certainly it was obvious he was not. Instead he chose what seemed to be the most courageous option, which was to clench his teeth and glue his lips together.

"Major Wynkoop?"

Through a haze of pain Silas heard the Indian translator John Smith address Ned. "Major, Black Kettle is recommending we remove the captain's shirt and pour cool water on the burn, sir. He says his tribe has often treated their children this way after they fall into fires, that they heal quicker."

"But sir, surely we should put butter on it," Cramer said.

Other officers began to chime in with advice. They fell silent when Silas began ripping off his blouse.

"For God's sake, do what Black Kettle says," Silas said through clenched teeth. "And hurry up."

Someone ran for a bucket of water and soon the water was running down Soule's arm. By this time the men forced him to sit back in the chair.

"Keep applying the water or take him to the creek and let it soak," Smith relayed from Black Kettle who stood by, speaking quietly. Soule got to his feet, waving off the men trying to help him. He made his way over to the tiny creek and put his arm in the water. Ned and Joe stayed nearby, as did Black Kettle and Smith.

After a few minutes, Black Kettle spoke softly to Smith.

"He says the captain should remove his arm from the water and dry it. He says he has a root with him to treat it, if the Captain approves."

Silas glanced at Ned, who shrugged. Silas sat upright, cradling his arm.

Black Kettle pulled out a deerskin pouch and reached inside. He crouched down and put the root on top of a rock. Taking a second stone, he mashed the root into a pulp.

"He says he'll need a cloth. I think he means a bandage," Smith said.

Ned dispatched a young officer who returned with a

roll of white gauze. Black Kettle gently applied the root pulp to the red section of Soule's arm, then wrapped the white gauze around the wound.

The Indian then placed a second piece of root in Silas's other hand.

"He says you should check the wound every day and reapply the mashed root for at least three days."

"What is it?" Silas asked.

Smith and Black Kettle conversed at length before Smith said, "It's from some kind of flowering plant. From his description and my memory of my mother's garden, it sounds like a four-o'clock, maybe."

Ned crouched next to Silas. "How are you feeling?"

"Much better. Hardly burns at all at the moment." Silas stood up somewhat shakily and looked at Black Kettle. "Thank you."

Smith translated, but Silas could tell Black Kettle didn't need the help. The Indian spoke to Smith, who smiled.

"What did he say?" Silas asked.

"He said, 'Better to thank the four-o'clock.'"

16

Faith wandered around Trish's living room. She had brought Polly with her, and now the plump prairie dog slept tucked into the crook of one arm. The sliding glass door stood open and the wind tossed ponderosa pine needles in the midday sun. There were traps to load in the back of Trish's van, preparations to make. And yet here she was walking in circles, ineffective and stupid and lost. The pressure behind her eyes signaled a budding headache. Faith gently put the prairie dog down on the couch and wondered how anyone could consider such a clean, social animal to be vermin. Not the Japanese. They happily forked over hundreds of dollars for a small, loving pet easy to care for in a tiny apartment. Meanwhile, the law forbade keeping prairie dogs as pets in the United States, but allowed killing them, or trapping them to ship off to foreign countries. In Colorado, the Division of Wildlife confiscated pet prairie dogs and promptly killed them. Trish didn't talk about her unusual pet to anyone beyond her circle. It was an accident anyway, a matter of fate.

Shaking off the memory of Polly's birth in captivity, Faith headed for the bathroom to search for aspirin or the like. As always, she paused when she entered to admire the glass-walled shower, the stone floor, the black marble counter. The woman looking back from the mirror needed a serious makeover. Faith sighed and opened a drawer, rummaging through the hair bands and spare change and combs. She moved to the next drawer. Razor blades and an old can of shaving cream and eye shadow. She moved to a free-standing cabinet made of wicker and looked inside. There. She picked up the bottle of aspirin and headed toward the door. A memory stopped her.

Faith turned back to the counter and set down the aspirin bottle. She opened the drawer holding the shaving cream and pulled out the can. Faith shook the can and something rattled inside. Holding the container in one hand, she put her other hand on the bottom rim and twisted. The bottom of the can came off, revealing the cavity inside. A roll of old-fashioned 35 mm film still in its metal canister fell into her palm.

Faith examined the roll of Kodak Kodachrome. No tongue of brown film sticking out. Why would Trish stash a roll of exposed film? And why in the one place that only Faith was likely to look? Faith had given the clever can to Trish on some Christmas long ago and far away. "For all your secret stuff," Faith had written on the tag. It was a longstanding joke between them, but in truth Trish's secretive nature had always been a sore spot for Faith.

That aside, the film seemed like an anachronism for Trish, the gadget-of-the-moment girl. Trish rushed to the store for a digital camera as soon as they hit the shelves, the better to send photographs by email. Faith had warned her not to send anything Faith's way. Her computer was too old and slow to digest hefty photo attachments.

Faith stuck the film in the pocket of her jeans. She tucked Polly back in her small kennel and grabbed the laptop in case she had some down time for editing. Traps to load and promises to keep.

***

"Unsung Hero"
By Faith O'Neill
Chapter 11

Sept. 23, 1864
Plum Creek, Five Days Out From Denver City

"He says it's going to snow."

John Smith kept the reins in his hands but lifted his chin toward the dark clouds bearing down on the caravan. Then he cocked his head toward Black Kettle huddled in the wagon with the other chiefs. "I'd reckon he's probably right."

Silas turned to Ned, whose horse was keeping pace with his.

"Jesus, Mary and Joseph. Last time I saw it snow this time of year, it was a damned blizzard," Soule said. "Doesn't seem to last long, goes right back to fall, but it's a miserable curse in the meantime."

"We can't make them ride in the wagon out in the open," Ned said. "We've got to get them to Denver in one piece."

Silas glanced at the buckboards, one full of Indians huddled deep in their blankets, the other where the children had been tucked under cavalry issue blankets next to the caravan food stores. Laura had taken on the role of mother to the two boys and to the little girl who had almost cost Laura her life. Belle's small arms rarely left their place around Laura's neck.

"Granted. Maybe it will blow over." Silas turned up his collar. "Damned sure getting colder, though."

"We're close to the old Coberly place. I think we should aim for that, hunker down if we need to."

The men fell silent, lulled by the sound of mules and harnesses and wagon creaks and the soft thud of horse hooves. Despite the early afternoon hour, the light dimmed by the minute and a cold wind gathered strength. Their route followed a small creek and the old cottonwoods rustled, their fading green leaves still attached and apparently determined to hold on to summer.

Thinking of summer, Silas found his image of Hersa had faded. He couldn't quite picture the color of her eyes, but he smiled remembering her fury at finding herself adrift in a sea of hay and cow dung. A blast of early winter smacked him in the face and wiped the smile away. He pulled up his bandana around his nose and mouth. The tiniest of snowflakes began drifting down on Delilah's sorrel mane, dim now but shiny as a copper penny in the bright sun. Funny, but he'd always had a soft spot for a redhead. Hersa, he recalled, had hair black as night. Night that shimmered and promised the mysterious feel of silk.

A loud crack and Silas was reaching for his firearm and reining his horse around searching for the gunman.

Instead he saw the buckboard carrying the Indians keeled over sideways and the men inside thrown against each other. The mules leading the wagon snorted and jostled one another, their ears back and their eyes rolling in fear.

"Damn it all!" The soldier driving the buckboard leaped off the crippled vehicle and stormed over to the wheel responsible. Silas and Ned stood beside him and all three saw the deep rut that had hidden in the failing light and falling snow. The weight of the wagon dropping in one corner had shattered the axle and broken the wooden wheel. Silas and Ned exchanged a look. Both men knew there were spare wheels, but the axle was another matter entirely.

As they stood there, tiny gentle flakes gave way to a crazed swirling dance of white. In seconds, a fine layer of snow began coating everything in sight, from mules to mustaches.

"We'll bivouac near the creek," Ned yelled into the wind to the soldiers who had congregated around him. "Cover for the civilians first, then tend to the mules and yourselves."

For the next hour the men struggled with tarps and wagons and nervous beasts. The wind tried to rip canvas from their hands and turn the cloth into flapping sails. The Indians worked with the whites to create a shelter by turning the remaining buckboard on its side, putting its back to a large cottonwood to cut the prevailing wind. The tarps they roped to the wagon's "roof" and staked to the ground a few feet in front of the structure, allowing room on the ground for a small fire.

Silas gathered the children and placed them inside at

one corner of the tilted wagon. The girl Belle wailed and shook as she clung to Laura. Wind whistled through the cracks in the wood of the wagon bottom, as if competing with the crying child.

Ned shouldered his way into the crude shelter and grabbed Silas's shoulder. "Stay with them," he said into the captain's ear. "We'll deal with the rest."

Soule and Smith—who had chosen to stay with the chiefs—cleared away a coating of snow and built a fire on the sandy soil, using their bodies to shield the small flames from gusts of wind until a decent blaze took hold. Despite the howling gale, the fire began to cast a spell of calm on the strange group. Belle's cries shifted from shrill to fretful as the flames took hold. Still, the children shivered with cold and anxiety. Silas took off his coat and draped it over the four waifs, who seemed to have turned into one big lump. He dug into his pack and found some strips of dried meat. Soule divided the pieces and handed one to each of the children, including Belle, who quickly began gnawing on the beef. Then Soule handed the rest to Smith to pass out to the chiefs.

"And so, the Shoshone people say that long ago, the chief of the animals, Black Bear, went out searching for food and found an anthill with many ants to eat."

Silas's head jerked up toward the speaker who sat among the chiefs. He didn't know this man, but the chief's English was as good as Left Hand's. He was a handsome man, not that much older than Soule himself. "Who is that," he mouthed to Smith, who replied "Neva. Kin to Left Hand. Left Hand's sister was married to a white man, a trapper. Taught 'em the lingo."

"Black bear was very hungry and so, she began to eat," Neva continued, and Smith began translating the story for the chiefs who didn't speak English. Silas noticed the children's attention was now riveted on the Indian, even Belle—who now sat quietly with wide eyes. "But then Grizzly Bear appeared. 'I will dig here,' Grizzly Bear told Black Bear. Black Bear said, 'I was here first. This food is mine, but there is enough for both of us to share.' Grizzly growled and said, 'I'll take what I want. Leave or fight me.' Black Bear shook her head. 'No. I need food also. I will share this food, but I will not give it all to you.' Grizzly Bear was angry. 'Then I will fight you,' he said. And Black Bear said, 'So be it. But if I win, then you will leave this place forever.' Grizzly Bear agreed."

Silas glanced toward the children. Belle was sucking her thumb and had relaxed her grip on Laura. Ambrose and Danny leaned toward Neva, all their attention focused on the storyteller sitting cross-legged at the other end of the shelter. Silas allowed himself to relax a little and began rolling a cigarette.

"Black Bear and Grizzly Bear fought very hard," Neva continued. "Grizzly Bear was much larger, but Black Bear was brave. Every time Grizzly Bear knocked her down, she got back up and kept fighting. Finally Grizzly Bear was too wounded and gave up."

Silas twisted off the ends of his smoke, struck a match and lit up. For a moment he was sitting on his grandfather's lap, listening to stories of the sea, feeling the swells, hearing the sails slap in the fierce wind and wondering how the crew would survive Poseidon's fury. The tip of the cigarette glowed orange as he inhaled.

Neva had stopped talking, but no one spoke. Finally, Ambrose said, "What happened then?"

Silas thought he detected a ghost of a smile on Neva's

face, the contentment of a teller of tales who knows his listeners have taken his bait and are now hooked on the line. The Indian shifted slightly before resuming the tale.

"Black Bear looked at her opponent and said, 'You must leave now, and never come back.' And so, Grizzly Bear began to climb the mountain slowly, very slowly, because he was hurt and in pain. And as he climbed, it began to snow, first one flake, then a few flakes, then many, many flakes of snow, until Grizzly Bear was covered up and looked all white."

Silas glanced at the children and was surprised to see Belle fast asleep, her head on Laura's shoulder and a bit of drool coming out of her mouth. The child looked more at peace than he had ever seen her.

"Still Grizzly Bear climbed higher and higher and higher. Finally he came to the very top of the mountain. In that moment Grizzly Bear gathered all the strength he had left and jumped into the sky. As he jumped, bits of snow fell off him and turned into stars. And Grizzly Bear himself turned into stars. The next night, the animals gathered in a council. Black Bear told them Grizzly Bear did one last good thing for the people by leaving a sky trail for them when they left this earth. That sky trail is what some call the Milky Way. And so it was."

Again Neva fell silent. Silas saw Ambrose lean forward. "But where is Grizzly Bear? Can I see him?"

"Yes, Grizzly Bear can still be seen in his place in the sky. White people call him 'the Big Dipper.'"

"Golly. But I think Black Bear was mean to make him climb up the mountain like that. Don't you think so?"

Silas studied Neva's face, wondering how the man would respond to the child's question.

"Ah. But Black Bear gave him a choice. Do you

143

remember?"

"Sure. She told him that if she had to fight him and he lost, he'd have to leave." The boy took his hands out of his pockets and held them out toward the small fire.

"She gave him a choice even before that, at the beginning. When they first met. Do you remember?"

Neva paused and Silas realized the man again reminded him of his grandfather, who often answered questions with questions of his own.

Ambrose frowned and his brow wrinkled.

"I know! She told him she'd share the food, but that he couldn't have it all. Is that it?"

"That's it," Neva said.

In the silence that followed, Silas realized the wind had slacked and no longer tried to rip the tarps from the wagon. It seemed the storm was passing as quickly as it had arrived. Strange, but he wished the winds would howl again and allow them to stay huddled by this little fire for a while longer, odd company and all. Somehow he knew this moment was unlikely to be repeated.

17

Faith knelt and positioned the forty-first trap about four feet from the top of the burrow. She wiggled it back and forth, roughing up the dirt under the wire bottom and disguising the mesh. Faith slid up two metal rings to allow the door of the cage to swing out and up. A ten-inch-long chain hung from the outside of the door, with a metal fastener at the loose end. She snapped the fastener onto the top of the trap, effectively locking the contraption open.

Slowly Faith got to her feet, picked up the small yellow plastic bucket and stood there, stretching her back as the sun slid behind Long's Peak. It was nearly 8:30 p.m. and the end of a very long, very hot summer day. She'd been on the move for twelve hours, since the meeting at the airport that morning. Trish could go 16 or even 18 hours a day on raw energy. Faith, on the other hand, enjoyed nine hours of sleep when she could get it, and at least two hours of down time before bedtime.

"Okay," she said aloud. "Stop feeling sorry for yourself. Get done and get out of here."

For the forty-first time since she'd started laying traps at

2:30 that afternoon, she took a handful of Sweet Feed out of the bucket and dribbled a Hansel-and-Gretel trail from the lip of the burrow, down the mound, and then into the trap. Now on her belly, she stretched to plop another handful of molasses-drenched grain in the very back of the trap, behind the trigger plate.

Faith knew acclimation was the trick to successful trapping. Prairie dogs are cautious—the key to a long life in prairie dog terms. Each trap sat several feet from the burrow's mounded entrance, allowing the animal to peek out and study the strange object below. Oh, and that heavenly sweet grain! Bite by bite, the prairie dog would eat its way closer to, and eventually into, the trap. She could place a tiny paw on the locked trigger plate and nothing would happen. But then one day, the trigger would be set and the dog would find herself trapped. She would then be transferred to a hay-filled kennel with some of her family members for company. Keeping families together was crucial for the next step—relocating the animals and having them remain in their new location.

"How's it going?"

Faith jerked and her arm—still partly inside the trap—knocked the lightweight structure on its side as she craned her neck.

"Sorry about that," said Open Space Director Stan Rodgers, crouching down to help her right the trap.

Faith scrambled to her knees. "I've got it," she said, working the mesh of the trap back over top of the grain bait.

As she got to her feet, Rodgers took her hand and helped her up. Heat surged into her face and she pulled her hand away, stunned by the electric pulse jolting her palm.

Only now she really noticed the man's attractive charm and crooked smile. She slapped at the dust on her grubby shirt and jeans, even as she registered the wedding ring on his hand and mentally shrugged. So it didn't matter that she was a lost cause on the fashion front, now did it?

"You know, if I didn't know you and Trish were sisters, I never would have guessed."

Faith sucked in some hot air to counter the punch to her gut.

"Sorry. That was a dumb thing to say."

"It's okay. I've heard it all my life. It's just that I..." Faith turned toward Long's Peak, where a pink-orange-purple glow backlighting the mountain top announced the sun had truly set. "I just miss her, I guess."

"Look, I'm really grateful for you taking this on at a tough time."

"Actually it's good therapy." Faith stole a look at the man near her. God, he practically sparkled in a white short-sleeved shirt over wide shoulders. The bottom half was just as good in tight-fitting jeans.

"I bet you haven't eaten today, have you? Why don't we grab something over at O'Shea's? My treat. To thank you for saving my butt on this project."

Faith's mouth watered at the thought of the Saturday night prime rib special at the best pub in town.

Even when she was at her poorest, she would occasionally bow to her carnivore desires and splurge on a meal there, comforted by the old red brick walls and the hum of happy people.

Then she remembered Trish, and how Faith recently had promised herself to reduce her meat intake in her sister's memory.

"Thanks, but I'm sure you've got a family to go home to and I'm exhausted."

"My wife's at a church function. I'll call her on her cell and let her know what's up. Besides, you've got to eat, don't you?"

Faith remembered the unfinished book waiting for her attention, her determination to get a few pages edited over a peanut butter sandwich before she collapsed into bed.

But in the end, she felt too tired to argue and too weak to resist.

***

"Unsung Hero"
By Faith O'Neill
Chapter 12

September 26, 1864
Governor's Residence
Denver City, Colorado Territory

"Tell Major Wynkoop I'm too ill to entertain visitors."

"Yes Governor."

The aide left the room. The governor's companion leaned forward in his red velvet chair.

"I told you he was a loose cannon. Sees himself as some historic peacemaker, no doubt."

The governor ran his fingers through the white hair that grew down to the top of his collar.

"Blasted awful timing, if you ask me. I need a drink."

The elder man stalked to the sideboard and poured

imported Irish whiskey into a crystal shot glass. He downed the alcohol in one gulp and refilled the glass. He glanced up at his guest. "Sure you won't join me?"

The big man sat back in the red brocade chair and waved off the offer.

"It will be quite a stir when the rest of the caravan gets here," the seated man said, fingering the shiny brass buttons on the coat of his dark blue uniform. "Bad enough he shows up with four children he's rescued, much less a wagon-full of Indian chiefs."

"At least he had the decency to ride ahead to see me before the circus arrives." The governor studied the amber liquid in his glass. "Do you know how much this whiskey cost me?" When the other man shrugged, the leader of the Colorado Territory continued, "Damn near three times what it was six months ago. Mercenary rum runners, that's what they are. And it's not just the whiskey. Flour. Sugar. Coffee. I tell you, I can't walk down the street without some irate citizen accosting me and giving me an earful about the cost of something. I don't know who I despise more—the damned Indians attacking the supply route or the goddamned traders taking advantage of the situation to rake in more profits."

The uniformed man nodded. "I'd say Wynkoop is a fool taken in by Indian schemers. You know the pattern. Winter approaches, Indians want to make 'peace.' "

The governor sighed and took another sip.

"How long before the Third is ready for action?"

"Three weeks. Four perhaps."

"Wouldn't I look the fool and a liar now, after all my reports to Washington about Indian depredations and the need to raise a regiment? You and I know this is all a sham, but you know Washington. They'll fall all over

149

themselves for this major and his peaceful chiefs."

"How quick they are to forget. Surely they heard the reports of the Hungate massacre?"

"Lincoln is too much thinking on the war and his own re-election." The governor sat down heavily in the chair opposite the army man. "Your own triumphs over the Rebs at Glorieta received scant attention in the eastern newspapers. The West is just a sideshow for them."

"Can't they see the advantages of Colorado statehood?" the colonel asked the governor. "Surely they realize that these Indian troubles can only discourage those who would settle this ungodly wilderness and turn it into a civilized, prosperous place."

At this the governor smiled. "Sounds as though you might be missing the pulpit a bit there, Colonel."

"I consider my men my congregation these days, sir."

"You've heard what they're calling your regiment."

The officer nodded grimly, unwilling to voice the slanderous nickname for his men, the 'Bloodless Third.'

"A decisive blow against the Indians would do much for your reputation and mine, don't you agree? Surely there are some Indian troublemakers ripe for the taking?"

The governor lifted his eyes from his shot glass and gazed at the military man before him. The other man met the politician's gaze. And nodded.

September 26, 1864
Two Days South of Denver City

In the fading light, Silas pushed past the tall coyote

willow stalks and nearly stumbled over the man sitting cross-legged on the ground. It was Neva.

"Are you all right?"

Neva got to his feet.

"Yes."

"I was just coming for some water." Silas gestured with his canteen.

"Yes."

Silas glanced at the rushing creek before them. The clear water ran shallow over the stones and sand. Tiny silver fish swam together against the current. A kingfisher flew low over the water, scolding the men loudly with his noisy rat-a-tat cry.

Silas worked his way a few yards upstream to a place where the water ran a bit deeper and to where he could position himself to keep the Indian in sight.

"It was a kind thing you did for the children during the storm the other day," he said, holding his canteen under the surface.

Neva nodded acknowledgement. Silas noticed that the red strips of cloth wrapping the man's long braids appeared wet. Perhaps he had been washing his hair in the frigid water. The braids had left damp spots on the Indian's white cotton shirt. Since the freak snowstorm, the weather had warmed to summer-like temperatures, making coats and blankets unnecessary.

"Do you have children?" Silas asked.

"Yes."

"Boys or girls?"

"Both. And you?"

"No. Although my mother keeps pressing me for a family."

"That is a mother's way."

Silas smiled. Neva smiled back.

"Does your mother also speak English?"

Neva did not answer. Silas wondered if he had offended him in some way.

"My mother is dead."

"I'm sorry."

"She was violated and scalped by three drunken white men who came across her. A child saw and ran for help but it was too late."

Silas stared at the Indian, who in turn gazed at the flowing water. Soule pulled the canteen from the creek. "What happened to the men?"

"Nothing."

Silas considered and rejected various replies, instead turning his eyes to the creek as well.

"The Dog Soldiers think we are fools to talk peace with white men."

Soule turned back to the Indian. The Dog Soldiers were younger braves who had a reputation of acting on their own.

"So why are you here?"

Neva turned toward him.

"The whites have killed most of the buffalo and left them to rot. Our hunting parties cannot find food and our children are sick and starving. My children are sick and starving."

Silas stood in the near darkness a few feet from this man, remembering the group of slaves he had accompanied northward in the Kansas darkness, remembering the woman who said her master had fathered all her children, then sold them off one by one. She had sworn she would find and free all her children someday, if it took the rest of her life. Silas had gladly followed his father's lead in the Underground Railroad. Amasa Soule had moved the family out to Kansas in hopes of joining those fighting to keep slavery out of that state.

But Indians weren't coloreds.

"The Dog Soldiers say the whites will lie to us and then kill us."

"What do you think?"

"I think I want my children to live. I want to live to see my children."

"Captain Wynkoop is a man of his word. If he says he will get you to Denver and home again safely, he will fulfill his promise."

Neva grunted and turned. He disappeared back through the willows before Silas could think of anything else to say.

18

Fox walked in his front door and dodged the cats who were overly interested in the brown paper bag in his arms. He stashed his Kung Pao chicken takeout in the cat-proof microwave, changed out of his uniform, grabbed Faith's manuscript and retrieved the food. His home phone rang as he was positioning himself in his favorite chair. Deciding it was a telemarketer, he let the call go to his answering machine and began spooning rice onto a plate.

"John. John, you there? C'mon John, I need you to be there."

The spoon froze in mid-air. Shit. The only time that voice made an attempt to reach out and touch someone was when there was bad news to deliver, or hard favors to ask, or both. For the briefest moment he considered not answering. Then he sighed and got up. Bad news never goes away, it just festers and gets worse unless you tackle things head on.

Fox stood at the phone and took one more breath before picking up the portable device.

"Hey there, Mar. I'm here. Good to hear from you," he lied.

"Johnny. Man, I am so glad I got a hold of you."

Cue the sobs, John thought uncharitably.

"I—I don't know what I'm gonna do. I just..." his half-sister's voice choked and ground to a halt. Fox began running down the list—boozy car accident? Bounced checks? Then the Indian side of him kicked in. Family was family, no matter what the self-help books said. He wondered if he'd ever find that middle ground of being loyal to family while staying loyal to himself. Then there was the leftover Catholic school guilt that said part of this was his fault for taking off to pursue his own life thirty years ago, and not being around when this woman needed him most.

"Arturo screwed me over, Johnny. He told me he loved me, you know, that he wanted to marry me."

Fox ran through a mental list, coming up short on any boyfriend named Arturo. And it sure didn't sound like a rez name. He found himself pacing around the living room, too antsy to sit back down. Rajul crouched in front of the arm chair, about to launch an assault on Fox's food waiting on the end table.

"Hey!"

"What? Are you yelling at me? Please John, don't yell."

Fox swatted at the cat and rescued his food, heading back toward the microwave where his supper could sit in safety.

"Sorry. One of the cats was trying to steal my dinner. Is it Ricky? Is Ricky okay?" Ricky, his eight-year-old nephew and only his favorite human on the planet.

"Of course Ricky's fine," Marlene said huffily before the sobs crept back. "It's not my fault, Johnny. We was smokin' some weed, good shit, and I was feeling good and he said I should try this new stuff, and I did and then like, I couldn't stop, you know? And he said if I helped him sell some he'd give me meth for free and I forgot to take my pills and all and now they busted me and the baby's due in a few weeks and—"

Fox closed his eyes and held the phone away from his ear for a second, letting the voice roll on in the distance. He put the phone back to his ear.

"…and they say I'll never see him again!"

He waited, but she seemed to have run out of steam.

"Arturo?"

"That asshole? No, no, Ricky!"

Fox paced to a side window and stood at the screen, listening to the wind blow through his neighbor's Chinese elm tree. "What about Aunt Rosie?" At the ripe age of seventy eight, Rosie was the main reason that Ricky was Fox's favorite human. She had stepped in to raise Ricky since he was born.

"I told you, she's in the hospital!"

Fox started pacing again. "What do you mean, she's in the hospital?"

"…so they said if there's nobody to take care of him, they're gonna put him in foster care or something and…"

"Marlene. Slow down. What's wrong with Aunt Rosie?"

He waited.

"They say she's got the lung cancer. From all those cigarettes."

Fox sat down hard.

"Where are you?" he demanded.

"County jail."

Not good, Fox thought. If the reservation cops had busted her, there would be more options. But she'd gotten caught off the rez.

"They're trying to make me talk and Arturo says his gang will kill me if I snitch. You gotta take him, Johnny. He's family. You gotta take him."

"Marlene, you know that's impossible. I work sixty, seventy hours a week. He needs someone around full time. He—"

Fox heard a strange woman's voice speaking in the background.

"They're making me get off the phone. The bus from Pine Ridge gets into Keyhole at three thirty tomorrow. This woman Sharon owed me so she got his ticket and packed his backpack and gave him a peanut butter sandwich so he'd have something to eat. Johnny, tell him I love him and—"

Fox was listening to a dial tone. He slammed the phone down and paced around his house cursing. Finally he sat down at the table to eat and grabbed Faith's manuscript. Anything to escape the complicated reality facing him.

***

"Unsung Hero"
By Faith O'Neill
Chapter 13

Sept. 28, 1864
Denver City

Delilah tossed her head before settling on a regal stance, as if aware she played a part in a historic moment. Up on a rooftop across the wide dirt street, a man fussed with a big camera on a stand and Silas wondered if he and Ned Wynkoop, astride his own horse next to Soule, would be in the photograph. Too small to be recognized from that distance, most likely. But the photographer was probably more interested in the caravan working its way down the street, especially the buckboard containing the Indian chiefs. Ned had arrived in town two days ahead of the group to inform the governor of the chiefs' visit, and word had spread. Now people lined the plank walkways and balconies of the wooden buildings, gawking at the spectacle. Children hung on to their mother's skirts, fascinated and afraid at the same time. Women stood arm-in-arm, as if to give each other courage.

"Fuckin' injuns! Kill 'em now! What're you waitin' for?"

The drunken man threw a bottle at the buckboard as a woman in blue-checked gingham clapped her hands over the ears of the little boy next to her. Ned looked over at Silas and cocked his head toward the man who still yelled in the street. Soule spurred his horse and trotted out to the man.

"Now sir, I wouldn't want you to get in the way of any of our army wagons and get yourself hurt."

The man looked up at the big red horse and the cavalry officer astride her. The heckler was young, maybe younger than Silas. He wore a tattered red bandana around his neck and carried the grimy look of a miner too long panning for gold that never appeared. He took a wobbly step backwards, then another. The horse moved forward. The man moved back.

"No sir, we definitely wouldn't want you to get hurt," Soule said, urging Delilah on and effectively herding the man back toward the saloon where he'd obviously been spending too much of his time.

As Silas reined his mare around to return to Wynkoop, there was Hersa standing on the plank walkway. She wore a maroon bonnet and held her mother's hand. Her mother stared fixedly at the wagonload of Indian chiefs, a scowl on her lips. Mrs. Coberly seemed much older than when he had seen her last.

Silas guided the horse to where they stood.

"Mrs. Coberly, Miss Coberly. I heard about your loss and I wanted to tell you how sorry I am—"

The older woman looked up at him, her eyes blazing. "How dare you even address me, when you have brought these savages here! Do me the kindness of not approaching my family again."

Silas turned toward Hersa, who had remained silent. He started to speak, but stopped when he saw a tiny shake of her head. She mouthed the word "Later" and his heart moved in his chest. Soule tipped his hat to the women and rode back to Wynkoop.

"Found her, did you?" Wynkoop said.

"So you knew she was here. When were you going to tell me?"

"You just arrived, remember? Besides, we're going to be busy enough the next few days."

The mules pulling the buckboard jostled past them. Neva stared over the side of the wagon directly at Silas as the vehicle rumbled by and the captain recalled their conversation by the creek. The two officers fell in behind the buckboard as rear guard for the town's controversial visitors. Behind them, a virtual wagon train of carriages and civilians on horseback followed the entourage,

Denver residents who had ridden out to meet the strange procession.

"I suppose we are giving them a stir," Ned said.

"I had to assign men to ride alongside the buckboard to keep the curiosity seekers back," Soule said. "I swear, one woman even threw an egg at the chiefs. Good thing she didn't have much of an arm. But the chiefs saw all right. Didn't bat an eye, far as I could tell."

"Any trouble the rest of the way up?" Ned Wynkoop asked.

"A broken buckboard. A snow storm. And one of the chiefs is feeling poorly, lots of trips to the bushes. Too much hardtack and too many worm holes, I suspect. We ran out of jerky."

"I talked to the manager over at Tremont House," Ned told Silas. "Had to use the authority of the U.S. Cavalry to persuade him to let the chiefs stay in their storeroom tonight. Tell the men to set it up as comfortable as possible for them. And let them get a little rest. We're meeting with the governor at Camp Weld at three this afternoon."

"Was the governor impressed when you told him the chiefs were coming?"

Ned laughed and adjusted the reins. His horse's ears flicked backwards.

"The governor was mighty ill when I got here, mighty ill. Had a miraculous recovery and arrived at my hotel the next morning," Wynkoop said. "Even then kept insisting the Indians were our problem, in our custody. And what would he do with the Third Regiment anyway if we made peace? I think he's afraid Washington will call him on the carpet for wanton spending."

"What is this Third Regiment?" Soule asked, shifting in his saddle. "Why haven't we heard of it?"

"Mostly drunks, thieves and miners who left their last dime with the folks who sold them shovels. Your friend is leading them up."

"Who?"

"The honorable Colonel Chivington."

"We wouldn't have won Glorieta without him," Silas observed.

"So you've said. You've also said that afterward when you became the man's assistant, you realized he was a glory hound."

"True."

"In any event," Ned continued, "I reminded the governor that I as a United States officer had brought these Indians 200 miles to meet with him in answer to his very own proclamation to peaceful Indians. That seemed to do the trick."

A young woman on the boardwalk gave a little wave. With a start, Silas realized it was Laura Roper, with two days to get cleaned up and find new clothes. Silas and Ned rode over to the former hostage. Silas now realized that Belle stood at Laura's side, holding onto her dress.

"Miss Roper." Silas doffed his hat. "I'm pleased to see you and Belle looking so well."

"Thank you. The women here have been most generous and kind. And everyone keeps asking me to tell my story. Of course, I tell them about the brave soldiers who brought me here."

Silas exchanged a quick glance with Ned, whose eyes twinkled. It wouldn't be the first time a girl had flirted with the two of them.

"We were just doing our jobs, Miss Roper. As we must

now. Please excuse us," Wynkoop said, touching his fingers to the brim of his hat.

The men kicked their horses to catch up with the buckboard. As they came closer, Silas saw bits of eggshell and yolk running down the back of the wagon, and a yellow stain on the white sleeve of Neva's shirt.

"Their aim is improving," he said.

***

Faith forked the last piece of prime rib and dipped it in the small cup of horseradish. The tender meat practically melted in her mouth and the horseradish added a pleasant tang. She leaned back against the padded booth of the pub and sighed.

"I had no idea I was so hungry," she said. "But then I haven't eaten much since…"

Her voice trailed off.

"In that case, I think dessert is in order. They've got a strawberry rhubarb cobbler special. And with ice cream, it's a killer."

Faith stared at Rodgers.

"What's wrong?" he asked.

"I think I need to go to the restroom."

Faith pushed through the crowd of men pursuing women and women pursuing men. The women smiled too much with lip-sticked mouths and finger-combed their hair away from their foreheads. Suddenly the noise and body heat seemed too much and Faith breathed in relief as she reached the back hallway leading to the bathroom. She was reaching for the doorknob when the back door of the restaurant opened and John Fox walked in. He wore a black T-shirt tucked into his jeans. It was the first time Faith had seen him in something other than a uniform. He was one of those men who actually looked sexier in civilian clothes, the better to see his muscles. Again Faith cringed at the picture of herself in dirt-streaked clothes and hair coming loose from the cloth band. However, the man stood ten feet away, and pretending she had not seen him was not an option.

"Hey there." Fox smiled and walked up to Faith. "You look like you've had a long day."

Faith tucked a strand of hair behind one ear and felt herself blush. What was wrong with her? She had spent the last few years determined to be happy without a man in her life and suddenly she was swooning over every male in sight. Actually, Faith admitted to herself she'd been fighting her growing attraction to Fox. She didn't want to humiliate herself over a guy who didn't seem that interested in her. And wasn't she still supposed to be numb over Trish's death?

"I was trying to get as many traps out as I could, but I'm not as fast as I used to be. Maybe I kept second guessing myself too much. Or maybe I'm just getting too old for this."

Fox nodded. "Give yourself a break. You've got a lot on your plate."

Faith studied her hands and wished she could hide her rough fingers and stubby nails. She sighed and looked up at Fox, who now stood two feet away. Faith could smell his aftershave. She felt an unwelcome tingle.

"You like to come here for a drink?"

"Nah," Fox said. "I don't drink. I come down here sometimes for a sugar fix. The Saturday night specials are the best."

"Any new thoughts about Trish?"

"Not really. I talked to Borsich and he definitely was not her greatest fan. But with all his money, I'm not sure he considered her anything more than an annoyance."

"Oh shit."

"What did I say?"

Faith shook her head. "Nothing. I just remembered the film. Shit."

Fox cocked an eyebrow, his question unspoken.

"I found a roll of film hidden at her house. I meant to drop it off at one of those one-hour places but I had to get some Sweet Feed for the traps and then I had a flat tire and shit. Shit shit shit. I can't believe I forgot." Faith shook her head in self-disgust. Tears burned in her eyes.

"Hey. Hey." Fox took a step and put a strong arm around Faith, who found herself leaning into him. And that was her mistake. In her exhaustion and grief, having someone actually hold her was the last straw. Before she could stop herself she was bawling, shoulders shaking and snot dripping. She pulled away, covering her nose with her hand.

"Sorry." Faith ducked into the restroom and staggered into a stall. Pulling toilet paper off the roll she blew, then blew again. She leaned against the wall and tried to get her breathing under control. Someone entered the bathroom, high heels clicking. Faith waited until the woman ran water at the sink and the door opened and closed again. Faith left the stall and went to the mirror. And wished she hadn't. Her eyelids were swollen and red, a nice shade to match her nose. She sighed, shrugged at her own image, and steeled herself to leave the sanctuary of shell-shocked women the world over. Maybe if she was lucky, Fox had decided to leave.

Outside the bathroom, he leaned against the opposite wall.

"Better?"

"Yeah," she said, secretly happy he had stayed. "You didn't have to wait."

"Sure I did. Look, you're pooped. Do you have the film with you? I can run it over to the 24-hour drugstore, get it to you tomorrow. You gonna be out at the airport?"

Faith hesitated, wondering if she could trust this man she barely knew. Then she fished in her pocket for the film and gave it to Fox.

"Faith, you okay?" Rodgers stood at the other end of the hall.

Faith watched as John Fox turned toward the open space manager in apparent confusion. Rodgers approached, hand outstretched to Fox. "Hey John."

"Stan. Faith and I were just chatting."

"We were about to have dessert. Why don't you join us?"

"No thanks," Fox said. "I'd better get home."

"Uh, but you—" Faith stopped.

"I think I left my oven on. I'll see you guys later."

19

The kid behind the counter looked so young he probably thought thirty-five millimeter film came from the dark ages. Nevertheless, the boy with the punk hair and ear plugs was the designated driver of the one-hour photo machine at the all-night drugstore. Life had probably gotten a lot more boring for these film jockeys, now that folks could take those racy nudie shots on their digital cameras and bypass the ogling of under-age, minimum-wage teens.

Fox filled out the necessary information and told the boy that he planned to wait. The kid shrugged and walked away with the thirty-six exposure film. The boy reminded him of someone. Fox watched him a few more seconds, searching his memory. Unable to make any connection, Fox shrugged off the feeling and wandered down a brightly lit aisle, surprised at all the foot traffic in the store at 10:30 on a Saturday night. He found what seemed like a relatively quiet corner by men's hair dye and fished in his pocket for his cell phone. He dialed the DOW headquarters number of his immediate supervisor, who thankfully left him to his own devices most of the time.

"I need to take two or three days of leave time. I've got a family thing going on I need to deal with," Fox said for the voice mail recording. The message wouldn't be heard until Monday, but no matter. He was essentially his own boss, able to craft his own schedule. Plus he had plenty of leave built up and there wasn't much happening this time of year. Lots of fishing licenses to check, but the main action was several weeks off when deer season would kick into gear along the Front Range foothills.

Fox cruised into the laundry soap section and grabbed a fresh bottle of bleach. The one he had at home was already a couple weeks old and he'd heard that bleach lost its potency quickly. With Ricky about to land on his doorstep, he had a lot of cleaning to do.

In any other circumstances, he would have flat told Marlene that he couldn't take the boy. Even though Fox had tried to be careful, the proteins or prions of chronic wasting disease had probably contaminated his entire house, especially with cats up and down on every surface. Regular cleaning products could not destroy the prions. Instead, Division of Wildlife brochures recommended soaking contaminated knives for an hour in fifty-fifty bleach and water. But the brochures didn't talk about what to do when your boots have been soaked by the blood of dozens of mule deer you helped slaughter because they might and probably did carry chronic wasting disease.

He tried to shake away the image of panicked animals running for their lives while he and other members of the culling team aimed their rifles and fired shot after shot after shot. Despite efforts by the DOW to explain that culling was the only logical way to try to cut the population and reduce the chance of the disease spreading, members of the public wrote angry letters to the local papers, decrying the "senseless slaughter" of the mulies. What about the live test for the disease, some argued. The DOW had not done a good job of explaining that technology did not meet the needs of fieldwork. There was no way to sterilize the equipment used to pull tonsil samples from tranquilized deer. In other words, the test aimed to determine whether an animal was infected could very well end up infecting additional members of the herd. So instead, he and his fellow game wardens violated every rule of ethical hunting by gunning down dozens of animals whose bodies would be left to rot. Humans had declared war against a strange disease and dead deer amounted to nothing more than collateral damage. Still, the bloody duty left critter cops like John Fox sick at heart and feeling like an assassin for hire. He'd decided to come up with some excuse to get out of any future culling duty.

"Excuse me."

An elderly man pushing a cart stood in front of him. Fox realized he had been standing in the middle of the aisle, holding his precious bottle of bleach, lost in his distasteful memories.

"Sorry."

Fox glanced at his watch. Forty-five minutes. He cruised back to the photo counter and discovered the punk rocker had an industrious streak. Fox forked over some cash and then wandered off with the packet to find a quiet corner. He found himself in the condom aisle, trying to ignore new flavor and texture varieties. Studying the photo envelope in his hands, he wondered if he should wait until he was with

Faith, but then she had asked for his help. Fox unpeeled the flap to pull out the inner package of photos.

Trish's van with a prairie dog town behind it.

A pet kennel standing on end, door open, apparently waiting for a prairie dog.

The allergic-to-the-sun woman, clad head-to-toe in white, kneeling at a prairie dog hole holding a green garden hose that gushed foam into the burrow.

Trish crouched near a burrow, her gloved hands clasped around a prairie dog that she was about to put into a kennel.

Fox flipped through the photos and sighed. Looked like Trish had decided to get some action shots of prairie dog relocation. He began shuffling the pictures more rapidly, wondering why he was standing in this drugstore on a perfectly good Saturday night, with his solo lifestyle set to expire in less than 24 hours.

His hands stopped in mid-shuffle. The photo now on top of the stack commanded his full attention.

Maybe he hadn't been wasting his time after all.

Faith looked out over the prairie dog town and panicked. The sun was setting and she had forgotten to lock open the traps. If a prairie dog got in a trap before dark, a predator could come along, work the trap open and eat the dog. Faith ran to the first trap in the fading light to lock the gate up, but she couldn't figure out how to work the fastener. Trish must have put on a new kind when Faith wasn't looking. Faith fumbled with the device, then realized she needed an old-fashioned skeleton key to work the lock. Did the hardware store still sell skeleton keys? Faith looked up and saw a giant prairie dog the size of an elephant staring down at her. Now the creature was indeed an elephant, with a tall wooden saddle on top. Trish was aboard, looking down on her.

"My elephant is sick," Trish said. "It's having trouble breathing."

The elephant seemed to be choking or gasping, and Faith backed away. If the elephant collapsed on top of her, she would die. Faith stepped backward and fell into a burrow. She slid down, down, down, faster and faster as if going down a toboggan run. Now there was nothing under her and she dropped in an endless fall, arms flailing in a futile effort to find something to hold onto. The folds of her long dress covered her face and she clawed at the material smothering her. She couldn't breathe!

Faith's eyes popped open. She was breathing hard and her hands were twisted in her thin cotton blanket. Sweat drenched the sheet beneath her.

Jesus. She couldn't even remember the last time she'd had the falling dream. As a child it had haunted her, returning night after night. What had come before the falling? She retrieved fragments of the dream, reliving the desperate hopelessness she felt trying to fix the traps before dark, the fear of being crushed by a huge beast.

An elephant?

Staring into the darkness, trying to calm her breathing, Trish's voice came back to her.

"If prairie dogs were the size of elephants, there's no way people would tolerate letting the developers slaughter them," Trish said. That was the day Trish had stood at a construction site watching huge earthmovers bite into the earth where she had been trapping prairie dogs. She hadn't gotten them all and time had run out. Now she had called Faith because she needed to vent. "I just kept thinking, 'What's going on down in the tunnels? Are they hearing the machinery rumble closer? Are they being swept up in an avalanche of dirt and smothering?' And that's the problem," she added. "People can't see them die underground. Out of sight, out of mind. No big deal."

Faith untangled herself from the bedclothes and stumbled to the bathroom to empty her bladder. When she was done, she stayed sitting on the toilet and put her head in her hands. Trish was dead. She was alone. What difference did it make how Trish died? Nothing would bring her back. An old thought came creeping in. How hard could it be, a knife along the veins or a bunch of sleeping pills? Now truly no one would miss her, no sister would be left behind to cope with the mess.

Minutes passed. Faith got up, flushed and headed back to bed, pausing to grab her lap top. She was wide awake and sleep wouldn't be back any time soon.

***

"Unsung Hero"
By Faith O'Neill
Chapter 14

Afternoon, Sept. 28, 1864
Camp Weld, outside Denver City

Black Kettle rose stiffly from his cross-legged position on the floor. Soule could not determine the age of the Cheyenne chief, but he estimated the man might be approaching forty years of age. Black Kettle had seemed fit enough when he had first presented himself. Ten days in the back of a buckboard could leave a person mighty sore, Silas figured, remembering the long trip from Maine to Kansas.

Translator John Smith had completed the formal greetings by the time Silas remembered to pay attention.

"...and so, when we received the white father's announcement that peaceful Indians should present themselves, we called for a council." Smith paused and exchanged some words in Cheyenne with the chief. "It took many days before we could gather the people for council," Smith continued. "At the council it was decided to answer your announcement and to come to your soldiers at Fort Lyon, to tell them of our desire for peace. We brought with us the white children so Major Wynkoop would know our hearts."

Black Kettle adjusted his blanket with the wide red stripe, making it more comfortable on his shoulder.

"Major Wynkoop proposed that we come up to see you. We have come with our eyes shut, following his handful of men, like coming through the fire. All we ask is that we may have peace with the whites..."

At this point, the governor's appointed note-taker interrupted, requesting time to catch up. Silas could understand how Simeon Whiteley—an agent to the Ute tribe—might be nervous, seeing as how Gov. Evans had warned him to make complete minutes because "upon the results of this council very likely depended a continuance of the Indian war on the plains." Then Black Kettle proceeded, saying how he wanted to take good news back to his people so they might "sleep in peace."

Funny, Silas thought. He had spent many a restless night camped on the plains, wondering if a band of Indians might be nearby. Sounded like Indians could toss and turn as good as the rest of them.

Smith took a sip of water from a glass and continued his translation, while Black Kettle stood regally, gesturing occasionally with his hands.

"I want the chiefs of the soldiers here to understand that we are for peace, that we have made peace, that we may not be mistaken by them for enemies," Black Kettle said. "I have not come with a little wolf's bark, but have come to talk plain with you. We must live near the buffalo or starve."

As Black Kettle continued, Soule glanced over at the governor, grim and stone-faced and perched on a high-backed chair. The Indian chief might have a golden tongue, but it seemed to have little effect on Evans.

Black Kettle finished with another reference to how good his people would feel on hearing the news that he Black Kettle had "taken the hands of all the chiefs in Denver," which Soule interpreted as shaking hands. The chief resumed his seat on the floor near the other chiefs.

At this point, Gov. Evans began to speak. He remained seated, Silas noted.

"I am sorry that you did not respond to my appeal at once," the man said sternly. "You have gone into an alliance with the Sioux, who were at war with us."

The chiefs on the floor shifted restlessly at these words as Smith translated. Silas glanced at Ned, who arched his eyebrows and gave him a tiny shrug. If this was so, it was news to the army officers. Evans continued on his tirade, accusing the Indians in front of him of stealing livestock and making war even while the U.S. government spent thousands of dollars to set up farms for them and prepared to "feed, protect and make you comfortable."

Evans accused the Indians of rebuffing him when he went out to the plains to meet with them. "Instead of this, your people went away and smoked the 'war pipe' with our enemies."

When the governor paused, Black Kettle said through Smith, "I don't know who could have told you this."

Evans stiffened and adjusted his jacket.

"No matter who said this, but your conduct has proved to my satisfaction that such was the case."

At this, several of the chiefs began to speak at once. Neva spoke in English, speaking directly to the governor.

"This is a mistake. We have made no alliance with the Sioux or anyone else."

Evans' eyes widened at the sound of such fluid English coming from the red man in front of him. During the exchange that followed, the Indians conceded that while they as individuals had worked for peace, their young braves at times were out of their control.

"So far as making a treaty is now concerned, we are in no condition to do it," Evans said. "Your young men are on the war path, my soldiers are preparing for the fight."

Silas and Ned exchanged another glance. Sounded like the "Bloodless Third" was itching for some blood before their hundred-days commission expired and they went back to being hungry civilians.

"The time when you can make war best is in the summer time," the governor continued. "The time when I can make war best is in the winter. I have learned that you understand that as the whites are at war among themselves, you think you can now drive the whites from this country, but this reliance is false. The Great Father at Washington has men enough to drive all the Indians off the plains and whip the rebels at the same time."

Silas looked down, seeing mule blood on his hands, hearing the gunfire, the cries of Johnny Reb dying at Glorieta Pass. He'd been the grateful recipient of many a free drink from settlers relieved that the Civil War had been kept away from their doorstep. He rubbed his hands on his pants. Silas felt eyes on him and raised his head. Chivington stared at him with a smile, his broad chest puffed out in the new colonel's uniform. We were there, his look said, you and I. Soule gave him a brief nod.

Silas heard the governor saying something about how the Indians had had the advantage until now, but that soon the plains would "swarm with United States soldiers."

"Now the war with the whites is nearly through, and the Great Father will not know what to do with all his soldiers, except to send them after the Indians on the plains," Evans continued. "My proposition to the friendly Indians has gone out. I shall be glad to have them all come in under it. My advice to you is to turn on the side of the government, and show by your acts that friendly disposition you profess to me."

The chiefs began speaking among themselves.

"What does this mean, to turn on the side of the government?" Neva asked.

Evans paused. "Well, this would mean obeying and assisting the military officers, in whatever manner they see fit."

Smith translated the governor's response and the chiefs all gave their assent.

Evans shook his finger at the Indians.

"The only way you can show this friendship is by making some arrangement with the soldiers to help them."

When Black Kettle replied that the chiefs would do their best and that he thought his young braves would go along with helping the troops, Ned Wynkoop jumped in.

"Did not the Dog Soldiers agree, when I had my council with you," Ned said, "to do whatever you said, after you had been here?"

"Yes." Black Kettle smiled at Ned.

At this point, a Cheyenne chief named White Antelope stood, fingering a medallion hanging around his neck by a striped ribbon.

"I am proud to have seen the chief of all the whites of this country. I will tell my people. Ever since I went to Washington and received this medal, I have called all white men as my brothers, but other Indians have since been to Washington and got medals, and now the soldiers do not shake hands, but seek to kill me. What do you mean by us fighting your enemies? Who are they?"

"All Indians who are fighting us."

"How can we be protected from the soldiers on the plains?"

Governor Evans cleared his throat. "You must make that arrangement with the military chief."

"I fear these new soldiers who have gone out may kill some of my people while I am here."

"There is great danger of it," Evans acknowledged.

"When we sent our letter to Major Wynkoop, it was

like going through a strong fire for Major Wynkoop's men to come to our camp," White Antelope said. Now Silas's eyes widened. If he had heard correctly, Ned and his men had just been credited for bravery by an Indian chief. "It was the same for us to come to see you. We have our doubts whether the Indians south of the Arkansas, or those north of the Platte, will do as you say. A large number of Sioux have crossed the Platte in the vicinity of the Junction, into our country. When Major Wynkoop came, we proposed to make peace. He said he had no power to make peace, except to bring us here and return us safe."

"Whatever peace you make must be with the soldiers, not with me," the governor repeated. "Are the Apaches at war with the whites?"

White Antelope listened carefully to Smith's translation. "Yes, and the Comanches and Kiowas as well," the chief said, adding that thirteen bands of Sioux had crossed the Platte River to fight with the Comanches and Kiowas.

Evans demanded to know how many warriors were involved, but White Antelope said he didn't know.

The governor began peppering the chiefs with questions. Which Indians attacked a train in August? Who murdered the Hungate family on Burning Creek? Who killed a man and a boy at the head of Cherry Creek? Who stole soldiers' horses and mules from Jimmie's camp in early September? Who stole Charley Antobe's horses? Who took livestock from Fremont's Orchard and then fought with soldiers north of there?

Neva tried to answer the governor's questions. But when he said a band of northern Arapahos killed the Hungates, Whiteley interrupted his note taking and leaned toward the governor. "This cannot be true," Silas overheard him whisper.

At the final question about Fremont's Orchard and the first battle of the ongoing fight between local Indians and whites, White Antelope again spoke. The chief told the governor that a soldier fired first, triggering the war.

The governor exchanged a mocking look with Chivington.

"The Indians had stolen about forty horses," Evans said. "The soldiers went to recover them and the Indians fired a volley into their ranks."

At this, the chiefs again conferred with each other.

"This is all a mistake," White Antelope said. He added the Indians had found a horse (which they returned) and a mule (which they planned to return) when they heard about soldiers fighting Indians nearby and fled in fear.

Now Neva, brother to Arapaho chief Left Hand, rose from the wood floor and addressed the governor.

"I want to say something. It makes me feel bad to be talking about these things and opening old sores."

"Look here, you—" Chivington said before Gov. Evans interrupted, "Let him speak."

"Mr. Smith has known me since I was a child," Neva said in his perfect English. "Has he ever known me to commit depredations on the whites? I went to Washington last year, receiving good counsel. I am determined always to keep peace with the whites."

Evans sat up straighter. "We feel that you have, by your stealing and murdering, done us great damage. You come here and say you will tell us all, and that is what I'm trying to get."

"The Comanches, Kiowas and the Sioux have done

much more injury than we have," Neva fired back.

The governor tapped his fingers on the wooden arm of his chair. "What are the Sioux going to do next?"

Now another chief spoke. "Their intention is to clear out all this country." Silas recognized the man as Bull Bear, who claimed his brother Lean Bear had been gunned down by soldiers as he approached them peacefully. "They are angry, and will do all the damage to the whites they can. I have given my word to fight with the whites. My brother Lean Bear died in trying to keep peace with the whites. I am willing to die in the same way, and expect to do so."

For a moment, no one spoke. Then Chivington cleared his throat.

"I am not a big war chief, but all the soldiers in this country are at my command." The big man paused to pull down the sleeves of his spotless dark blue uniform jacket. "My rule of fighting white men or Indians is to fight them until they lay down their arms and submit to military authority. You are nearer to Major Wynkoop than anyone else, and you can go to him when you get ready to do that."

When Smith finished translating the colonel's words, the chiefs smiled for the first time that afternoon. Soule smiled too, happy that Chivington had finally tossed the ball to Wynkoop. The meeting over, the chiefs stood and eagerly "took the hands" of everyone present. Soule clapped Ned on the back and turned in time to see a stone-faced Chivington exchange a handshake with Neva. Silas felt his smile evaporate.

Chivington looked like a man going through the motions, and that worried Silas Soule.

20

Fox sat on his bed, staring at the phone in his hand. Then he tapped out the numbers.

"Sam? It's Fox. Were you asleep?"

"I wish," Sam Gary responded.

John wasn't at all surprised to find the man wide awake late on a Saturday night. "I can deal with the wheelchair, but the insomnia is a curse from hell," Sam had once told him.

"I've got a weird question for you." Fox paced, the phone in one hand and a photograph in the other. "You were the small mammal guy for years. What's the latest on black-footed ferrets in Colorado?"

"What's up?"

"Humor me for the moment."

"I don't think I know any more than you." Sam Gary paused, and Fox heard a snapping sound, followed by a deep inhale and exhale. In other words, the man continued to ignore Fox's urging to quit smoking. "But anyway. We put out about two dozen near Dinosaur a couple years ago. No sign of successful reproduction yet. We just had some night crews out spotlighting a couple weeks ago and no eye shine.

Maybe they all croaked."

Ah yes, the agonies and ecstasies of relocation. The DOW had taken a big public hit in the shorts over their early attempts to relocate lynx from Canada back into Colorado, where they had been hunted out. The biologists had rushed to get the cats back in the wild in the snowy spring, but the animals didn't adjust to their new territory as well as expected and most of them starved to death. After that public relations disaster, the next year the Division fattened up the beautiful predators with the tall ear tufts and waited until closer to warm weather to let them go. Those cats did much better.

Black-footed ferrets had their own issues. The species had the misfortune of hunting one animal almost exclusively—the prairie dog of the short-grass prairie. And when European settlers trudged Westward in their quest for land, things went downhill fast for both the prairie and anyone who lived there, whether Native people or prairie dogs. The federal government became an expert on extermination—smallpox-tainted blankets for the Indians, poison for prairie dogs despised by ranchers and farmers. And as the prairie dog population crashed, the ferret population crashed harder. Without a prairie dog, what was a self-respecting black-footed ferret to eat?

"Fox? You there?"

"Sorry. How long have ferrets been extirpated on the Front Range?"

"Hard to say, but the last documented sighting was decades ago. Gotta figure they're hard to spot in the best of circumstances. Okay, cough it up. What's up?"

"Probably a wild goose chase." Fox paused. How easy

would it be to rig a photo? "Heard a rumor about a recent sighting, but you know how these things go."

"I suppose it's possible they had a breakout over at the farm, but they run a pretty tight ship over there, I hear." Sam paused for a puff and exhale. "Know anybody over there?"

"Actually, I don't. Been wanting a tour but got busy and distracted."

The black-footed ferret recovery program included a new, state of the art breeding facility up near Fort Collins, which DOW types had dubbed the "farm." When you raise baby black-footed ferrets to release into the wild, you have to teach them how—and what—to hunt. The folks at the farm were always looking for live prairie dogs trapped off of construction sites. They put the animals into a fake prairie dog burrow system and then sent the ferrets in behind them. The whole venture was costing taxpayers millions of dollars—another good reason why it made sense to protect species before they end up on the endangered species list, Fox thought. There'd been many a time when he'd heard folks say about some animal or another, "there's plenty of them" to justify killing something dubbed a 'varmint.' Fox wondered how these folks would react to his own fantasy version of a Gary Larson cartoon, in which giant bacteria discuss humans and say, "It's okay if we take out a few thousand—there's plenty of 'em."

"...so give him a call and see if he can help you out," Sam was saying.

"Sorry Sam. Getting too close to my bedtime, I guess. What was that name again?"

Sam huffed. "Geez man, you really are starting to lose it.

And I thought I was getting old. Carmichael's the guy's last name, don't remember the first. Nice enough guy, bright red hair. He's running the show over there. Tell him I sent you, but don't tell him I didn't remember his first name."

"Deal."

Fox hung up and nudged the cats aside so he could get under the covers. He turned off the light. Thoughts battered him, unexpected thoughts. Why was Faith hanging out with Stan Rodgers, and why should that bother him anyway? He tossed and turned until he finally sat up and switched the light back on. The manuscript was close to hand on the bedside table.

***

"Unsung Hero"
By Faith O'Neill
Chapter 15

Evening, Sept. 30, 1864
Parlor of Tremont House, Denver City

Ned patted his stomach.

"Real food, by God. Although that second piece of apple pie may have sized me right out of my uniform."

"That'll be the day," Soule said. "I swear I never met such a pole of a man who could eat as much as you and not change a whit."

Joe Cramer grinned at Silas sitting on the red velvet chair across from the major and himself. They had made the most of their meal, then retired to the parlor for an evening smoke.

"Captain, I do believe you sound a bit jealous," Cramer said, taking a puff off his cigar—a town treat.

Ned cocked his head and eyed Silas. "My, my, Soule. Don't tell me you're worried about your girlish figure. I thought—"

The major stopped in mid-sentence, his eyes caught by something behind Soule. Silas turned in his chair and stood up so fast he banged his knee against the side table.

"Are you all right, Captain?" Hersa stood a few feet away, wearing a very fetching green dress and matching bonnet. Then she did a quick curtsy as all three men stood and bowed.

Silas bent down and picked up his hat, which had slid off his lap in his haste. "I'm fine, thank you," he said as he brushed off the wide brim.

Into the awkward silence, Ned Wynkoop cleared his throat.

"If you'll excuse us, miss, Lieutenant Cramer and I were just leaving."

"But..." Cramer started. "Of course. Please excuse us."

Silas turned his head and flashed Ned a small smile before the two men departed, headed for the saloon across the street, no doubt.

"Would you like a seat?" Silas crushed his cigarette out in a silver tray and gestured toward the sofa the men had vacated. After they had positioned themselves, Silas looked into Hersa's green eyes and wondered how he could ever have thought he preferred redheads. "It's been a long time."

"Yes." Hersa dropped her gaze to her hands. "Mother doesn't know I have come to see you."

"Is there anything I can..."

Hersa was already shaking her head. "Her heart's broken. She believes you are consorting with the enemy, that you're a traitor."

"They brought us back white children who had been kidnapped," Silas said. "They are trying to find others who are lost. We brought the hostages home."

Hersa looked up. "The problem is, you didn't bring my father home."

Silas felt his face burn. "You must miss him terribly."

"Yes," she said. Her gaze dropped again. "I have missed you as well."

Soule's mouth went dry.

"So—"

"So, what can I say? My mother is grief stricken. How can I add to her pain?"

"Why have you come here then?"

"I wanted you to know that you have remained in my thoughts, that I do not bear you ill will."

"And am I to be satisfied with that? That you bear me no ill will?"

Hersa stood. Silas followed suit. He took her hands in his and she met his gaze. Her lips parted as if she wanted to speak. Tears slid down her cheeks. Silas had just begun to bend toward her face when she pulled away and rushed out of the front door into the evening beyond.

Soule drained the shot glass in one gulp. As he put the glass back on the saloon table, he saw Ned exchange a look with Cramer, but thankfully neither one said what they were thinking.

"Deal me in," Silas said to Lieutenant Cannon, who

was shuffling. "And none of that silly faro business. I'm wanting some serious five card draw."

Cannon cut him a sideways glance, with his cigar drooping from his mouth. "Better get your poker face on then, Captain. On the other hand, what am I saying? As I recall, last time we played poker you took a tidy sum from me."

"Last I heard, you could afford it, with that fine Kentucky family of yours."

Cannon laughed harshly as he dealt cards. "Far as they're concerned, I might as well be dead. My father swore he'd never rescue me from another fix. The old bastard."

Soule shut up at that. His own father, Amasa, had been dead several years, but he still thought of the man as a hero. "You have to take a stand somewhere, and it might as well be here," Amasa had told the young Silas when the boy finally arrived from Maine to the Kansas territory, part of his father's quest to make sure Kansas would be slave-free when statehood came. They stood in waist-high prairie grass, rippling in a soft morning breeze. Silas thought of ocean waves lapping at the Maine shoreline and stood amazed at the total lack of trees. "Don't be fooled, there's black gold under this grass, best soil you ever saw. And by God, as I live and breathe I'm determined to keep this black Kansas soil free."

Silas studied his hand and tossed in three cards. He wondered how Hersa's mother would feel if she knew Silas had schemed to rescue anti-slavery men from the gallows, men who had joined the great abolitionist John Brown. And a rescue there would have been, if the jailed men hadn't instead chosen to nobly meet their fate.

He rearranged his new cards. A pair of sixes. Mediocre business. Silas went to pour himself another round but only drops came out of the bottle. He signaled the bartender for a new one.

"I was eager enough to get to Denver," Soule said. "Now I cannot wait to leave this place and head south."

***

Faith turned off the engine and got out of the pickup. The airport was deserted early on a Sunday morning, so she had the view all to herself. The rosy glow of dawn blossomed on the mountains of the Front Range to the west. She knew from experience that the incredible color the locals called Alpen glow wouldn't last long, so she leaned against the fender to take it in. Probably the native people had been stopping to take this sight in for thousands of years—before they got killed or relocated by the whites.

The thought made Faith remember her book, the one she couldn't seem to finish.

"Sorry, Silas," she said out loud.

The earth turned a bit more toward the sun and the rosy glow faded into memory. "Okay, show's over. Stop lollygagging."

She tucked one trap under each arm and then grabbed the handles of three traps with each hand, sad to disrupt the Sunday morning silence with the clatter of metal.

Over the next couple hours she dropped forty more traps near burrow entrances, leaving them haphazardly as they fell. She would set them up later. The first stage of the process involved just getting the traps to the burrows. What took the most time was going back to bait the traps and then label them by location of coterie and burrow—A1, A2, A3... B1, B2, B3... etc. When an animal was trapped, the prairie dog would be placed in a kennel with the location info taped to the outside so that it could be reunited with family members at the holding site. She was walking back to the truck for her bait bucket and a big roll of yellow duct tape for labeling when she saw a black Toyota truck pulling up alongside Trish's pickup.

"Tried to call you," John Fox said as he climbed out of his vehicle. "Figured I'd take a chance and look for you here."

Faith pushed back the hair from her forehead. It was only 7:30 in the morning, but she could feel the sun cranking into gear. Over at the row of light planes tied down to the tarmac, a motor sputtered to life and a nose prop began spinning.

"What's the matter?" Faith yelled over the noise.

"Let's get inside." Fox gestured at his vehicle.

Inside with the windows rolled up and the plane motor muted, Faith watched Fox reach inside a camouflage-colored backpack on the seat between them. The pack was shaded in faded tans and greens—a design favored by hunters in the Rocky Mountain West rather than the dark shades more suited to jungles. Fox pulled out a white photo pack.

"You got them!"

Fox handed her the package. She yanked the photos out of the envelope and began flipping through them. Faith stopped at the first one that included Trish, sighed, and then kept flipping until she found herself back at the first one of the series.

"I don't get it. There's nothing here. I mean, nothing worth hiding."

The game warden looked at her. "I saved one until last, just in case there was something I missed in the other shots." Fox reached in the pocket of his denim short-sleeved shirt.

Faith stared at the photo, then leaned closer to the image.

"What is that?" she said. And then, before he could answer, she breathed "Holy shit."

21

"So why wasn't Trish shouting about this from the closest mountain top?" John Fox asked. "Assuming, of course, that this is legit."

Faith pulled her gaze away from the photograph.

"I don't know." Faith looked through the windshield of Fox's truck out over the prairie dog town and toward the Western horizon with its ridgeline of the Southern Rockies. A few puffy clouds tinged with silver floated over the jagged ridges, hinting at the possibility of an afternoon thunderstorm. In the section of the dog town where she had baited traps yesterday, she could spot a few animals poking partway out of their burrows. She tried to see the scene through prairie dog eyes—the odd and scary wire shape a few feet from the doorstep. But oh! The luscious smell of those morsels of molasses-covered grain. Sneaking out just far enough to munch the first piece, then a little farther for the second... Those were the burrows she'd worked on yesterday. At the holes where she'd begun staging traps today, the animals were still too spooked by the sounds they'd heard above ground to venture out.

"Trish was one of the smartest people I've ever known. Almost scary smart," Faith said. "My guess is she decided to lay low and consider her options. I mean, she had to know people would attack her, accuse her of rigging the shot. Just like you did."

Faith looked back down at the photograph. At first glance it was nothing special. The lighting was poor, either just pre-sunup or post- sundown. In the foreground, a blue sign announced "Future Home of Borsmart Mega Store!" In the background, a long, slinky creature stood upright at the foot of a burrow, looking toward the camera from perhaps 20 feet away. Despite the dim conditions, the black mask across the narrow face and the black feet were clearly visible.

"Yeah, I admit it. I'm really suspicious of that." Fox cocked his head toward the image in Faith's hands. "I think there's a good chance she staged this somehow. I mean, she was determined to foil Borsich one way or another, don't you think? If she could prove he had an endangered black-footed ferret on his property, his development would grind to a stop. Assuming someone would believe her 'evidence' despite the fact that wild ferrets haven't been seen in this area in decades. On top of which, ferrets need huge prairie dog towns. This is a postage stamp in those terms."

Faith sighed. "I wouldn't put it past her. On the other hand, at one point, black-footed ferrets were already considered extinct until a handful were found somewhere in Wyoming or the Dakotas. Some rancher's dog brought home a dead one and the man didn't know what it was, that kind of thing. So it's possible, isn't it?"

Fox shrugged. "Like they say, anything's possible. But

191

why didn't she get the film developed?"

Now it was Faith's turn to shrug. "Maybe she took the picture just before she died and ran out of time. Trish was always behind schedule and she worked pretty much non-stop."

Fox rubbed his eyes. "All I know is, if I thought I had a shot of a black-footed ferret alive and well on the Front Range, I would head straight to the first place I could and get it developed. I'd want to know that I actually could see it in the photo, prove to myself that it was real."

Faith nodded.

"On the other hand," Fox continued, "If I had staged something, I'd already know it wasn't real."

"Okay. But if I staged something like that, I'd take more than one photo. Wouldn't you?" Faith asked. "Wouldn't you want to make sure you got a good shot of the fabulous ferret?"

"Agreed. So we're back where we started. Who else do you think knew about this?"

"Trish was incredibly secretive. Maybe no one."

"How about the lady in white?"

"Who?"

"You know, Miss Sun Allergy. I forget her name. She's in some of the photos."

"Oh, that's Hope Packard," Faith added. "I've been meaning to call her, see if she can help me out here."

"Do you have her address? Maybe I'll drop in on her."

"I thought yesterday you said you had a lot of cleaning to do?" Fox looked away and Faith backed off. "Sorry, none of my business."

"It's okay. My nephew is coming for a visit and—aw,

shit, who am I kidding. The kid's coming to live with me for the indefinite future."

Faith felt her eyebrows rising. "Whoa. Do you have any kids of your own?"

Fox shook his head. "Two marriages, no progeny."

"Gee. I've never had kids either, but let me know if I can give you a hand with him."

"He's a good kid. I just have some juggling to do."

"When is he getting here?"

"Three this afternoon."

"Whoa," Faith said again.

"Yup. So if I'm gonna see your friend Hope I better get going."

Faith fished her wallet out of her pocket and handed him a scrap of paper with Hope's information scribbled on it. "She gave me this at the memorial service. But I don't think she would have hurt Trish. She's the meekest person I've ever met."

"I'm just hoping she can give us more information about who Trish had been talking to." Fox looked down again at the photo in Faith's lap. "All I know is, that picture right there might provide a pretty good motive to go after Trish."

Fox pulled up in front of the address and sat staring in wonder. He felt as if he had fallen into a fairy tale. The miniature cottage sat in old town Green Mountain, where a shack could sell for close to a million bucks. Location, location, location. Critics might scoff and call the liberal stronghold the "Republic of Green Mountain," but Fox wondered if they were secretly jealous because they hadn't been foresighted enough to buy in when the place was just a refuge for hippies and before home prices skyrocketed. This cottage with all its curb appeal would go for a pretty penny, square footage be damned. Lush xeriscape landscaping added to the charm, with stalks of purple penstemon complementing the yellow blooms of coneflowers—native stuff that didn't require coddling and tons of water. He might not have time to work in his own yard, but Fox knew what he liked when he saw it.

Hope Packard answered the door almost immediately and Fox suspected she'd seen him from a window. Up close and without her Lawrence of Arabia garb, the tall woman was presentable enough, but she'd never been beauty pageant material. Her jaw was a little too long, nose a little too big, eyes a little too wide apart. Still her makeup was impeccable and subtle, her chin-length brown hair shiny and styled, and the scarf around her throat looked like silk. She wore a brown T-shirt over new-looking blue jeans and Fox realized she was one of those rare people who could make casual clothes look chic.

She cut off his introduction and apology for intruding on a Sunday morning. "I was about to leave, but come on in," Hope said in the whispery voice.

The inside was as good as the outside. An overstuffed sofa with a green chintz design sat by the many-paned window overlooking the garden. A gray butterfly tabby with green eyes inspected Fox from its perch on the back of the sofa. Fox approached slowly and the cat let him run a hand down its back, raising its rear end in appreciation.

"Who's this?" Fox asked.

"Miramar."

"Cool name. Where'd that come from?"

"She used to sit in the window of my San Francisco townhouse and stare out at the bay. Mira-mar?" Hope eyed him, testing his Spanish language IQ.

"*Ocean view*. Nice."

Hope waved at the couch with long fingers and short manicured nails painted a soft peachy pink.

"Can I get you a cup of tea? I'm afraid I don't do coffee."

Fox picked a flavor and watched as Hope disappeared toward what he presumed was the kitchen area. He wished he had simply declined her offer. A glance at his watch confirmed his bleach cleaning time was ebbing away. Still, Fox found himself intrigued by another of Green Mountain's eccentric types.

"So you're off duty, I presume?" Hope handed him a dark blue mug. Fiesta Ware, Fox knew from one of his practice marriages. Miramar climbed down from her perch and settled onto his lap.

"Yeah. I'm trying to help Faith understand what happened to Trish, figure out how the accident happened."

Hope shifted her gaze to the cat. "You have good cat karma. She doesn't usually do that."

"Cats know I'm a sucker," Fox said, wondering at the change of subject. "Did you work with Trish for a long time?"

"Off and on, over the last couple years, when I could. I teach some classes over at Milarepa and I do some landscaping around town."

"I noticed your garden. I have a brown thumb but I

appreciate those of the green-thumbed species." Hope laughed as he held up a real brown thumb.

"What kind of work did you do with Trish?" he asked.

"Little bit of everything. Mainly I helped when she flushed, even though she could do it single-handed. I got pretty good on the hose while she would catch," she said.

"Good on the hose?"

"I know it sounds silly, but it takes a little practice to fold the hose and keep the right pressure. You want to mainly get foam down the hole instead of water."

Fox nodded. He'd watched Trish a couple times.

"Plus I helped clean out kennels at her place, feed the dogs, that kind of stuff."

For a moment Fox thought Trish had dogs as pets, then reminded himself Hope was talking prairie dog lingo.

"Sounds like you did a lot. What did she pay you?"

"Nothing. I volunteered."

One of those Green Mountain things, everybody trying to save the world. Especially those everybodies not worried about paying the rent.

"She must have really appreciated that." Miramar purred and pushed her head under his hand.

Hope grimaced and looked away.

"No?"

Fox watched as a struggle played out on the woman's face.

"Trish was… complicated. She could charm you into doing almost anything, but after awhile she seemed to forget you were giving up your own time to be there."

Fox waited. He raised his eyebrows in a question.

"Well, she chased away a lot of good volunteers. You

know, they'd spend hours cleaning kennels and then a prairie dog would escape into the room and she'd give them hell. Or she'd ask someone to help her flush and then she'd show up an hour late."

"Hmm. A little weak on management skills?"

"Yeah. To give her credit, though, she knew it."

"So why did you stick around so long?" Fox asked.

"I decided early on to work short stints, set strict boundaries. I told her if she was more than fifteen minutes late, I'd be gone."

"Anybody ever get really pissed at her?"

Hope stood and walked across the room to a big water color painting of lush flowers in a porcelain vase. She straightened the frame, which already looked straight enough to Fox. She turned around, chewing her lip.

"One. A hippie throwback, complete with an old VW van. He traveled around the West, taking up causes. He worked for Trish about five months, seven days a week, probably ten or twelve hours a day. Became her right-hand person."

"So?"

"Aside from the fact she never paid him or said thank you? I don't know. I was cleaning kennels one day when he stormed in, dumped traps and grain and yelled that he was fuckin' out of there. The gossip was he asked for a day off and she acted like it was the end of the world."

"And his name was…?"

"Jeremiah Johnson."

Fox looked at her. "You're kidding, right?"

"I know, I've seen the movie too. I don't know if that was his real name or not."

Fox pulled out a pen and small notebook and wrote down the name of the famous mountain man/possible prairie dog volunteer.

"So," Fox said, meeting Hope's eyes. "How did you feel about Trish?"

"I thought she had a lot of guts, standing up for animals considered disposable. And…"

"And?" Fox said when she didn't continue.

"She was kind to me."

Interesting, Fox thought.

"How so?"

Fox watched as a pink flush crept up the woman's face.

"She helped me through a difficult time."

He waited, but her mouth was set firmly. Fox took a last sip of tea, put the mug on the table and the cat on the floor.

"Thanks for your time." Fox stood, took a couple steps and then stopped. "I almost forgot. Faith showed me a few photos of you and Trish working. Did Trish ask you to take a lot of photos for her?"

Hope's face froze for a half second before she smiled. "We were usually up to our eyeballs in prairie dogs."

Fox waited, but the woman had stopped speaking. "Well, I better get going. I've got to take care of some stuff and I don't want to make you late for church."

"Meditation," Hope whispered.

"Right," Fox said.

Back in his truck, Fox wrestled with his conscience and pinned it to the mat, opting for a cup of strong coffee and a Silas Soule fix before heading home for a bleach fest. Soon he would be a family man, at least for the foreseeable future. He craved some solitude in a crowded coffee shop.

***

"Unsung Hero"
By Faith O'Neill
Chapter 16

Oct. 8, 1864
Fort Lyon, Colorado Territory

Left Hand looked thinner than Silas remembered. He wondered what ailed the chief, but decided it was impolite to ask. It was truly a shame the Arapaho chief had been too ill to travel to Denver with the other chiefs. Left Hand was a gifted speaker and might have made a stronger impression on the stubborn governor than the other Indians.

"And so tell them to bring in their villages to near the Fort, so I can keep them under my eye until I hear from my department headquarters," Wynkoop was saying, with Smith again interpreting. Black Kettle, Neva, White Antelope and others had gathered in the Major's office for another council. Silas wondered why Left Hand himself didn't translate, then decided that this strategy allowed the Arapaho leader to focus on all that was said without distraction. And since everyone knew he spoke English, it would keep them on the up-and-up.

"Please tell Black Kettle I need him to bring in the three other white prisoners as soon as possible," the major added.

When Black Kettle heard the translation, he spoke rapidly to Smith who said, "He says this will take time, as the group is at a distance. He will send Bull Bear to bring them here as quickly as can be done."

The Indians got up off the floor and Wynkoop passed out small bags of tobacco to each of them.

"I am sorry I could not be there with you," Left Hand said in English to Wynkoop. "It sounds as if everything went well."

"I am waiting for word from my superiors, but yes, I do think things went well," Wynkoop said of the Denver trip.

Left Hand reached out to take Wynkoop's hand, then turned and took Soule's as well. "I want peace for my family before I die," the man said before he turned away.

Soule caught Ned's eye. The major gave a little shrug. When the Indians had left, Wynkoop gestured at a chair. "Join me for a drink?"

Silas accepted the whiskey Ned poured and clinked glasses with him before downing the fiery stuff. He must have grimaced slightly because Ned smiled and said, "Not quite up to Denver standards, eh?"

"It will serve."

"Mmm."

They were sitting quietly there five minutes later when Joe Cramer appeared.

"Excuse me, sir, but there is a telegram from General Curtis that just arrived." Cramer handed over a folded piece of paper. Silas stood to leave, but Ned waved him back down and gestured for Cramer to remain in the room. "You may as well be party to what the general has to say about our exploits."

Ned scanned the letter quickly and Soule watched as a red flush crept up his neck. His hand balled into a fist, crushing the paper. Silas flashed a look at Cramer. Ned still refused to speak.

"Not good news then?" Soule finally said.

Ned jumped to his feet and stomped over to the window that looked out into the yard of the Fort, leaving his back to them. Silas gazed past Ned, his eyes settling on a young Mexican wash woman scrubbing a uniform on a washboard in a metal tub. Her black braid lay against a shoulder left bare by a slack white blouse, clothing that led men to call such girls "loose women." Finally Ned sighed heavily and turned.

"General Curtis says he has been informed by Colonel Chivington about our trip to Denver, that the Indians are claiming they want peace because winter approaches and the Third Regiment is full," Ned said. He laughed harshly. "Ah yes, the 'cowardly savages' are quaking in their moccasins about the ragtag Bloodless Third."

Straightening out the crumpled paper, Ned began to read.

"'...as such, I require the bad Indians delivered up, restoration of equal numbers of stock, also hostages to secure. I want no peace till the Indians suffer more. No peace must be made without my directions...'"

"Jesus H. Christ," Soule said, as Cramer shook his head.

"What do you think it means for us?" Cramer ventured.

"Don't worry Joe, it's my head on the block, I fear," Wynkoop said. "I suspect Chivington is only telling Curtis bits and pieces. What am I supposed to do, chase down Black Kettle and Left Hand, tell them everything I said was a lie? God damn Chivington, anyway."

Soule got out of his chair and went over by Ned.

"If Chivington isn't presenting all the facts, then you

need to do it, Ned." Silas pulled out his tobacco pouch and began rolling a cigarette. "Curtis is an egotistical bastard, probably thinks you should have consulted him." Soule finished the cigarette and handed it to Ned, who accepted it with a slight smile. Soule struck a match and Ned inhaled deeply.

"Doesn't he know that Evans is the de facto Indian agent for Indians in the Colorado territory?" Ned said. "That's not even part of Curtis's jurisdiction."

"Since when did logic rescue a man from himself?" Soule quipped.

Ned sighed again. "I certainly can't lay things out in a telegram. And Black Kettle's people will probably be here in a matter of days."

"So write a letter. Send some men with it to Kansas, let them hand it to him in person," Silas said, licking the edge of the rolling paper for his own smoke.

"Sile is right, major. Lay out all the facts," Cramer said.

"This is idiotic," Ned said, blowing out a puff of smoke. "What's going to happen to those three white women if we renege on our word now? And doesn't Curtis understand that we can make these people our allies against the Kiowa and Comanche? We certainly don't have enough troops to take on a general Indian war."

"Major," Soule said, deliberately invoking his friend's rank. "You are among the best of men with a pen in your hand. Put it all to paper."

Ned finished his cigarette and ground it out on the wooden window ledge. He looked at Silas.

"What man can you spare that is reliable and fast on his horse?"

Soule considered. "Lieutenant Denison would be a good choice."

"Tell him to prepare himself to ride to Leavenworth with three other men. Tell him to be ready in three hours time and to report to me at that time."

"Ned, what do you think Curtis will do?"

Wynkoop turned back to look out at the dirt yard where soldiers ambled about on their various tasks.

"Whatever it is, I'm the one who made the decisions, and I'm the one to face the consequences. Let's hope Curtis can see the sense in everything we've done."

"I'll drink to that," Soule said, retrieving his glass and gulping the last of the whiskey.

22

Fox unlocked his front door and pushed it open for the child next to him.

"This is it, buddy." Fox walked in behind the boy, who had stopped in the middle of the living room, blue backpack on his thin shoulders. Fox bent down to take the backpack. The boy had an odd look on his face. "What's the matter, Ricky?"

"Why does your house smell bad, uncle? Are you cooking?"

For a moment Fox felt completely disoriented until a light bulb went on. "Cooking" could mean different things in a house of drug addicts. A wave of shame flooded him—good intentions gone awry again.

"It's okay, Ricky. I was cleaning before you got here. You're smelling the bleach I used."

All the windows of the small house stood open and exhaust fans propped in the frames blew inside air to the outdoors. Still, the smell of bleach permeated the dwelling. Fox had booted Abby and all the cats outside while he frantically scrubbed counters and mopped floors with a very strong bleach-water solution. He was terrified that his home was contaminated with chronic wasting disease proteins that would sicken his cherished nephew. But now as Ricky stood there, Fox wondered what was worse—a strange protein not proven to affect humans, or bleach fumes that sickened you on the spot. How could he possibly bring a child into his warped, obsessive-compulsive world?

"Tell you what, guess who's in the backyard?"

Ricky looked up, the hope shining in his eyes wrenching Fox's heart.

"Abby?"

"Let's go see."

Back in fresh albeit very hot air, Fox watched the boy lying on the ground wrestling with the German shepherd, who slobbered him with doggie kisses and left Ricky giggling breathlessly. Abby knew this was the one human where all rules were out the window—she could jump and lick to her heart's content. Frankly, Fox couldn't tell who was having a better time, the boy or the dog. The two began to chase each other around Fox's overly large back yard— the one he struggled to keep mowed and watered in the scorching summer heat. If the place hadn't come with built- in sprinklers and he had more money, the green grass would have been replaced with a mini-prairie of blue grama and buffalo grass a long time ago. Now, though, he could see why some people fought to maintain a lawn in this part of the world—what could be better for a kid and a dog at play?

"Watch out for dog poop," Fox hollered at Ricky, who was running through the grass toward the yard gate and the old tire swing hanging from the poplar outside the fence. Leaving the gate open for Abby, Ricky put himself through the tire on his belly and spun himself in all directions as Abby trotted around him, catching a pat on the head every so often. Fox had never had the heart to take down the tire swing when he moved in. The poplar and his old Granny Smith apple tree stood beyond the edge of his fenced yard. The tire swing and the apples had been enjoyed by folks in the old neighborhood for decades, so he left them in place when he moved in. The swing and community apples reminded him of his childhood and a freer, if perhaps riskier, time. Hopefully his sentimentality would not be rewarded by a lawsuit.

Fox found himself pushing the tire swing up and around, with Ricky yelling "Higher! Higher!" Finally when his arms began to complain, Fox grabbed the tire and spun Ricky around to face him. "I'm getting hungry, kid. How about a burger?"

"Yeah! McDonald's?"

Ah, the power of corporate advertising and manipulated taste buds. "I know a better place. And hey, would you mind if I invited a friend along?"

"I really shouldn't have let you talk me into this," Faith said, digging in for another scoop of her raspberry ice cream with chocolate sprinkles. Across from her, Ricky shoveled in some kind of pistachio ice cream concoction. It was clear he remained skeptical of the merits of a burger made from grass-fed Coleman Beef, the specialty of Good Times—a liberal, politically correct version of a fast food joint. But by dessert, Ricky seemed to have let go of comparisons.

Faith studied the child, noting a trace of Fox in the thoughtful dark eyes and wide mouth. No doubt about it—the kid was gorgeous. A little like the child she had carried in her womb for five months, probably, with the dark Hispanic features of her ex. Tears welled and she focused back on her ice cream, rubbing her eyes with the back of a finger.

"Yup, I can see you weren't hungry," Fox said to her.

Faith looked up, catching a teasing glance from Fox.

"Okay, okay. A girl's gotta eat, after all." She smiled.

Flirting. Is that what they were doing? Was flirting like riding a bicycle? She flashed on a poster that Trish purchased when she and her husband had gone splits-ville. A cartoon goldfish in a pond looked down with puzzlement at a little bicycle stuck in the sand. "A Woman Needs a Man like a Fish Needs a Bicycle," the poster proclaimed. At least Faith had lived long enough to know that she couldn't look to some guy to provide happiness, despite all those Sleeping Beauty and Cinderella stories of her childhood to the contrary. How had that one shrink of hers put it? Happiness is an inside job? Still, without a little human companionship now and then, where would the species be? On the third hand, a little human companionship usually led to a lot of broken heart that took her months to get over. As she'd gotten older, she had begun to think that a few days or weeks of bliss weren't worth the price. Better to stick with dead guys like Silas.

"Penny for your thoughts?" Fox said.

Faith laughed, nearly choking on the last mouthful of ice cream. "I don't think they're worth that much." Seeing Fox smile, she caught herself thinking there might be something worthwhile about hanging out with a live guy, even if Silas was a handsome devil in those old photographs. In one, he reminded her of a young and rakish Colin Firth...

***

"Unsung Hero"
By Faith O'Neill
Chapter 17

Oct. 18, 1864
Two miles outside Fort Lyon, Colorado Territory

"God in heaven. They are about the scrawniest lot I ever saw." Silas sat astride his horse, watching gaunt women in leather dresses leverage some lodge poles upright. Beyond the lodge Soule could see horses inside a rough corral of sticks. "I don't know who's thinner, them or their ponies."

"Look at that child," Ned said, nodding toward a toddler perhaps two or three years old.

Silas decided that for an Indian, the boy was quite handsome. He was unnaturally thin, however, playing in the dirt. Presumably his mother was among the group setting up housekeeping.

"Shouldn't they be well fattened up after the summer?"

Ned took a puff on his cigarette. "I'm hearing the buffalo are getting harder and harder to find, what with the government encouraging every fool with a rifle to shoot them and let them rot."

Left Hand walked out of a lodge that was already in

place. The buffalo skins making up the walls of the lodge were decorated with crude pictures of people and horses, in shades of blue and orange and red. Silas wondered how they made the paint.

"My friends, it is good to see you," the chief said. He smiled slightly, but Silas thought the man looked much worse than he had even 10 days ago. Still, he didn't bear the marks of small pox that was taking down many of the Indians over Texas way. Silas had heard rumors that the U.S. Army was giving some Indians blankets contaminated with the pox virus, but it seemed unlikely to him; wouldn't that jeopardize the troops themselves?

The officers dismounted and shook hands with Left Hand.

"We heard word you had arrived," Wynkoop said. He told the ten other soldiers they could dismount. "How many do you have with you?"

"I have my band, and Little Raven's band is with us. Altogether there are more than 100 lodges, perhaps more than 600 people." Left Hand invited Wynkoop and Soule to his lodge, and the three of them sat on buffalo robes laid on the ground outside the entrance. The weather was warm and the sky stretched blue and cloudless. The once green leaves of the cottonwood trees now shimmered a buttery yellow. Although Silas missed the red and orange autumn leaves of Maine, he had to admit that October in the Colorado country was a spectacular time of year, a welcome pause after the blazing heat of summer and before the brutal winter cold.

A middle-aged woman appeared with a tin plate containing a few small pieces of dried meat. Silas exchanged a look with Ned, but each of them took a small piece. They already knew that refusing the food—even on the best of intentions—would cause shame to their hosts. Then each of them protested mightily that they had eaten recently and could eat no more.

The three men sat quietly for several minutes. Finally Left Hand spoke.

"Major, my people are near to starving. We have found no buffalo. We need your help."

Ned removed his leather gloves and laid them across one leg.

"I will issue you provisions. I will send out some wagons with flour, sugar, coffee, tomorrow. How was your journey here?"

"We have too many children dying," Left Hand said, glancing toward the youngster playing in the dirt.

"I'm sorry to hear this," Ned said.

"Have you heard from your military commander yet?"

"Yes. He wants all stolen stock returned and the culprits turned over to us."

"And then there will be peace?"

"I am doing all in my power to make it so," Wynkoop said.

There was another pause.

"My people would like to come to the fort, to trade."

"Of course. As long as they remain well behaved, they may come and go at will," Wynkoop said. "But tell them my men are under orders not to provide liquor at any price."

"I understand. Sometimes I think the liquor is the worst enemy."

"We have brought a few things for you today." Ned reached in the saddle bag he had brought over to the meeting. He laid out packages of tobacco, sugar and flour, as well as a small package wrapped in brown paper. Left Hand opened the paper and smiled at the small pile of beads inside.

"My daughter will be pleased with the beads to decorate her dress," Left Hand said.

"How are your people taking to our agreements?" Ned asked.

"Well, overall." Left Hand took a small piece of meat from the tin plate. He held it in his hand and studied it as he spoke. "My people know how to make war, but for many years the Arapaho have been known as the best traders. We have made friends with many tribes because of this. So it is not strange for us to seek peace with whites."

Ned nodded. "And your young men?"

"If some buffalo appear that they can hunt, this will do much to calm them."

Left Hand reached into a leather pouch and removed a small stone pipe carved from cream-colored rock.

"Major, please take this pipe as a thank you for all you have done for my people. It was a gift from my father and I would like you to have it."

Silas watched Ned hesitate.

"Chief, I am still waiting for word from my commanding officer. Why don't you save this until later?"

"My friend, we never know what comes tomorrow. We only know what we see today."

Ned looked over at Silas, then put out his hand to accept the beautiful pipe from the chief.

"I will cherish this always," Ned said.

Silas could have sworn he saw a tear in Ned's eye.

23

The boy held the tiny pink creature in his cupped hands, oblivious to the two men standing near him.

"Normally we try not to handle the kits—the last thing we want is for them to imprint on humans," Carmichael said.

At this Ricky looked up with a question in his eyes.

"That means they would grow up thinking they are humans instead of black-footed ferrets," Carmichael said with a smile. "But this little guy hasn't opened his eyes yet, and anyway we have to feed him because we had to take him away from his mom. That's why we have him here in the nursery." Carmichael waved his hand to encompass the small room where they stood. A row of rectangular, clear-fronted containers lined the metal shelf against the wall. Carmichael had pulled the baby ferret out of one of the containers, which he informed them were called animal intensive care units or AICUs.

"How come?" Ricky said, his eyes back on the squirming, nearly hairless being.

"Well," Carmichael paused, looking at Fox. Fox

shrugged and nodded. "His mom isn't too happy in her new digs, she's pretty stressed. She ate her other two kits."

"Gross," the boy said.

"Actually, stuff like that happens in nature," Fox said. "Sometimes a female prairie dog will eat her sister's babies. Even housecats sometimes eat their kittens."

"Why?"

Now it was Fox's turn to look at Carmichael, who returned the shrug.

"We're not sure, really," Fox said. "With prairie dogs, we think the moms who kill someone else's babies may be trying to get more protein so their milk is better for their own babies. With housecats, it may be young cats who don't know what they're supposed to do with their babies."

Fox watched Ricky talking softly to the infant ferret exploring his palms with tiny pointed nose and clawed feet.

"Would you like to feed him?"

Ricky looked up at Carmichael with such a wide-eyed expression of hope and wonder that Fox felt tears welling in his eyes. The big, red-haired man walked over to a small refrigerator and took out a small glass container holding a milky liquid. He unscrewed the metal top and set it aside as he put the small jar into the microwave on the counter. After a couple seconds, the scientist pulled out the jar and swirled the liquid inside.

"We have to let it cool a little," Carmichael said. After a couple minutes, he opened a drawer and brought out an eyedropper still in its plastic wrap. Carmichael un-wrapped the dropper and used the tip to stir the liquid. Then he filled the eyedropper and squeezed out a drop on his wrist.

"This little guy has already gotten used to this. Let me

show you." He took the baby in one hand and with the other, brought the dropper to the creature's mouth. Suddenly the ferret began sucking on the tip of the dropper. "The trick is to just squeeze a little bit at a time, so he has time to swallow."

Carmichael handed the tiny ferret back to Ricky and watched the boy carefully feed the baby as instructed.

"You're a natural! You're an honorary conservation biologist!" Carmichael said.

Fox watched the two and realized that beyond providing Ricky with a great experience, asking if he could bring the boy with him to the ferret recovery center was a stroke of genius. Carmichael seemed to love kids.

"Thanks for letting us come on such short notice," Fox said.

"Not a problem. Our usual Monday morning meeting got canceled and I always love to show this place off."

Carmichael diplomatically left out a reference to "professional courtesy," but Fox had no illusions. If he had been Joe Blow Public and not a game warden for the State of Colorado, there would have been more hoops to jump through and more of a delay. This new facility set up by the U.S. Fish and Wildlife Service was part of a multi-million dollar effort by the federal government to save the black-footed ferret from extinction. The biologists here were more focused on breeding ferrets for placement in the wild than on giving tours. Not to mention that there were so many variables in this business. When the last few ferrets were discovered in the wild in the mid 1980s, biologists rushed to the scene to study them. Many of them brought their faithful doggy companions along, and one theory was the dogs carried canine distemper. Of course, local coyotes also might have been carriers. Regardless, disease killed off many of the last remaining ferrets.

"He's probably had enough," Carmichael said, helping Ricky replace the little ferret into the aquarium and capping it with a screen he locked into place. "Wanna see our pretend prairie dog town?"

Carmichael led them outside to an area fenced with metal mesh. The ground was fairly bare, although they could see holes in the ground rimmed with black plastic. "How'd you set this up?" Fox asked.

"We took a cue from Trish O'Neill, the relocator," Carmichael said. "We put some wooden boxes in the ground with connecting drain pipes that come up to the surface. This is how we train the kits to hunt."

"Hunt what?" Ricky asked.

"Prairie dogs," Carmichael replied. "Remember, the babies born here have never lived in the wild. If we don't teach them how to catch their food, they won't do very well when we put them out."

"How do you do it?" the boy asked.

"Well, a BFF mom and her kits spend at least 30 days in this pen," Carmichael said. "When we think they've got the hang of the burrow system, we bring a prairie dog to the pen so the kits can learn how to hunt."

"That's not fair," Ricky said.

"You're right. But it's also not fair that because of humans, the ferrets are almost gone. Remember, if these ferrets had been born in the wild, they'd be eating prairie dogs on a regular basis. And once they learn to hunt, we take them out to big prairie dog towns out in the country and release them so they can live the life they were supposed to."

Ricky went in the enclosure to look down the artificial burrows, leaving Fox and Carmichael at the gate.

"Dr. Carmichael—"

"Please. Call me Paul."

"Paul, do you happen to know when the last documented sighting of a ferret on the Front Range might have been?"

"How about this morning."

Fox turned to the man, eyebrows raised.

"Sorry, it's an old joke of mine. We have a pet domestic ferret at home. I trapped him after we got reports of a black-footed ferret in a vacant lot in our neighborhood. He's a dumpee. You know, the 'Born Free' syndrome."

Fox nodded. He knew of many domestic critters put into the wild by misguided and/or stupid folks who could no longer handle the rabbit/snake/guinea pig they'd bought their kids for Christmas. The animals usually died quickly in the wild because of predators they had never learned to avoid. Domesticated ferrets evolved in Europe and were a completely different species than the black-footed ferret, which evolved in North America.

"Last documented account I know of anywhere in Colorado goes back to the 1940s," Carmichael said. "That doesn't count the calls I get from folks who swear they've seen one in their backyards."

"What would happen if you verified an actual sighting? At a place where a development was going in?"

Carmichael stared at Fox.

"What's going on?"

"Probably a hoax. I'd rather not get into the specifics just yet. You guys haven't had any breakouts lately?"

Carmichael shook his head. "Security at this place is tighter than Fort Knox." He rubbed his chin. "I assume I can trust you to let me know as soon as you can? If there's any chance…"

"I know. I will, but I don't want to send people off on a wild goose chase if I can help it."

Carmichael sighed.

"Okay. Well, we'd look for a way to have the development suspended until we had a chance to verify the animal's presence. If we confirmed one or more BFFs on the site, we'd capture them and relocate them to an established release site. Although—"

"Yeah?"

"It could get political, I suspect, with folks using this as an excuse to try to permanently stop the development," Carmichael said.

Ricky wandered back toward them.

"Seems like everything's political these days," Fox said, putting his arm around the boy's shoulders. "Ready to go, sport?"

Fox guided Ricky out of the facility, thinking that perhaps things had always been political. Certainly it had been just as true in Silas Soule's time as in his own.

***

"Unsung Hero"
By Faith O'Neill
Chapter 18

Nov. 5, 1864
Fort Lyon, Colorado Territory

"What do you think?" Silas said in a low voice to Ned.

They stood side by side on the wooden porch outside Wynkoop's quarters, watching troops ride into the fort. The sun had vanished behind clouds and the afternoon had turned cold. Small groups of Arapahos gawked at the riders, pausing in the business of trading decorated buffalo robes for some of the soldiers' rations of coffee, hardtack, beans and bacon. Watching the cavalrymen approach, Soule recognized the officer at the front of the group. He should have felt the man a kindred spirit, but he did not.

"Looks like Curtis sent the great Scott Anthony to do his dirty work," he muttered. Ned sent him a warning look.

Major Scott Anthony rode straight up to Ned, dismounted, and tied his horse off. The men straightened and exchanged salutes.

"Major Wynkoop, Captain Soule."

Silas noticed the man did not smile, and that his eyes were as red as ever. Amazing what a good case of scurvy could do to a man.

"Good to see you, Major Anthony," Ned said.

"I have orders from General Curtis. May I speak with you in your quarters?" Anthony shot a glance in Soule's direction. "Privately."

Wynkoop escorted Anthony inside and Silas wandered into the yard and found Cramer near a group of Indians. He had a buffalo robe slung across one shoulder.

"So who is that?" Joe said, pointing with his chin

toward where Silas had recently been standing.

"You mean you've never met the great Major Anthony?"

"Isn't he the one who fought to keep Kansas a free state? Just like you?" Cramer asked.

"The very one, cousin to Susan B. Anthony herself, if she claims him."

"I take it you don't like the man?"

"He's a good soldier," Soule admitted. "Fought well at Glorieta. And apparently he's a shrewd businessman. Prospered with his general store up north in gold country, before he got his appointment."

"But?"

"But I don't trust him."

As if on cue, Anthony came out of Ned's office. He looked around, spotted Soule and waved him over.

"Captain Soule, assemble the troops please."

His heart sinking, Silas found the bugler and within minutes the men had gathered in the yard in formation. Around the fringes of the fort, Indians, trappers and wash women stood silently.

"Good afternoon," Anthony said, standing in the same spot Ned had been only a few minutes earlier. "I'm going to read orders from General Curtis."

Anthony cleared his throat.

"*30 October, 1864.*

I hereby order Major Scott J. Anthony to report to Fort Lyon in the Colorado Territory and assume the position of commander of the post. Major Edward Wynkoop is hereby ordered to report to District Headquarters at Fort Riley, Kansas.
Signed, General S. R. Curtis."

Anthony folded the order and tucked it inside his dark blue coat, ignoring the stir among the troops. He dismissed the men and summoned Soule.

"Please see that my men are fed and quartered, captain."

"Yes sir."

Soule went through the motions and it was nearly an hour before he could slip back to Ned's quarters. He found the major bundling up books and papers.

"Jesus, Mary and Joseph and all the saints," Soule said.

"We knew this could happen."

"I didn't think they'd relieve you of your command!"

Ned paused, looking down at his desk.

"At least Curtis gave me three weeks to get my affairs in order before leaving for Kansas."

There was a knock at Wynkoop's door.

"Yes?"

Cramer peeked in.

"Come on in, lieutenant."

"Sir, it's just not right!"

"Stand down, Joe. There's nothing we can do about it except to try to smooth things along."

"Ned, what did he say?" Soule leaned against a wall.

"Apparently the word is that we are giving supplies to hostile Indians."

Cramer started to splutter and Soule pushed away from the wall.

Ned raised his hands. "I know. I know. When I get there I'll be able to go into more detail, help them understand."

"Are they crazy then? To think you would do something like that?" Cramer slapped away a fly that hadn't yet succumbed to colder weather.

Ned walked to his favorite position at the window, as if taking in the sight for the last time.

"Anthony is moving in here in half an hour." He shook his head, then turned back to his officers. "I'll do everything I can to keep you two out of the soup. What I need you to do now is to talk to the men, assure them we'll do everything in our power to make this a smooth change."

"Yes sir." Silas clenched his fists. "Dammit, Ned."

"Go on, now."

Outside in the yard, Cramer turned to Silas.

"We've got to do something for him. He doesn't deserve this!"

"Whatever we do," Soule said, "I wonder will it be enough."

***

Faith bent over the prairie dog trap to write "G-13" on the yellow duct tape label. She capped the black permanent marker and began rising from her crouch, only to freeze—paralyzed by pain in her lower back.

"Fuck." She worked to control her breathing, to sweet-talk her back muscles into relaxing and freeing her from the spasm. "Okay, body, this is not the time for you to go on strike." As she spoke, the pain seemed to ease and slowly she brought herself upright. She let out a long breath. The last thing she needed was a repeat of a few years ago, when she had pulled a muscle in her back. Her walk had become a hobble, and pushing in the clutch on her standard transmission became damn near impossible. Back then, the library had let her stick to desk work for a few days, but she doubted the airport would postpone any poisoning on her behalf.

Her scalp prickled with sweat under her baseball cap and the tops of her ears felt like they were roasting. She glanced at her wristwatch and wasn't particularly surprised to find it was only 9:30 a.m. The monsoon season usually had kicked into gear by now, but was late starting this year.

Deciding she had earned a break after three and a half hours of work, Faith headed for the airport office and its bathroom facilities. One time when she and Trish were out on the open prairie setting up artificial burrows for a relocation project, the two of them ended crouching with their pants down on opposite sides of the truck, only partially shielded by the open truck doors. Treeless grasslands didn't offer much privacy when a girl just had to go, and the two of them had ended up giggling and gasping for breath. In this case, with light planes coming and going on a regular basis, she preferred the walk to the office.

Faith smiled at the woman behind the counter of the otherwise vacant room. "How's it going, Lisa?"

The attractive woman with short strawberry blonde hair returned the smile. "Peachy. Potty run?" She turned toward the radio microphone as a pilot asked for local weather conditions.

Faith hadn't even stopped on her way to the bathroom. "Bladder the size of a pea," she quipped, quoting from the movie "Paper Moon." She'd always felt a little sorry for the floozy character, since they both shared a need for frequent bathroom breaks.

Minutes later Faith stood drying her hands with a paper towel when she heard voices coming from the short hallway beyond the bathroom door. The man's voice she quickly pegged as belonging to Stan Rodgers, but his words were hard to make out. Not so the woman's.

"I'm so glad I caught you," the voice said. Faith stood quietly, trying to place the speaker. "Of course, we were so sad to hear about Trish. Then we got to talking and realized you folks might need some help."

Faith shook her head and sighed. Becca Whiteman. Co-operator of Prairie Solutions and the subject of many a rant by Trish.

"Relocation is so time-consuming, but in our case we could come in and flush for you and take the dogs over to the Ferret Recovery Center. Less time and money for you, and the animals go to a good cause. Everybody wins. Plus we've done the research to make sure our methods work."

Ah yes, the drum the Whitemans had been beating for the last 10 months since they'd gone into direct competition with Trish and began to lure away some of her clients. If nothing else, the line succeeded in pushing Trish's buttons, since she did not have a biology degree. "I guess a biology degree counts for more than working with dogs in the field for six years," she'd say bitterly. "I'd like to ring Becca's pretty little neck." Faith wondered if Becca's feelings toward Trish fell in "the feeling's mutual" category.

"Actually, Trish's sister Faith stepped in to finish the work for us. At this point we wouldn't have any grounds to change over," Rodgers said.

"Oh, okay," Becca said. "Faith seems like a nice person.

Works at the library, doesn't she?"

Faith snorted and opened the door.

"Oh, hi there," she said to the two of them. "Actually, Becca, I'm in my second career. I got tired of wildlife biology after ten years in the field. You know how it goes."

Faith was gratified to see Becca struggle to process this information and mold it into her world view.

"Actually, I taught Trish a lot of what she knew, although I never met anyone who could flush better than she could," Faith said, liberating a bit of her inner bitch. One thing she had learned from her own life was that it was unwise to make assumptions about people based on appearances. A drunk homeless man may have been a lawyer. A woman cleaning houses in Green Mountain might be working on her doctorate degree. A librarian might have fled to the sanctuary of the book stacks when the world of science let her down.

Becca at least had the grace to look embarrassed. She twisted the oversized diamond on her ring finger.

"Todd and I, we just thought you might be overwhelmed with your sister dying and all."

"How thoughtful of you," Faith said.

Rodgers cleared his throat. "I appreciate you stopping by, Becca. I'll let you know if we have stuff coming up."

After some quick handshakes, Becca walked off with her brown ponytail bouncing.

"And I thought the world of city politics was cutthroat," Rodgers said, eyeing Faith.

"Sorry," Faith said. "Trish wasn't a saint, but she sure had a helluva lot more experience than these slime balls who whispered about her behind her back. And who're in it for the money more than for the animals."

"Whoa there. Take it easy."

"Sorry," Faith said again. "My compassion levels are low these days."

24

Through the binoculars, Faith checked on the three prairie dogs already inside traps, standing on their hind legs scratching at the wire. At the third trap, another dog approached the outside of the Tru Catch trap and sniffed at the one stuck inside. Not kissing, as people usually thought, but acknowledging each other as relatives through smell. No matter how often she had seen this, the exchange still made her heart ache. No matter that her efforts were aimed at giving these animals a second chance, and that with luck these two would be reunited soon. Most people didn't realize how social prairie dogs were, living in tight family units. In fact, a big prairie dog town was more like a big city suburb. Each family group defended its own territory, defined perhaps by a tiny fence of taller grass. Neighbors were fine at a distance, but not welcome into the family home. Instead, the colony's families lived near each other more for protection than for socializing. Your odds are better if a prairie dog a quarter mile away spots the badger coming and sounds the alarm for *her* family—because you'll hear the alarm also.

Faith leaned back in the driver's seat. She had decided to start trapping in the area where she'd staged traps two days ago, even though she knew at least three days of pre-trapping was a better way to go. Becca's appearance that morning had spooked her a bit. Faith wanted to stay on the scene, not only for the prairie dogs, but also to remain in Trish's world awhile longer in hopes of gaining insight into her death.

She looked at her watch. The first dog had gone in the trap about 15 minutes ago. When Faith had taught Trish to trap, she'd recommended checking the traps two or three times a day. But Trish had come back once and found a trap overturned, allowing the gate to open and a housecat to reach in and snag the trapped prairie dog. She had discovered said cat still munching on the unfortunate rodent. After that, Trish tried to stay on site and not leave a dog in a trap more than 20 or 30 minutes. The problem was that by going out into the field to collect one animal, you scared dozens of others down their holes—sometimes for an hour, sometimes for the rest of the day. Trapping was a balancing act of compassion and efficiency. Faith picked up the antique Zeiss binoculars and scanned again. Yup, the relative of the trapped dog was working his way into another trap near the burrow entrance, munching on the irresistible Sweet Feed.

A light plane cruised in and lowered itself to the runway, sliding past the traps perched on the runway's edge. The dog near the trap paid no attention. Instead he took a step inside the trap, then another. A little more. Come on now. That way I can put you two together in the same kennel and your buddy won't be lonely. Come on. You can do it.

A chorus of prairie dog yips echoed through the colony. The prairie dog backed out of the trap at high speed and vanished from Faith's field of vision.

"Damn." Faith lowered the binoculars.

A red-tailed hawk circled over the burrows, ignoring the warning barks below. Most of the dogs in the area were at the lip of their burrows, barking at the enemy above.

"Good thing I'm not a pilot," Faith said to herself. "I'd be so busy dodging hawks and prairie dogs I'd be up shit crick."

Deciding to use the interruption to make a collection run, Faith turned the ignition key of Trish's van. She made a U-turn on the road overlooking the runways and worked her way around to enter the airport grounds.

Faith pulled down the lane between two airport hangars and stopped the car short of the runway. She got out and opened the side door. She put the green towel over her shoulder and set off with two small plastic kennels under one arm and a third under her second.

After making sure the runway was clear, she trotted across the tarmac as prairie dogs yipped even more frantically. By the time she reached the dirt, all the dogs were down except for the three in traps. She slowed down as she approached the first one.

"It's okay," she said quietly, as the panicked animal banged against the mesh. She set down the hay-filled kennels and spread the towel over the long rectangular trap and the animal inside. The dog quieted. She lifted the trap overhead, noting a broad space between the anus and genitals—a big male.

Faith set the trap down and propped a kennel on end

between her knees, with the door open at the top. She reached for the trap and angled it downward so the doorway rested inside the kennel opening. Faith slid up metal rings alongside the trap door, allowing the gate to swing open. When the dog refused to move, Faith peeked under the towel—prompting the prairie dog to plunge into the hay below. She closed the kennel and removed the bracelet roll of yellow duct tape around her wrist. Faith ripped off some tape for a label, stuck it on the kennel and used a Sharpie to write "A-31." Coterie A, trap 31. Plus the date of the dog's capture.

Faith stood slowly, coddling her back, and brushed hair from her forehead. One dog down. About 250 to go. No sweat.

She repeated the procedure for the two other trapped animals. Sweat slid down her spine as she trudged toward the car with the loaded kennels.

Above and behind her she heard the whine of engines. Turning her head, she saw a light plane landing on the runway she had to cross. A breeze blew hair into her face. Faith set down the three kennels and reached up to re-do her hair band as the aircraft coasted down the runway. Something wasn't right. The wheels of the plane seemed to wobble and jerk.

Then the plane veered toward her.

Faith grabbed two of the kennels and stumbled back toward the burrows. Behind her the thrum of the twin engines roared in her ears. She sucked in hot air and her thighs burned from the strain. Then her back seized and she fell face forward into the dirt.

***

"Unsung Hero"
By Faith O'Neill
Chapter 19

Nov. 6, 1864
Fort Lyon, Colorado Territory

At the sound of the shot, Soule stuck himself with the scissors he was using to trim his mustache. He ran to the window in time to see three Arapahos fleeing out the gate of the Fort. Sidearm in his hand, he ran outside clad only in his red undershirt and uniform pants. And stopped short when he heard men laughing.

Thinking they were amused by his disarray, Soule looked toward Ned's—no, Maj. Anthony's—quarters. The new fort commander stood on the wooden porch, chortling so hard that he wiped tears from his oh-so-red eyes. One of his guards stood nearby, grinning like the Cheshire Cat itself. The guard was putting his pistol back into his holster.

Soule saw Ned coming from the other direction.

"Major, are you all right?" Wynkoop said to Anthony.

"Oh," Anthony said, gasping for air. "Fine." This seemed to trigger another round of laughter. When Anthony finally caught his breath, he pulled out a pouch and began rolling a cigarette. Occupied with shaking just the right amount of tobacco into the rolling paper, he said, "My guard was simply carrying out our new orders. As you recall, Gen. Curtis made it quite plain that the Indians are to be kept out of the fort. This seems to be the only way to get their attention."

Soule watched Ned's face and sure enough, he saw the twitch. He'd only seen Wynkoop angry a handful of times, but each time the major did a masterful job of hiding his rage—except for the twitch of his right eyelid.

"Actually I have found them quite compliant with my spoken requests, Major Anthony. I would have been happy to relay your wishes to them."

"Frankly, Wynkoop, I think it needs to be made clear to them just who is running this fort, since I believe they may have been under the impression that indeed they themselves were in charge."

Soule waited for Ned to explode. Instead, Wynkoop seemed to clamp his lips together as he gave Anthony a cursory salute and barely gave the other officer time to respond in kind before turning on his heel.

Silas found Wynkoop in his new quarters, adjusting his hat.

"I'm going out to talk to them. Want to join me, captain?"

Soule did not point out that theoretically they ought to ask for permission to leave the fort. He did, however, need to finish dressing.

"I'll meet you at the gate in 10 minutes."

They left on horseback, even though Left Hand and Neva had positioned their people just across the river from the Fort—"river" being a misleading term. Soule could never get used to how people in this country called a sandy creek bed a "river" just because water flowed for a few months of the year. The rest of the time, there might be a trickle or not even that.

Left Hand and Neva greeted the men shortly after the cavalry officers rode into their camp among the now leafless cottonwood trees. Left Hand kept his blanket tight around him and invited the men into his lodge. The women left the dwelling as the men arrived.

After the customary greetings, Wynkoop started in.

"Chief Niwot," he said, using Left Hand's name in Arapaho, "I understand there was an unfortunate incident this morning."

Left Hand stared into the small fire burning at the center of the lodge.

"Three of our young men came to me and said your troops had fired upon them when they went to the fort to trade."

"They are no longer my troops," Ned said as Left Hand looked up. "I have been relieved of my command as of yesterday. A new officer, Major Anthony, has taken charge. I am here to tell you I will explain all that has passed between us to try to make sure that our agreements will be upheld and that you will be told of the military's decisions."

"We have seen this before, you know," Left Hand said. "I believe you are a man of honor. But who is this new man?"

Silas watched Ned, wondering how he would respond.

"He is an officer who fought bravely in the war of the states."

"Can we trust him?"

There was a pause, broken by new voices outside the lodge.

"You brought more soldiers?" Left Hand asked.

Wynkoop said, "No, no. Just Captain Soule and myself."

All the men got to their feet—Left Hand slower than the rest—and went outside to find Maj. Anthony and several of his guards riding into the center of the camp.

"Well, well, Major Wynkoop. Fancy finding you here," Anthony said as he dismounted. "In the future I expect you to request permission before you sally from the fort. This time I'll overlook the omission as a lapse of memory. I'm sure you simply forgot that you are no longer the commanding officer."

"Yes sir."

"Is this the famous Left Hand?"

"I am Niwot or Left Hand, as the whites call me."

Anthony had to have known that Left Hand spoke English. Still, he appeared somewhat shocked at the chief's complete fluency.

"A pleasure to meet you, Chief Left Hand. I am Major Scott J. Anthony, and I have been ordered to Fort Lyon to assume command of the post and make some changes. I hereby order your people to surrender all their weapons, as well as any horses or mules that you possess that belong to the U.S. military or to white settlers."

Left Hand turned to Neva and the two men exchanged a long look. Neva left. "My brother will carry out your wishes," Left Hand said.

Anthony looked around the camp.

"Major Wynkoop has informed me that he has been issuing provisions to your people."

"My people are very hungry. We wish to have peace with the whites and to help them however we can. We have no desire to fight. We have said as much to your Governor Evans, and we have turned over many white prisoners to prove we are of good heart."

"So I have heard."

Anthony turned to watch several young braves approach, leading four gaunt horses and several mules.

Other young men appeared one or two at a time with a few weapons and laid them on a blanket on the ground. Soule found the assortment rather pathetic—three rifles, a pistol and dozens of bows and arrows still in their quivers. Silas suspected not all the weapons had been presented. Under similar circumstances, no doubt he himself would have kept a few things aside.

Soule guessed Anthony had reached the same conclusion, but wondered if the man would have the temerity to order some kind of search.

"Have you heard from Black Kettle's people?"

Left Hand nodded. "Yes. We understand about 600 of our Cheyenne brothers are to the north, perhaps three to four days away. Another 2,000 are perhaps twice as far. They are coming here at the invitation of Major Wynkoop."

"Yes, yes, I understand the circumstances," Anthony said, sounding impatient. "I suppose they would expect us to feed them as well."

Left Hand did not reply.

Anthony huffed. "Well, Chief Left Hand, considering your arrangements with Major Wynkoop, I will issue your people some rations for the immediate future. Bear in mind, however, we will have to re-evaluate the situation in the coming days."

When the troops returned to the fort, Anthony immediately ordered Wynkoop and Soule to his quarters.

"If you ever break the chain of command again, I will have you court-martialed," Anthony said the moment the three of them were in the room with the door closed. "Is that understood?"

The two officers said yes and Anthony dismissed them.

Wynkoop and Soule walked out in silence, but Silas would have sworn they both had one word on their minds.

Bastard.

25

The roar of the propellers deafened Faith. Her heart thudded in her chest. Air churned by the aircraft's blades buffeted her body. Then the noise and gale passed over her, like a motorized tornado.

Raising her head just a fraction, Faith saw the plane jerk to a stop in the dirt some twenty feet beyond her. The engines coughed and died.

Faith put her face back in the dirt. There was a moment of silence. She smelled the earth, clutched at it with her fingers. She choked back a sob but her effort at self control sent a shudder through her body. Her back went into another spasm and she froze, unable to move.

A sound like a plane door opening. Running footsteps.

"Oh my God. Oh my God. Are you alright?"

A woman's voice was in her ear, a hand was on her shoulder.

"Oh God. Are you alright?"

Like something from a home video, an image of herself falling and a plane rolling over her caused her to giggle into the ground. She couldn't stop. The idea was hysterical. Then her giggles abruptly morphed into sobs.

"Faith? Faith? Are you okay?" A man's voice. Stan Rodgers.

"I don't know what happened," the woman said. "My wheels had just touched down, everything was fine. I must have hit something. I don't know what happened."

"Faith?" Stan's voice was in her ear.

"Can't," Faith mumbled into the dirt.

"Can't what?"

"Can't move. Back hurts."

"What did she say?"

Faith could see the woman's brown leather hiking boots near her face.

"Her back is hurt."

"Oh God!"

At the note of panic in the woman's voice, Faith decided she better do something. Taking deep, slow breaths and trying to keep her spine as straight as possible, she pushed with her right hand until she was lying on her left side. And looked right into the gray eyes of Keyhole's madam mayor.

"Don't move! Don't move anymore. The EMTs are coming."

Faith wiped her mouth with her hand and swallowed. From a distance she heard the wail of a siren.

"It's okay, really. It's just my back."

Violet Brady put her hand over her mouth. "Oh my God."

Faith stifled another giggle over the mayor's limited vocabulary. She eased herself to a sitting position. Her back did not complain.

"No, no. I just had a back spasm. I'm okay, really."

"Are you sure?" The mayor's brow wrinkled with concern. Maybe she feared a lawsuit?

"No, really. My back seized up while I was running and—" Faith jerked upwards.

"Easy, there sport," Stan said. "Take it easy."

"Where are they?" Faith said, her voice rising. Now she sounded panicked to her own ears.

"Who?"

Faith twisted away from Stan Rodgers and stood up shakily. The two kennels sat only a few feet away. One sat as if Faith had simply put it down. The other leaned on its side. Walking up, Faith could see the metal door remained in place. She let out a breath of relief. Then she remembered the third kennel. Looking toward the asphalt of the airstrip, she saw the wreckage of plastic, metal and hay strewn along the edge of the tarmac.

"No," she breathed.

Faith walked slowly, scanning the debris. The kennel had broken apart in pieces. Tufts of green hay lay scattered. No blood. No body. The dog had apparently run for cover in a stranger's hole.

There were worse things.

***

"Unsung Hero"
By Faith O'Neill
Chapter 20

Nov. 26, 1864

Fort Lyon, Colorado Territory

"**We have sumpin'** for you to take with you, sir." Cramer spoke first as he and Soule stood in front of Ned. The major was packing the last of his things. Cramer handed him the two letters. Wynkoop stood looking down at the paper. "Go ahead, sir," Joe urged. "Read them out loud."

Silas watched as Ned unfolded the first letter, which Cramer had solicited from the local farmers and ranchers. No less than 27 area residents had signed the letter Wynkoop stood reading:

Major E.W. Wynkoop:

We, the undersigned, citizens of the Arkansas Valley, of Colorado Territory, in view of your recent action in taking certain chiefs of the Arapahoe and Cheyenne tribes of Indians to Denver to have a consultation with the governor of this Territory, and your efforts thereby to effect a treaty of peace and restore pacific relations between us and those tribes who have threatened our peace and safety as settlers of this country, desire to express to you our hearty sympathy in your laudable efforts to prevent further danger and bloodshed, and sincerely congratulate you in your noble efforts to do what we consider right, politic and just, whether those efforts on your part prove successful or not, sincerely hoping they may prove successful, and peace instead of war reign throughout our land.

In consideration of the danger and risks you

have incurred in achieving the rescue of prisoners from those tribes, the hazard to your own life and the lives of the men under your command, we desire to further express our appreciation of your bravery, as well as your sense of right, and earnestly express the hope that the merit which is justly your due may not go unrewarded in official preferment as well as the gratitude of private citizens.

As Ned silently read the list of signatures, Silas watched him shake his head.

"Amazing," Wynkoop said, looking up from the paper in his hand.

"Read the other, sir," Cramer urged.

As Ned unfolded the second letter penned by none other than Joe, Soule—who had read the letter earlier—remembered marveling that Second Lieutenant Joe Cramer, who spoke like a backwoods country boy, could write like a true gentleman. Silas had decided that Joe was a humble man who had hidden a quality education in exchange for a more relaxed relationship with the soldiers around him. Once again, Ned read aloud:

Dear Sir:

Having learned with regret that you have been relieved and ordered to Fort Leavenworth to report your official proceedings in regard to Indians while in command of this post, I cannot let the opportunity pass without bearing testimony to the fact that the course adopted and carried out by you was the only proper one to pursue, and has been the means of saving the lives of hundreds of men, women and children, as well as thousands of dollars' worth of property.

No one can doubt that the lively aid rendered by you (at the risk of your own life as well as the lives of your small command) to the captives among the Arapahoes and Cheyenne Indians, was also the means of saving their lives. For this act alone (even if you had not done more) you should receive the warmest thanks of all men, whether in military or civilian life.

Your visit to Denver with some of the principal chiefs of the Arapahoe and Cheyenne tribes was productive of more good to the Indians, and did more to allay the fears of the inhabitants in the Arkansas valley, than all that has been done by all other persons in this portion of the department. Since that time no depredations have been committed by these tribes, and the people have returned to their houses and farms, and are now living as quietly and peaceably as if the bloody scenes of the past summer had never been enacted.

Hoping that in all things your course will be approved by the commander of this department, and that you will soon be restored to your command in this district, I remain your obedient servant,

> *Joseph A. Cramer,*
> *Second Lieut.,*
> *First Cavalry of Colorado,*

All seven of the other officers at the fort had also signed the letter, including Silas and First Lt. James Cannon of the First New Mexico Volunteers.

But it was when Ned read the postscript to this second letter that Silas saw his eyes widen in apparent surprise.

Respectfully forwarded to headquarters district, with the remarks: That it is the general opinion here by officers, soldiers, and citizens that had it not been for the course pursued by Major Wynkoop towards the Cheyenne and Arapahoe Indians, the travel upon the public road must have entirely stopped and the settlers upon the ranches all through the country must have abandoned them or been murdered, as no force of troops sufficient to protect the road and settlements could be got together in this locality.

I think Major Wynkoop acted for the best in the matter.

Scott J. Anthony

"Well, I'll be damned," Ned said.

"You see?" Silas said. "Our long speeches served their purpose. He's acknowledging you made the right choices."

"That seems to be so," Ned said. "It eases my mind. What with Left Hand and Black Kettle waiting for word."

Wynkoop walked to the window of the small room, taking in the yard of the fort.

"Looks like Smith's headed out to do some business."

Beyond the major, Silas could see a wagon loaded with trade goods. The translator John Smith was strapping down the crates of coffee, sugar, rice, flour and bacon with the help of Private Dave Louderback and a teamster.

"Anthony asked Smith to go out to the Indians, see how many are already out at the creek," Wynkoop said. "John told me he was glad of the opportunity to do some trading, see his wife and son again."

Some men in the fort looked down on Smith for wedding an Indian woman and producing a half-breed son, but it was common enough among men long in this territory.

"I'm going to miss this God-forsaken place," Ned said.

"You did the right thing, Ned. I'll always be proud of what we've accomplished."

"That goes for me too, major," Cramer piped in.

Ned carried his bags outside, where soldiers loaded them in the stagecoach. The troops serving as an escort were already mounted and waiting.

The three men shook hands in the dirt yard, then Silas and Joe took a step back and gave Ned a formal salute which he returned smartly.

With a last adjustment to his dark blue uniform, Ned climbed up into the stage, which lurched forward the second the major was inside.

"Haw!" the driver hollered at the team of horses and the wooden wheels threw up a small cloud of dust as the vehicle traveled out the gate of the fort and turned left. At almost exactly the same time, the buckboard wagon carrying Smith, Louderback, the teamster and all the trade goods, lumbered out the gate and turned the opposite way.

"What will happen to him, do you think?" Cramer asked.

"Ned's a good man. Not even the army is so stupid as to lose an officer like him."

Silas reached for his cigarette fixings, feeling the urgent need of a smoke and wondering if he had given the army more credit than it deserved.

26

Odd, Fox thought as he and Ricky walked back to his personal truck in the parking lot of the black-footed ferret recovery facility. There was no reflection off the passenger side window. Then he realized there was no passenger side window. Instead, small chunks of glass covered the gray cloth of the seat.

"Uncle, look!" Ricky exclaimed.

The facility behind him might be tighter than Fort Knox, but obviously the parking lot was not. Fox held Ricky back and unrolled the cuff of his long-sleeved shirt, using the material to cover his fingers as he opened the door. He reached behind the truck seat for the box of latex gloves he kept there and slid on a pair. There was always a chance that someone had put a finger down in just the right way and left a clue.

A glance told him his car stereo had survived to play another day. His CDs rested undisturbed in their cloth container attached to the visor. Fox reached for the glove box and felt underneath his insurance paperwork. Blocking

Ricky's view with his body, he held his breath until his fingers touched the hard plastic body of his Glock 357 Sig. Proverbial sigh of relief. Everything well with the world. Perhaps someone interrupted the thief.

"Did they take anything, Uncle Johnny? Up on the rez, the guys say you should ditch hot stuff as soon as you can. We could ask at some of the pawn shops around, maybe get it back."

This was way too much knowledge for a eight-year-old.

"Nah, looks like everything's here, so—"

A thought occurred to Fox.

"Uncle?" Ricky looked worried.

"Hang on a sec." With a sense of dread and grim expectation, Fox again opened the glove box. He patted at the papers serving as camouflage for the weapon beneath, but the white envelope from the drugstore was gone. Along with the negatives he'd forgotten to give Faith when he handed her the snapshots.

Shit.

The sheriff's deputy who responded was polite but brief. He had bigger fish to fry than some lowlife snatch-n-grab car thief, especially one who only took some photo negatives. Fox reported the theft as a formality for his insurance and as a professional courtesy (after all, he liked to keep track of stuff on his own turf.)

He drove back to Keyhole, pissed and determined to make some connections when it came to Trish's death. Why would someone search his car? Did someone know about the photos, or had it been a lucky find? Whoever it was, they weren't street-savvy enough to make the break-in look like a real burglary by taking the gun and the CD player. No, this had to be someone on a mission, suspicious of something Fox was doing. And the only thing Fox had been doing differently in recent times was hanging out with Faith. The break-in gave Fox a bad feeling. It made Trish's death look more suspicious.

Fox stopped by the house to pick up Abby before driving to nearby Roosevelt Park. He parked at a spot where he knew he could get an unsecured wireless signal and let the two-legged and four-legged youngsters out to play. Through his windshield, he watched Ricky and Abby tussling in the grass of the park, a sweet expanse of big trees and peace in the up-and-coming eastside neighborhood. He turned on his personal lap top, putting in his security code for a little off-duty snooping. Fox started with Borsich, the one with the most to lose if a little ol' black-footed ferret showed up on his would-be construction site.

As he waited for the computer to churn out the background check, Fox heard little-boy giggles and looked up to see Ricky pinned to the ground by a grinning German shepherd. Ricky hugged the dog, who let herself be rolled over. Now it was a grinning boy pinning a supposedly subservient dog. If there was ever a match made in heaven, it had to be these two. If Fox wasn't careful, Abby would soon be demanding more treats for her work as babysitter. Fox only had a vague idea of the kinds of things this boy had had to deal with, but dog therapy could only be good.

Information had appeared on the computer screen. Fox was somewhat disappointed to find that Borsich had a clean record. Not even a speeding ticket. Still, people with money could always hire someone else to do their dirty work.

Fox yawned, paused, then typed in "Jeremiah Johnson." He got a list of 276 people nationwide. Hmm. Musta been a lotta women with a crush on Robert Redford. Unfortunately many of them were born about the time the movie came out, like in the 1970s. Scanning the list he found only one who'd ever had a Colorado driver's license. A few more keystrokes and he was looking at the driver's license photo. Handsome guy with scraggly dark hair and a Peter Pan smile. He had the look fitting the character that Hope Packard had described, but he'd have to show Hope a photo to be sure.

"Uncle, Abby's thirsty." Ricky stood by the side of the car, the dog panting heavily at his side.

"See over there?" Fox pointed at a water spigot at the edge of the park. "Take her over and if you cup your hands, she'll drink out of them. Meanwhile, you might want this." He reached under the seat and pulled out a dirty, lime green tennis ball. "Just don't throw it near the street, okay?"

"Cool!" Ricky grabbed the ball and was gone.

The Jeremiah Johnson who Fox focused on came back with speeding tickets from multiple Western states. Fox sat up straighter. There was a domestic violence conviction in Utah with a short jail stint, and a marijuana possession charge in Green Mountain, Colorado that was resolved with community service—right about the time the guy would have been working on the prairie dogs for Trish. Fox thought back to the memorial service. He couldn't remember anyone who looked like this. And wouldn't Hope have mentioned if the guy was there?

Fox pursed his lips and typed in Hope Packard and her

address. He leaned back and closed his eyes. Fatherhood, or whatever it was he was doing, took some energy. He was sliding into a dream where he was back on his father's ranch—except the location of the barn and corrals was all wrong—when a child's scream and a screech of brakes ripped through his heart. He was up and out of the car before he was fully awake, running toward the sound of Ricky's voice.

"Abby! Abby!" The boy raced toward a red Subaru stopped in the road. A woman was getting out of the car. The German shepherd was nowhere in sight.

"Abby!" Ricky cried again and the dog came around the backside of the car, green ball in her teeth, tail wagging and a smile on her lips.The elderly woman was holding a hand on her heart as Fox ran up. "Did I hit him? I heard a scream and saw the dog run toward the road and the little boy right behind and I slammed on the brakes and—did I hit anybody?"

Fox inspected the boy and the dog and decided that the real casualty was the woman, who looked like she was about to pass out. "They're fine. Everyone's fine."

The woman leaned back against the side of her car. "Praise the lord and pass the biscuits," she said.

Fox laughed, nearly overwhelmed with relief. Ricky had his arms around Abby and was hugging her so hard the dog was getting restless.

"I had just looked down at some directions," the woman said. "If it hadn't been for the boy yelling I wouldn't have seen them. Oh Lordy."

"It's okay, ma'am. Just take it easy. I'm so sorry. I told him not to throw the ball in the street. Ricky come over here and apologize to this nice woman."

Ricky reluctantly let go of the dog. "Thanks for not running into Abby," he said. "I'm sorry."

"Ricky, I told you not to throw the ball into the street," Fox said.

"I didn't!" the boy protested. "I threw it and Abby bumped it with her nose and then she chased it and—"

"Okay, okay, sport. It's all right. I should have been out here with you. Hopefully we all learned something today."

Fox made sure the woman was calm enough to drive away, then he and Ricky headed back to Fox's vehicle. Fox noticed his hands still shook. Maybe he was making a huge mistake. What did he know about taking care of kids? But would Ricky be better off in foster care? Surely not.

Back in the vehicle, the screen of his laptop had gone black. While he waited for Ricky and Abby to settle in, he hit a key to bring the image back and found himself looking at a background check for Hope Packard. Her history went back three years, and then nothing. No driver's licenses from other states, nothing.

Hope Packard had apparently sprung to life full grown three years ago, like some kind of Greek myth.

***

"Unsung Hero"
By Faith O'Neill
Chapter 21

Morning, Nov. 28, 1864
West of Fort Lyon, Colorado Territory

"No, sir, no injun trouble. No injuns, for that matter." The driver of the mule team spat out a stream of tobacco juice, just missing Silas's knee as he sat astride Delilah. Behind Soule, nineteen other troops looked on. Nearby, a small thread of water in the Arkansas River murmured behind coyote willows, bound for the Missouri.

"We've been sent to scout the territory," Silas said. "Last night, I and another soldier spotted some campfires in the area. We were thinking maybe the Kioways were getting riled up. The Arapahoe and Cheyenne are peaceful, staying on a reservation. If they had come that close to the fort, they would have come on in the whole way to do some trading."

"Well." The muleskinner paused to spit again, "I said I didn't see no injuns. 'Sides, you got nothing to worry about with them soldier boys coming in anyways." The man gestured with his head toward the northwest.

Silas studied the teamster. "What soldier boys?"

"Colonel Chivington, o' course, outa Denver with his 'hundred daysers.' You saying you didn't know?" The teamster looked at Silas. "Seems like you fellas in blue ought to know what the other hand is doing."

"How many men?"

"Some ten, maybe twelve companies, I reckon."

Soule looked off in the direction the man had indicated, but saw nothing untoward. What the hell was Chivington doing down here? Showing up without notice, and with that many men?

Soule thanked the man and signaled his troops to put their horses into a trot. They only rode a couple miles when they crested a small hill and saw below them the spectacle of hundreds of mounted troops, riding four abreast. At the front was a man so big he appeared to be some kind of mythic figure.

Silas urged his men on, and his small group rode up to where the body of troops had stopped, apparently awaiting them.

"Well, well, if it isn't Captain Soule. How are things, Silas?" The big man sported an odd smile that made Soule uncomfortable.

"Fine, sir. We saw your campfires last night, but we didn't know it was you."

Chivington rubbed his chin.

"So they are not expecting us back at Fort Lyon, then?"

"No, sir. I didn't know you were coming until we came across a mule team driver a few minutes ago."

"I see. Any Indians at the fort then?"

Silas paused. "Not at the fort. Black Kettle's people and a few of Left Hand's are camped some miles away, but as you know sir, they're not dangerous. They continue to petition us for peace and are waiting for word from Gen. Curtis, as we have told them. We consider them prisoners."

An officer to the left of Chivington guffawed. "They won't be prisoners after we get there," he said, and the men near him laughed. Silas felt a chill go down his spine.

"I don't want that mule train to reach the fort before I do. Major Downing, you will accompany me. Captain Soule, you will escort my command to the Fort." Chivington kicked his big gelding and he rode off with his major before Soule could respond.

Silas led the command toward the fort but barely noticed his surroundings. He was too busy thinking.

It was noon when Silas and Chivington's command of volunteers reached the fort. Chivington rode out from the fort to meet them and then ordered his men to set up camp below the commissary. Soule sent his own men into the fort for the midday meal, while he stayed to watch the proceedings.

"Major Downing," Chivington called to the man who apparently stuck close to his side, "Station pickets around this post immediately. And read my order please."

Downing positioned his horse in front of the troops and held up a piece of paper.

"General Field Order number 2: One: Hereafter, no officer will be allowed to leave his command without the consent of the colonel commanding, and no soldier without a written pass from his company commander, approved by the commander of his battalion. Two: No fires will be allowed to burn after dark, unless specially directed from these headquarters. Three: Any persons giving the Indians information of the movements of these troops will be deemed a spy and shot to death."

Silas felt stunned. He looked toward Chivington and found that the big man was staring directly at him. Then the colonel faced his troops.

"Gentlemen, we will march at 8 o'clock this very night. Officers, see to it that your men are provisioned." With that, the colonel turned his horse and rode back into the fort. Immediately there was activity in all quarters, as Chivington's officers directed soldiers in the commissary to issue rations of bacon and hardtack, as buckboards were loaded with hay and sacks of corn for the horses.

Silas left Chivington's encampment, rode into the fort and headed straight for Cramer's quarters.

"Find Baldwin," Soule said, speaking of the other lieutenant that had served under Ned. Silas took off his hat and paced Joe's tiny room, slapping the hat against his thigh. "Chivington's going to attack the camp with Black Kettle and Left Hand. I need your counsel."

Cramer returned with Baldwin in the space of minutes and Silas outlined the situation.

"What did he say when you told him that the Indians he wants to attack are in Black Kettle's group?" Joe asked. "That they want peace."

"He said nothing. I believe he was planning to attack them all along."

"But why?" Cramer asked.

"Simply put? Because he can," Soule said. "I think the colonel has visions of being the next Kit Carson. I aim to find Anthony and enlist his help, but I wanted to know if I had your support before I do so."

Cramer shook his head. "Major Wynkoop would be furious if he knew."

"I agree," Baldwin said. "After all Major Wynkoop has done. These men are nothing but cowards."

Silas replaced his hat. "I'll find you as soon as I speak with Anthony."

The post commander responded immediately to Soule's knock and bid him enter. Silas found Anthony leaning forward in his chair, putting a knife and fork to a tasty looking piece of beef. Soule wondered where he had gotten such a meal.

"Excuse me, sir."

"No problem, captain," Anthony said, chewing. "You won't mind if I finish my dinner."

"Of course not, sir," Silas said, as if it had been a question in the first place. "Sir, I believe that Colonel Chivington plans to attack Black Kettle and Left Hand's people."

"I believe you are correct," Anthony said matter-of-factly, this time around a chunk of potato.

Soule stared at him in disbelief.

"But sir, you yourself pledged to uphold the agreements made by Major Wynkoop. These people are peaceful, they are no threat to us."

"Frankly, Soule," Anthony said around a mouthful of food. "Some of those Indians need killing for their transgressions. Indeed, I have only been waiting for enough forces to make it possible to pitch into them."

Anthony looked up. He swallowed the food he'd been chewing and pointed his fork at Soule.

"You'd do well not to look at me that way, Captain," Anthony said, adding, "Besides, Chivington has told me the goal of the attack is to punish the bad Indians in the camp. Those to whom I have pledged peace will be left alone, as well as the whites and the soldiers currently in their camp. Rest assured, you will not compromise yourself by going out and you can protect that lily white conscience of yours."

Soule stood speechless.

"And if you have it in mind to approach the colonel himself, I'd advise against it. He's none too pleased with your belligerent attitude. Indeed, he has threatened to take action against you if you continue to try to obstruct this campaign."

Anthony stopped chewing and stared at his officer.

"Is there anything else, captain?"

27

Faith pulled up to her house and her heart sank. She had hoped for an hour of rest and recuperation after her close encounter at the airport. Instead, the presence of her brother-in-law's Cadillac SUV at the curb told her that rest was not in the game plan.

"Good God, Faith, you look like you were run over by a truck," Tom Baker said. Strange, but his teeth looked grayer than she remembered. His pearly whites had been one of the things that had attracted her in that long ago, far away.

"Close, but no cigar," Faith said.

"Huh?"

"Just tell me what you want, Tom." She was in no mood for long explanations or reliving what had happened less than an hour ago.

"Can we go inside?"

"No. Tell me here."

Faith wanted to keep the conversation short. When she got inside, she was heading straight for the shower and a few minutes of warm bliss before heading back to the airport. Faith figured if they stood outside, Tom would make quicker work of whatever he had in mind.The man shifted uncomfortably.

"Uh, well, I figured I should let you know that I'm moving back to the mountain house soon. I know you've been going up there now and then. I didn't want you to be surprised, you know."

Faith stood speechless. A cloud passed over the sun, erasing the stark shadows of a moment before.

"I'm trying to finish Trish's airport job. What'll I do with the prairie dogs I'm holding up there in the shed?" Trish had long used the large shed at the mountain house as a temporary holding facility for the animals she was relocating.

Tom paused. "Maybe I can rent some kind of warehouse space in town. Just until you finish this job."

Faith rubbed her eyes.

"C'mon, Faith, this isn't some big surprise. Trish and I were married. She didn't have a will. Don't worry, I don't want Trish's personal stuff. Take what you want, I trust you. I'll probably give most of it away anyway."

Tom Baker stopped, apparently reading something on Faith's face.

"In name only," Faith said. "You were married in name only."

"Faith, be reasonable. Trish left me for her prairie dogs a long time ago. I was just a money tree to support her habit."

Faith choked on her disgust. "So you were a poor little victim, I guess. You had choices too."

"I loved her. I wanted it to work."

She snorted. "Right. Look, you're gonna do what you're gonna do. How much time do I have?"

"Well," again Baker paused. He looked off beyond Faith's shoulder. Was it her imagination or had he lost weight in the couple days since she'd seen him last? "We'd like to move in in three days."

We. Not *I.* Faith bit back the retort on the tip of her tongue. He was perfectly within his rights. Technically, he could have just moved back without telling her. But the image of his new woman in Trish's bed made her want to vomit.

"There're only a few things I want. Some jewelry that belonged to our mother. And I have Polly already."

She saw a look of relief wash across Tom Baker's face. Had he been planning to call the Division of Wildlife about the illegal animal that Trish loved, even though he knew Polly would be immediately killed? Then again, the new woman wouldn't want to share her mountain hideaway with a rodent.

"Is that all?"

Baker heard the frost in her voice.

"That's all. Sorry Faith," Baker said, backing away toward his car.

She stood watching him drive away and turned to go into her house. Then on some strange impulse, she turned and jumped in her own car, leaving Trish's van parked at the curb.

A few minutes later she realized that following someone in real life was a lot different than in the movies. She had to drive several car lengths behind Baker and so watched helplessly when he cruised through a green light just before the signal changed. She was stuck three cars back at the red light.

"C'mon, c'mon," she said, trying to stare the stoplight into compliance.

Three minutes later she drove ahead, speeding up in hopes of catching sight of Baker's vehicle. His car wasn't visible and she shook off feelings of insecurity.

She was about to give up and go home to her shower when the gods answered her. Faith spotted Tom Baker's car in a strip mall parking lot, in front of the town's Dunkin' Donuts. Waiting in a parking space a couple rows over, she watched him emerge about 10 minutes later. One hand held a plastic bag with the distinctive red markings from the drug store next door, while the other held a large white paper bag apparently full of sugary goodies. Interesting. Trish had often complained about how her husband hounded her for eating junk food. It was one of the few things Faith had continued to admire about her sister's husband—his discipline when it came to eating and staying healthy. Maybe his new woman was a doughnut junkie?

Baker's car pulled out of the strip mall parking lot and headed north. The stoplights were fewer now and Faith managed to keep him in sight. He turned left on Highway 60, heading west toward the Front Range mountains and Lyons, the village some 10 miles west of Keyhole.

Along the highway Faith stayed even further back since there was little traffic to provide camouflage. She passed by some outlying suburbs and then some farms that belonged to Green Mountain County Open Space. A quaint barn here and there, reminders of a much slower time.

Baker was picking up speed. As he approached the last intersection before Lyons, Faith fully expected him to get in the left lane and head south on Highway 36 toward Green

Mountain. Instead he zoomed straight west toward Lyons on a green light.

Puzzled, Faith slid through the intersection under a yellow light and immediately slowed down. As she figured, Tom Baker's SUV was stopped at a signal in old downtown Lyons. The quaint town sat wedged in a canyon, its narrow streets lined with artsy-fartsy shops and art galleries. Slower speed limits gave the town an opportunity to distract tourists bound for Rocky Mountain National Park.

She pulled into a restaurant parking lot and pretended to be considering where to park. When the light changed and Tom's SUV drove forward, Faith followed, still wondering where Baker was headed.

On the far edge of the small community, Baker turned left. Faith had thought he might go right on the well-used road to Estes Park, the gateway town to the national park. Instead, Faith's car was the only one behind him on the narrow, curving road that snaked between rocky bluffs. She eased off the gas and hoped he was too involved in his own world to be interested in her vehicle. For once she was glad her Honda Civic—like many others on the Front Range— was painted silver. Just another silver car, she said, mentally sending the message to Tom's brain.

On they went this way for another 20 minutes before Baker's SUV pulled off on a dirt driveway and disappeared down into a forested area by the creek. Faith took her foot off the gas, ignoring the angry look of a driver whose speeding car had appeared suddenly in her rearview and now passed with a throaty engine roar of road rage.

She pulled onto the shoulder and cut the engine. Why had Tom come to this isolated place? And what now? Wait in the car? Faith felt too antsy for that. She took a deep breath and got out of the car as quietly as she could, then left the car door ajar rather than risking a noisy slam. If a thief wanted her CDs, he could have them.

She found herself in the shade of a big old Douglas fir and felt a stir of gratitude. In the middle of a hot Colorado summer, the foothills could offer quick relief. Faith stood by the tree's trunk and pondered. She'd never considered Tom Baker to be a violent man. However, her sister was dead and he had the leavings. Her brush with death earlier in the day had left her oddly awake, angry and charged up. If she got caught she'd talk her way out of it. Right Sherlock?

Staying in the shadows, Faith spotted the SUV parked in front of a dilapidated cabin nearly hidden by old overgrown lilac bushes—remnants of some easterner's attempt to remember home. Lilacs did pretty well on the Front Range, but the blooms on these bushes were long gone along with the spring. Instead, their leafy bodies offered the promise of camouflage.

A branch cracked under Faith's foot and she stopped, waiting for Baker to come out of the cabin and confront her. When that didn't happen, she kept moving while conscious of her heart pounding. "Wuss," she castigated herself under her breath.

She worked her way to the lilacs near the cabin and found a small gap between a couple of the shrubs. Faith ducked her upper body and eased between branches, her goal a smudged window. Leaving some leaves between herself and the cracked glass, she peered inside the dim room, trying to get her bearings. And smelled something wretched, a burned chemical odor. Good God, what was that stench? Cupping her hand over her nose and mouth, she fought the impulse to flee and focused on seeing inside.

Baker stood with his back to her, facing an old kitchen counter. There was plastic tubing and some metal pots on the ancient gas stove. At first she was surprised that the stove would work, then realized there might be a propane tank on the far side of the building.

He couldn't be cooking something, could he?

And with sudden understanding, Faith realized Tom Baker was indeed cooking. Emphasis on something.

***

"Unsung Hero"
By Faith O'Neill
Chapter 22

Afternoon, Nov. 28, 1864
Fort Lyon, Colorado Territory

Lowly Second Lieutenant Joe Cramer stood his ground.

"Sir, perhaps you have not heard all the details of our interactions with these Indians. Frankly, I believe it would be murder to kill them." Joe was very aware of losing his backwoods accent in this context.

Chivington reared back in his camp chair. "How dare you accuse me of such a thing, lieutenant. These savages have killed white women and children. They need to pay the price."

"Sir, these 'savage' Indians saved our lives up at Smoky Hill. There were only some 120 of us and we were outnumbered at least five or six to one."

Chivington took out a cigar and carefully clipped an end. He struck a match and puffed for several seconds before raising his eyes to Cramer.

"Are you such an idiot that you cannot see these Indians have been using you to survive the winter before launching new attacks?"

"Sir, they are in pitiful condition. Even come spring they would have little chance. Major Wynkoop pledged his word as an officer and a man to these people. All the officers under him indirectly made the same pledge."

"Then you are all fools," the big man said, fixing Cramer with a hard stare.

Joe took a deep breath. "Sir, you are placing us in very embarrassing circumstances. You are asking us to go after the very same Indians that saved our lives."

At this Chivington rose to his feet from his camp chair. Major Downing watched from the side as the Colonel approached Cramer and towered over him.

"Lieutenant, are you aware that I have served as a minister of God?" Chivington took another puff. The end of his cigar glowed red.

Cramer swallowed. "Yes sir."

The colonel removed the cigar from his mouth and gestured with it in his right hand. "Then let me put it to you plain, young man. I believe it to be right and honorable to use any means under God's great heaven to kill Indians that would slaughter innocent women and children. Indeed, damn any man that is in sympathy with the Indians."

Chivington moved closer to Cramer until Joe could feel the heat of the cigar near his cheek.

"Such men as your precious Major Wynkoop and yourself had better get yourselves out of the United States service. Do you hear me?"

Cramer stood very still. What Chivington didn't know was that despite Joe's relatively small stature and good education, he had also been a scrapper all his life—a fairly common response to having been bullied. He had taken on men the size of the colonel and come out the winner. Staring up into the fiery green eyes of the colonel, Joe found himself thinking how he could use his leg to trip this man and bring him to the ground, to use the glowing end of Chivington's own cigar against him. To the colonel's credit, he seemed to pick up on Joe's thoughts, for at this moment he turned and walked back to his camp chair.

Sitting down, he turned to Major Downing.

"Major, you will escort the lieutenant back inside the post. We would not want anything to happen to the young man before he has the chance to vindicate himself in battle tomorrow."

"I don't know what else we can do, captain." Joe Cramer leaned against the wall in Soule's quarters. "Cossitt and Minton got some of the others together including some of the civilians and had another go at him. Even Colley was there. They said Chivington went livid with anger, storming around the room and yelling at them, the same as what he said to me. Damn any man in sympathy with an Indian."

Soule shook his head in amazement, not at Chivington, but at the fact that Ned Wynkoop was such a leader that so many people believed in him and would stand up for him. Not only Soule himself, not only lieutenants like Cramer, Cossitt and Minton, but civilians as well. Even that reprobate Indian agent Stephen Colley. William Bent had accused Colley of selling the Cheyenne and Arapaho the very annuities the government had granted them for free, trading the flour and coffee and blankets for valuable buffalo hides. Indeed, the word was Mrs. Colley even used annuity flour to bake those tasty apple pies with the flaky crust that she sold to Fort Lyon troops. And yet even the corrupt Colley was there, arguing for the Indians. All for nothing, apparently.

"Joe, I think it's going to happen. We need to think about what our choices are."

"Not good, any of them. I have a wife and a child on the way, sir. I don't want to be shot for a traitor by my own people."

Silas walked over to his desk and fingered the last letter he had received from his mother in Maine. He had planned to write to her tonight. His letters were always cheerful and carefully bland. What would she think of him, a leader in the Underground Railroad to save runaway slaves, if he willingly slaughtered these people who had turned themselves over to the whites? What would his dead father think? Yet he had worked hard to become a respected cavalry officer, sworn to do his duty and obey the chain of command. There had to be something they could do short of outright mutiny, short of killing Chivington and his officers. How could they live with themselves doing that? But how could they live with themselves gunning down Left Hand and Black Kettle and Neva and...

"Joe, gather our officers here as quickly as you can, and quietly. We need to put our heads together."

"Yessir."

Cramer left and Soule began rolling a cigarette. He remembered the time as a boy he had turned to his father, not long after Silas began taking part in the Underground Railroad.

"But Poppy, aren't there a lot more slaves still down south?" he had asked. "What about them?"

His father had turned to him with a gentle smile and put a hand on his shoulder. "Sile, son, we save the ones we can. That's all we can do. We save the ones we can."

28

"Did he see you?"

Faith rubbed her eyes in response to Fox's question. After her brief fling with espionage, she had left her brother-in-law to his strange devices and put in six more hours at the trap site. She was exhausted. Faith remembered something a friend had said years before, how different people have different personal ecologies. Trish could go 16 hours a day with practically no food or sleep. Faith got cranky if she didn't get at least nine hours of shuteye, plus several hours of downtime to read or write. Write. Oh God, the book. Sorry, Silas. Maybe you should haunt someone else.

Faith brought herself back to the man in front of her. "Not that I could tell. I just backed out of there and drove home. I guess I should have called the cops right away, but I wanted to talk to you first."

Ricky was in the bathroom at the Pizza Hut and Faith had used the opportunity to give Fox a quick rundown on her private-eye work.

"I have news for you too. Someone broke into my car

today and grabbed Trish's negatives from the glove box."

Faith stared at him. "Should I be freaking out? What's happening?"

"My guess? This is still a small town. We're asking a lot of questions. Someone's getting nervous."

"Speaking of nervous, forgot to tell you the mayor almost killed me today."

"What was she pissed off about?" Fox asked, smiling.

"No. Really. She almost ran me over with her twin-engine Cessna."

Fox listened to the tale without interrupting.

"So you're okay?"

"I'm fine, but I thought the mayor was gonna have a heart attack on the spot." Faith tried to grin, then found her lips trembling.

"Shit," she muttered, wiping her eyes. "Why is it I always seem to end up crying around you?"

Fox reached across the table and took her free hand, placing it between his two large paws. The warmth and electricity flowed up her arm. Heat surged into Faith's face as she looked across at the game warden. And watched the kindness in his dark brown eyes shift to something else, something fearful.

"Look Faith, I really like you, and I don't want anything to happen to you. I—I'm attracted to you. But I don't do relationships anymore. One wife thought I was too Indian, the other didn't think I was Indian enough. I still have PTSD from Vietnam. And I'm a dry drunk. You don't want to know what I was like when I was drinking. I took myself out of the game a long time ago. I just want us to be friends."

"Friends," Faith repeated, trying to read his face. Was he

looking for a bedroom buddy? Frankly, she'd been with enough men happy to bed her, but unable to love her. Now she chose to believe what a guy said, instead of hoping to change his mind between the sheets. And to think she'd started to fall for him.

"Agreed. Friends, no benefits. Now please let go of me."

He released her and sat back as if he'd been slapped.

"I'm sorry," Fox said. "I thought maybe you were getting, I don't know, kind of attached and—"

"Well, excuse *me*. I'll just *de*tach and get out of your way."

Faith jumped to her feet, ignoring the paper napkin that fell to the floor. She turned to go and found herself in front of Ricky, who stood very still with a stricken look on his face. She knelt down in front of him.

"It's okay, Ricky. Your uncle and I just had a little disagreement. You're a great kid." She gave the boy a quick hug and walked away, feeling somewhat satisfied that she was sticking Fox with the bill. And who needed him anyway? She had the perfect dead guy waiting for her at home.

When they got home from the pizza place, Fox checked his messages and heard Sam Gary's voice. "Call me," the assistant DOW director said, and Fox knew the man well enough to know he meant "now," not later. He tucked Ricky into bed and as he walked out of the room, Abby slipped by him. Fox never let the German shepherd sleep with him, but he couldn't bring himself to keep her out of the boy's bed. A kid needed something to hang onto, and the dog probably provided more comfort than Fox anyway.

Fox sat in his favorite chair, holding the phone and looking longingly at Faith's manuscript. He wondered if he'd ever get time to keep reading. With a pang, Fox realized he might never see the author again anyway. He punched in Sam Gary's number.

"What're you stirring up, John?" Sam Gary said at Fox's hello. "The director's getting phone calls from the Keyhole Chamber of Commerce claiming you're trying to sabotage development in the city with tall tales of photos of black-footed ferrets. No beating around the bush, just tell me straight."

For some reason, Fox thought in that moment that Sam Gary was the closest thing he had to a friend. He pictured him sitting on his back deck, a glass of rum and Diet Coke perched in the cup holder attached to his wheelchair.

"No secrets in a small town, I guess," Fox said.

Gary didn't respond but Fox heard the sound of ice clinking in a glass.

"Trish had some undeveloped film and when we got it developed, there was a shot of what looks like a live black-footed ferret at the Borsmart site." Fox ran a hand over his hair. "I'm guessing it's a hoax, but I figured it was worth asking around. Guess the Fish and Wildlife Service has a lot of friends around town."

"We who?"

"What?"

"You said 'we' got the film developed?"

"Oh, Trish's sister and I."

"Trying to get laid?"

"Huh?"

"There are easier ways than playing the white knight rescuing the fair damsel, you know. The director's pissed. He's planning on running for governor next year and Keyhole is a key part of his campaign plans."

"Well, goody for him," Fox said, still stinging from Gary's crass assessment of his attempts to help Faith. "Besides, I thought you were above all that political bullshit."

"Look, I ran interference for you. Told the director you probably had no idea what a stir you were kicking up. But unless you can find proof that there's any validity to this photograph, you need to back off. Let this go. You already have a reputation for ruffling feathers."

"Feathers need to be ruffled."

"Maybe so. But don't I recall you have an extra mouth to feed these days?"

With a jolt, Fox realized that being Ricky's caretaker entailed certain baggage he hadn't considered. Although he loved his job and didn't know what he'd do if he lost it, Fox had liked the idea of being free to stay or go.

"Okay, I'll back off," Fox said. Would he? What would he be without this job? And what would happen to Ricky if Fox lost his career? Think about it later. "Meanwhile, I need some help with a background check."

The game warden ran through Hope Packard's name, description, birthday and got off the phone. John Fox wondered if Hope could hide her past from a computer whiz like Sam Gary.

Only when Fox was lying in bed sliding into sleep did he realize Sam had referred to Trish's photograph before Fox did. He tried to think. Who other than himself and Faith knew the image existed?

Ten a.m. and already the heat was blasting from the sun. Faith wiped her brow as she sat in the beat-up van watching the traps down below. July first and no sign of the monsoons that swept into Colorado during the late summer. She had slept poorly after the argument with Fox and was on site by 5:30 a.m., using the dawn light to set traps in the first area and finishing up placing more traps in the new area.

Since she'd started trapping she had caught sixteen animals. Not bad, but the number would have been much higher if she'd had more time to acclimate the dogs to the traps. She had the critters stashed in kennels in Trish's storage shed. It would be a hassle to transfer them to another site just because Tom was in a hurry to move home.

However, if Tom was truly manufacturing meth, maybe a simple phone call would simplify things. Or maybe Fox had already taken action. She had hoped he would give her advice, but she had stalked off before they'd gotten that far in the conversation. Faith might not like her former brother-in-law, but he had been married to Trish and she wasn't sure about what she'd seen at the shack. If he was really making meth, did he kill Trish in a drug-induced haze? Or more likely, maybe he was running out of money and wanted Trish gone so he could get the insurance money, the house and whatever else. On the other hand, if it was meth, and if he had not done anything to Trish, would she want him thrown in jail, or give him a chance to clean up his act? On another hand—she had lost count—if he had killed Trish and she reported him for possible meth making, he would probably be out on some kind of bail and free to do to Faith as he chose. The whole thing was giving her a headache.

Faith leaned her head back against the seat. She jolted forward some time later at the sound of a car pulling up next to hers. Open Space Director Stan Rodgers got out of his pickup and walked up to her driver's side window.

"I have bad news, Faith."

"Let me get out of the car." She groggily got out and shaded her eyes against the blinding sunlight. "What's up?"

"Plague. The county has confirmed it in prairie dogs five miles south of here, and there's a little girl in the hospital with a suspected case. Haven't you read the paper lately?"

Distracted and distraught, Faith shook her head. Plague was much more of an issue for prairie dogs than for people. There was almost no risk for people, unless they actually held a prairie dog. Like herself. Even then, plague was usually curable and she knew enough to alert a doctor if she got really sick.

"So how does this affect me?"

"The City Council voted to shut down the relocation."

"What? Why?"

"For one? They don't want the liability if you get sick. For two—"

"For two?"

"They voted to exterminate prairie dogs on the south end of town to try to make sure there's no outbreak. And they left open the possibility of exterminating all the prairie dogs in town—even these."

"Shit. Tell me you're joking."

"No joke."

"And there's no law to prevent them from doing it." She wasn't asking a question. She already knew the answer.

"This is ridiculous. There's almost no risk to humans, just to the dogs," Faith said, hearing the heat in her voice. Plague, likely introduced by rats on ships docking in San Francisco around 1900, could wipe out entire prairie dog towns in days. "This isn't a health issue, it's a political issue. There's no reason for them to kill all these animals. Can't you explain?"

Stan Rodgers put a hand on hers. "Faith. I'm sorry. I tried to tell them that Green Mountain simply closes off trails when this stuff comes up, but one of the councilmen shouted at me that Keyhole isn't Green Mountain with its 'animal rights freaks.'"

She took a breath to steady herself. "So how long do I have?"

"I was able to persuade them to give you until Friday to shut down. Any animals left behind will be gassed. They plan to start the extermination on the south end of town as soon as they can get the contractors on the ground."

"Just on public land?"

"Public and private. They're calling it a health emergency."

"Holy shit." Well now. The new Borsmart would be on the south end of town. Wouldn't that just tickle Borsich to no end.

"'Course there won't be many official types around on Friday, so you might able to squeeze in a few hours then."

Faith rubbed her eyes. "Why won't they be around on Friday?"

"'Cause it's the Fourth."

July Fourth. Independence and freedom and an excuse for fireworks.

"Right."

"I'm sorry. I know it doesn't seem fair." Rodgers looked over across the airport runways. "We'll pay you for all your time up until you finish, including the relocation time. I did tell them you wouldn't be able to get the animals into the new location by Friday, so at least you can keep trapping until then, do the relocation after."

Faith nodded numbly.

***

"Unsung Hero"
By Faith O'Neill
Chapter 23

Dawn, Nov. 29, 1864
The Big Sandy, Colorado Territory

The horses' hooves broke through a small patch of ice on the mostly dry Big Sandy creek bed as D Company galloped to a position southeast of Black Kettle's camp. Capt. Silas Soule signaled for his men to dismount, along with the other two companies of the Colorado First under Anthony's command. The horses shifted restlessly, chewing on their bits. Steam rose from the mouths of both horses and men, breath turning to fog in the cold morning air.

"Easy now, girl," Silas muttered to Delilah, putting a gloved hand on her neck. Silas watched his men. Their eyes shifted from the view of the lodges standing in the sun a quarter mile away, to him, and then back again.

Looking behind his men and others of the Colorado First, Silas saw the "Bloodless Third" approaching with the big colonel at the front on his gelding. Chivington stopped his crew in the sandy bed of the river below the village. Silas saw the men take off the overcoats that had kept them warm on the 45-mile overnight ride from Fort Lyon. As men of the Third rode up behind Anthony's command, the sound of Chivington's voice began to reach Soule.

"...and remember the murdered women and children on the Platte!" the big man yelled. Silas groaned and watched as Chivington's hired guns dismounted and fired toward the lodges, over and through Anthony's men positioned between the shooters and their target.

"Goddamned idiots!"

As the two companies under Anthony's command spurred their horses to get out of the way of Chivington's bullets, Cramer pulled his horse alongside Silas. "Anthony sent us along the creek bed. Company D is ordered to the south bank."

Soule nodded in understanding and the two companies parted ways as the level of gunfire and cannon blasts increased. Apparently the cannons of Chivington's Third were now in operation, and some of that shot was landing among the lodges. Silas glanced behind him and was gratified to see his men in strict formation, as disciplined as if they were on a parade ground.

The old Indian woman in a beaded leather dress and

holding a bundle of sticks pushed aside the flap of leather at the lodge entrance and spoke rapidly.

 Private Louderback, who'd escorted the trade wagon to the Indian camp, looked up from his breakfast jerky.

"What did she say?" asked Louderback, still half dressed in his long johns and cavalry pants.

The translator John Smith turned to him. "She says she heard rumbling and there's a heap of buffalo coming."

Louderback might be new to this country, but he'd been there long enough to understand that he was among hungry people and that any chance of hunting buffalo might mean the difference between life and death.

The private, Smith and teamster Watson Clark continued chewing. But a couple minutes later, an older Cheyenne man pushed into the lodge and addressed Smith. The man looked agitated.

"What's happening?" Private Louderback looked at Smith, who had risen to his feet. The private stood also, sensing the charged atmosphere.

"Lots of troops headed this way," Smith said. "They want me to go out and see who it is."

"Troops?"

"Must be Blunt's men from Fort Riley in Kansas," Smith added. "I've gotta get out there and let them know they're about to attack the wrong damned Indians."

The private stared at the old weathered man in front of him. Smith had been ill and still wasn't in the best of health. Louderback said, "Look, if your son Jack can catch me a horse I'll ride out and see what they want."

The men rushed outside the lodge and saw that the troops were between the village and the horse herd. Gunfire split the morning and Louderback heard a child crying. The private pulled a white handkerchief out of his cavalry pants pocket and tied it to a stick.

Smith took the lead walking toward the troops, telling Louderback "They won't be likely to mistake me for an Indian," with a gesture at his hat and coat. But when the translator had closed the gap to about 500 feet of the soldiers kneeling on the ground, Private Louderback heard someone yell, "Shoot the old son of a bitch. He's no better than an Indian anyway."

Smith ducked and crouched, covering his head and trying to dodge bullets. Louderback shouted, "Smith! Smith!"

The private saw a real cavalryman race his horse past the lines of shooting men and head toward the old man. The private's heart rose at the sight of George Pierce of F Company under Joe Cramer. Pierce had earned a name for himself at Glorieta by dashing forward from the line to capture a couple of Confederate officers. Surely now the troops would stop firing, with the gallant soldier passing in front of them on his mission to save Smith.

"Attaway, George!" Louderback yelled, just before George Pierce's horse stumbled and fell, apparently brought down by the troops shooting at John Smith. Private Louderback watched as Pierce worked his way free from the saddle of his fallen mount. Almost the moment Pierce stood, a gun fired and the cavalry man collapsed. "No!" Louderback yelled.

Miraculously, Smith and Private Louderback ran unhurt back toward the lodge.

"The flag!" Black Kettle told his wife as the sound of

gunfire increased. The woman found the large American flag given to them in 1860. Together they took one of the lodge poles and attached both the U.S. flag and a white cloth. By this time White Antelope had appeared. The three of them raised the pole as Cheyenne women and children ran nearby.

"Come here! Stand by us," Black Kettle shouted. "Don't be afraid. We have protection!"

Many of the women and children gathered by the chief. There was only a handful of men—most had left the camp in recent days to search for buffalo. "Stay calm. When they see the flag, we will be safe."

Babies cried in their mother's arms while older children clung to the women's legs. "Come here. Stay by the flag!" Black Kettle yelled. More and more people gathered near the chief.

A group of soldiers rode toward the group. Black Kettle, his wife and White Antelope supported the lodge pole, waving it slightly.

The men dismounted their horses, crouched, and began shooting. A woman near Black Kettle collapsed, blood on her head.

"Stop! Stop!" Black Kettle yelled, using one of the few English words he knew. "Peace!" He switched to Cheyenne. "Stay calm. Stay near the flag," he said to the group still huddled near him.

The shooting intensified. A boy to the side screamed and held his bloody arm. In the next instant, a bullet struck his chest and he fell. At this, the group disintegrated. People scattered under a hail of bullets.

Black Kettle, his wife and White Antelope stood firm.

They had to hold the flag.

29

"I'd like to speak to Henry, please." Fox adjusted the portable phone at his ear while he poured milk over Ricky's cereal. Fruit Loops. Sugar and more sugar, the drug of choice for an eight-year-old, but Ricky had begged and Fox figured the sugar detox work could wait a few days. Fox shooed Rajul off the table before the cat could paw Ricky's glass of milk off the edge. Worried that Rajul might have contaminated the table with chronic wasting disease prions, Fox headed for the kitchen for paper towels and bleach.

"This is Henry."

"Henry, John Fox. How's life on the res?"

It was a running joke between them. Henry Grayfeather ran a Green Mountain relief fund for Native Americans, and the gathering place for Indians was an anomaly in the urban setting.

"Hot. Red hot. We're planning a protest up your way over that whole Chivington Road thing."

"Oh yeah? When?"

"Friday. These folks need to wake up."

Fox had heard this line of thinking before. The Fourth of

July might celebrate the birth of a country, but it ignored the fact many Native people had died in the process.

"The whole thing is crazy, man," Grayfeather continued. "I mean, don't these people know what Chivington did? I mean, and they call themselves Christian? How's life, dude? I haven't seen you in forever."

"Hey man, history's written by the winners." Fox liked Grayfeather, but sometimes got tired of the Christian message emails Henry liked to send, and his quasi-Hippie lingo—which Fox ruefully found himself falling into when he spoke to the man. Grayfeather, like Fox, was a Vietnam vet. That controversial war had dropped off people's radar quickly, and folks often thought Fox was too young to have served there. But he'd been 19 years old when he enlisted in 1971, and was thrilled to get chopper training. He served two years, flying Hueys as one of the youngest Army pilots until the U.S. officially pulled out troops. But after the war, Grayfeather veered toward Jesus and love beads, while Fox steamed toward a biology degree on the government's dime. These days, Henry was big in the Indian born-agains, and even did a little preaching now and then.

"Say Henry, I was hoping you could help me out." Fox wiped the table where the big white cat had been. Ricky wrinkled his nose at the bleach smell, even though Fox had diluted it with a bit more water than normal. The kid held his nose with one hand and shoveled cereal in his mouth with the other. Ability to adapt—a true mark of a survivor. "I have this great nephew who's staying with me, kinda unexpected, and I've taken a few days off but I need some help. You guys have any cool summer programs going?"

"Hey, you've got good timing, man. AISES has a kids'

science camp starting next week up at NOAA. I heard they've still got some scholarships left, too."

This was good. The American Indian Science and Engineering Society worked to educate Native youth, and it sounded like they had partnered with the National Oceanic and Atmospheric Administration, which had its headquarters in Green Mountain. NOAA was probably a thorn in the side of the Bush administration, since the government agency continued to insist that global warming was real. From the corner of his eye, Fox saw Ricky surreptitiously letting Abby lick the dregs from his cereal bowl. Fox turned his back on the scene, so as not to give official approval.

"Man, who can I talk to about that?" Fox wrote down the contact information on a piece of scrap paper. "Cool," he said, then immediately grimaced at his own choice of words.

"So Fox, if you're not working maybe you could come out for the protest. We're gonna gather in downtown Keyhole about seven Friday night, march through the suburb where the street is and end up out by the airport where folks gather to watch the fireworks."

"Can't. Even when I'm off duty, people know I'm a critter cop for the state. It wouldn't look good. But I'll be with you in spirit."

"I hear ya. You take care and God bless."

"Thanks Henry."

Before Fox could click off, he heard a crash and the sound of breaking glass. Rajul had won another round.

The chatter of prairie dogs ceased the moment Faith

opened the door of Trish's storage shed. Despite how she felt, she smiled briefly. The animals were like birds in a forest, twittering away until the predator shows up. In this case, the prairie dogs kept trying to communicate with each other, despite being divided into small groups in kennels stacked two and three high.

She made trips to the van and back until she had all the small transfer carriers inside the building. Faith upended one of the containers and sat it on the floor, with the door on top. Reaching into the hay with gloved hands, she fished for a prairie dog and popped it into the larger holding kennel. "No messing around," she told herself. The more she empathized with the animals, the more likely she was to drop one and have to spend time chasing it down—much more stressful for the prairie dog in the end.

"I've got you, big guy," she said, transferring a large male into the holding container with his two coterie kin. All three animals tucked themselves into the hay and disappeared, hiding motionless. Faith put a bowl of water inside and made sure the plastic food bowl attached to the door was full of grain.

She worked methodically until the last batch of dogs was situated. Faith sat down on a bale of hay, exhausted. One of the prairie dogs who'd been in the holding area a few days sounded a jump-yip call. All's well. Right. Suddenly, she was crying again. What a god-damned basket case.

A car door slammed outside and Faith jumped. She wiped her eyes and used the bottom of her shirt to clean her nose. Her heart pounded. Maybe Tom had come calling, to check the place before he moved back in. She went to the door and cracked it open, peeking outside. Fox and Ricky were climbing out of Fox's Toyota truck. Her first response was relief. Her second was panic. She had to keep Fox out of the house. Worried that Polly wasn't getting enough attention, she had picked up the prairie dog on her way up to Trish's place and had stashed her in a back-up cage while she worked in the storage shed.

Fox stood at the side door of the house, knocking.

"Faith?"

"I'm here," she said, coming up behind them.

"I'm sorry to bother you," Fox said, hat in hand. "I tried to call your house, left some messages. I remembered you were keeping the prairie dogs here, so I took a chance. I wanted to make sure you knew what was happening."

"You mean with the city and the extermination?"

"So you do know."

Faith nodded and sighed. "I spent all day trying to figure out what to do. In the end I just kept trapping, waiting for inspiration. I know you can't help me trap, but can't the Division of Wildlife ask the city to postpone the extermination?"

Fox shook his head. "Not until the state legislature changes the status of prairie dogs from varmints to something else. And we'll all be dead and gone before that happens. Look Faith, about last night—"

Faith gestured with her head toward Ricky, wandering by the house a few feet away. "Ricky, would you like to see the prairie dog hotel?"

She walked the two of them over to the storage shed. In obtaining her relocation permit from the Division of Wildlife, Trish had to state where she would hold the animals in transition. The storage shed set-up was no secret.

Faith stood in the doorway as Ricky wandered inside. "Where are they?" the boy said.

"Hiding in the hay. Just don't open any doors."

While Ricky toured the stacks of kennels and peered inside, Faith turned to Fox. "Don't worry about last night. I'm sorry I gave you the wrong impression. I have a book to finish, not to mention these guys."

She gestured toward the kennels. "I've been thinking. You know when you talked about systems theory, that day up on the butte?"

Fox nodded.

"Maybe that's why we kill prairie dogs now, and fought Native people when Silas was alive. We believe in a system of private land ownership, and if animals or people get in the way, too bad for them. And then there's capitalism…"

Faith heard a phone ringing inside Trish's house.

"Do you need to get that?" Fox asked.

"I guess," Faith said. "Stay here. I'll be right back."

Faith ran to the house, pulled the door closed behind her and grabbed the phone in the kitchen.

"Hello?" Faith waited, but there was no response. Then she heard heavy breathing. Her spine tingled. An obscene phone call? Tom trying to send her a message?

"Faith." The voice was whispery and faint.

"Hope? Is that you? What's the matter?"

"Loved her."

"Who, Trish? Hope, are you there?"

"Betrayed. Me."

Faith heard a clatter, as if the phone on the other end had been dropped.

"Hope? Hope!"

286

Behind her Faith heard footsteps and turned to see Ricky and Fox next to the floor cage where Polly had her nose to the bars, luxuriating in Ricky's fingers scratching her head.

Fox drove quickly en route to Hope's house, but held it to five miles above the speed limit. Faith tapped the passenger door with her fingers while Ricky jabbered between them.

"Polly is the coolest! She's just like a little puppy!"

Faith stayed silent.

"Tell me what Hope said again?" Fox said.

I'll throw her in a kennel and leave the state, Faith thought. I can't believe I didn't make sure the door was completely closed.

"Something about loving someone and betrayal."

"Did she and Trish—" Fox stopped with a glance at Ricky. "Uh, were she and Trish close friends?"

"Trish never told me, if they were. Can't you go any faster?"

"We're almost there," Fox said.

They pulled up in front of the Hansel and Gretel cottage. "Stay in the car," Fox told Ricky.

The front door was ajar.

"Hope? It's Faith."

Nothing.

Faith pushed the door in a few inches. "Hope?"

From inside came a low moan.

"I'm going in," Faith said, not waiting to see if Fox was behind her. Faith glanced in the living room where furniture was overturned and broken glass decorated the rug. She

287

went down the hallway and heard another moan.

Hope sprawled face down on the bedroom floor, her head in a pool of blood. Near her right hand, a portable phone lie on the rug. A blue kimono with red and yellow flowers partially covered her body, leaving a shapely leg exposed. Faith saw a fireplace poker on the bed, one end of the dark iron covered in blood.

Faith crouched near the woman and touched her shoulder.

"Hope, it's Faith. Can you hear me?"

"I'm calling 911," Fox said as he came in behind her.

"She's gurgling!" Faith said. "What should I do?"

Fox quickly told the dispatcher he had a woman with a severe head injury and gave the address before hanging up. "She may have blood in her airway. Let's reposition her on her side."

The game warden directed Faith to hold Hope's head until he was able to bring the woman's body in alignment. Then the two of them began positioning Hope on her side to help her breathe. In the process the kimono opened across the front of Hope's body, exposing two beautiful full breasts.

And a shaved groin area that included a penis.

30

Morning, Nov. 29, 1864
The Big Sandy, Colorado Territory

All the Indians near them had fled and the bullets were whizzing past when Black Kettle finally said, "We must run!" Dropping the lodge pole in the dirt, Black Kettle and his wife ran off through the camp. White Antelope, however, ran toward the creek bed where most of the Indians had fled. A group of mounted soldiers were galloping down the stream bed chasing the rag tag group of Indians.

White Antelope stumbled to the middle of the sandy creek bottom, holding his arms high above his head and shouting "Stop! Stop!" in plain English. But the soldiers kept riding toward him, sand flying under the hooves of their horses. White Antelope crossed his arms. He stood still. He opened his mouth and sang the Cheyenne death

289

song: "Nothing lasts long except the mountains and the sky."

The bullets dropped him like a stone.

Major Scott J. Anthony watched White Antelope fall. Behind the Cheyenne chief, Anthony saw women and children racing around a creek bend and out of sight.

Except.

There was a small boy, maybe three years old. Perfectly naked. Running on the sand. Following after the adults. From behind Anthony watched the little boy's legs pumping, making little headway. The child looked just like Anthony's son when he tried to run away from the bath his mother planned for him.

To the side, Anthony saw a soldier of the Bloodless Third dismount and draw up his rifle. "No!" Anthony cried, but the man fired. The shot, fired from a distance of perhaps seventy-five yards, went astray. Anthony breathed in relief. But too soon.

A second soldier rode up and said, "Let me try the son of a bitch. I can hit him." Too far away for Anthony to stop him, this man dismounted, knelt and fired. And still the child ran. He was nearly at the bend in the creek.

"I'll get him." Anthony saw a third man get off his horse, raise his rifle and fire.

The little fellow went down in the sand.

Lieutenant James Cannon tried to contain his men,

but some had caught the fever. He watched as two of them rode down a young squaw, jumped off their horses and pinned her to the ground. Another soldier was crouched over a dead Indian man and was methodically cutting off his fingers to get at the silver rings adorning them. From some lodges nearby Cannon saw men carrying out finely worked buffalo robes worth perhaps fifty dollars each.

"Hey lieutenant! They's good ones here, plenty for all."

The soldier threw a buffalo robe up at Cannon, who caught it and found himself thinking that here was the money to buy a real winter coat.

About that time, Cannon saw two young Indians burst out of a nearby lodge. He couldn't tell if they were girls or boys, what with their long hair down their backs. They ran holding hands, sprinting toward the creek.

"Don't worry sir, I'll get 'em."

A soldier on horseback spurred his horse after the pair as Cannon turned his own mount to and fro, yelling commands that his men ignored.

Private Dave Louderback stood at the entrance of the lodge, paralyzed by what he saw. Fifty feet away, a soldier pinned a struggling Indian girl on the ground while a second one yanked up her leather skirt and mounted her. Troops rode past on their horses as if nothing was happening, shooting at Indians Louderback couldn't see.

Off to the other side, the private saw a soldier struggling to cut off the scalp of an older Indian. Louderback could see a long silver ornament in the

Indian's hair. Finally the man cut off most of the scalp and the private watched as the soldier waved his trophy high in the air.

Hearing a scream, Louderback looked back at the young squaw on the ground and saw one of the soldiers plunge his knife into her chest as she struggled. Finally she lay quiet and the soldier kept working the knife. In shock Louderback watched, trying to understand what the man was doing. The next moment he saw the man thrust his free hand into the bloody mass of the girl's chest, while the soldier next to him handed him a stick.

The first man pulled his hand out of the girl's body and impaled her heart on the stick.

Private Louderback doubled over and heaved, watching his partially digested breakfast spill onto the ground.

First Lieutenant James Olney of the Colorado First was leading his men up the creek toward the fleeing Indians. He looked back and saw a few of his troops had captured three women and five children. Olney turned his horse and began riding back to the group when he saw Lieutenant Harry Richmond of Chivington's "Bloodless" Colorado Third ride up. Richmond dismounted and addressed Olney's men. Although Olney could not hear what was said, he saw his men move away from the Indians and Richmond draw his revolver, shooting a squaw in the face.

The other two squaws grabbed the screaming children to their breasts and faced Richmond. Olney could hear their voices and knew they were pleading for their lives. Richmond gunned them down one by one.

Olney's men stood to the side, aghast and paralyzed.

John Smith ran alongside the caisson pulled by horses of Lieutenant Baldwin's command. If Chivington had not come along and recognized the old translator calling out to him, Smith figured he would already be a dead man.

Baldwin's men moved up the creek until they came upon an odd scene. Smith could see perhaps 200 troops in position, firing at Indians dug into the sand banks of the creeks. Smith counted maybe some 30 braves shooting arrows and firing rifles, and shook his head at their courage. There was nowhere for the Indian fighters to go, but every minute these boys and old men kept the troops busy was another minute for their women and children to escape. About fifty feet in front of him, Smith saw the body of a young soldier, an arrow protruding from his neck. Further along the creek, he could see the bodies of Indians, mostly squaws and children. He studied the bodies, but did not find his Indian wife and adult son Jack.

The troops seemed determined to stay until every last Indian in the sand was dead. The old man Smith watched, his heart numb.

Silas Soule halted his company of thirty men a couple miles upstream from the village and turned his horse to face his troops. In the distance he heard cannon shell and rifle fire.

As he looked back in the direction of the village, a group of six or seven Indian women and children ran around the corner of the creek and stopped suddenly at the sight of the soldiers. His men started to turn their horses toward the handful of Indians, who now began a sideways dash toward the creek bank and the prairie beyond.

"Gentlemen, you will face forward." Soule's voice brooked no opposition. Although the men glanced at each other, they turned their horses to face the officer leading them, and turning their backs to the Indians running for their lives.

To the side of the creek, three more Indians stumbled past, one a squaw holding a papoose. The Indians kept looking back at the soldiers, as if waiting for them to begin the chase. The young cavalrymen watched them go, but kept their horses facing Silas Soule.

"So gentlemen, have I ever told you of the time I played a drunken Irishman in a plot to save some of John Brown's men from the hangman? No? Well now, this would be as good a time as any," Silas said in a thick Irish brogue, as four squaws and two children burst out of a clump of willows and fled toward the horizon.

The fringe on the women's leather dresses whipped against their legs as they ran.

31

"So you never even suspected?"

Fox spoke in a low voice. Ricky was across the hospital waiting room, carefully studying the contents of the vending machine before inserting the coins Fox had given him. The police had stayed at Hope's house to investigate. Presumably detectives would make their way to the hospital soon.

Faith shook her head. "We knew she was a little odd, but this is Green Mountain, after all."

Fox nodded in agreement. "Do you think Trish knew?"

"I don't know. They spent a lot of time together, but Trish seemed to know more about the individual prairie dogs she was handling than the people helping her."

"So she—he—" Fox stopped. "Hope said she had relatives in Trinidad?"

"I think so, but I didn't pay much attention."

Trinidad, Colorado, on the state's southern border carried the distinction of being known as the sex-change capital of the world. Fox had been assigned to the southern town nestled against the signature Fisher Peak Mesa for a few weeks to help monitor turkey hunting when the district had been shorthanded. He'd been grocery shopping when he'd come around the aisle and almost run into a woman pushing a cart. She stood over six feet tall and must have weighed 200 pounds, without an ounce of fat. Her hair was carefully styled, her nails perfectly done. She apologized profusely in an odd falsetto. Fox had passed her and glanced back. Only then, when he saw the size of her feet, did he get it.

"I think that's why I couldn't find her to do a background check. Probably changed her legal name."

"You're disgusted, aren't you?" Faith looked at him accusingly.

"C'mon, admit it. You were shocked too."

"Yeah, okay. Well, I've never seen anyone with both—" Faith stopped. Fox watched as she turned to verify Ricky's status. Milky Way or Starbursts. Decisions, decisions.

A doctor came in wearing purple scrubs.

"You're here with Hope Packard?"

Faith nodded.

"Are you related?"

"No."

"We need to find her relatives," the woman said, sitting down across from Faith and Fox. "She's in a coma."

"I don't know. I don't know much about—her."

The doctor smiled slightly. "I understand the two of you saved her life."

Faith looked at Fox and shrugged.

"Crimes against transgender people are fairly common, actually," the doctor said.

"Transgender," Faith repeated. "I'm confused. Why does she have—" Faith stopped abruptly. Ricky was returning.

The doctor stood up and smiled at Faith. "Let's just say that major change is a process and takes time. The staff will keep trying to find her next of kin. Thanks for all you've done."

Fox glanced at his watch. It was approaching eleven at night. Ricky was munching on a bag of potato chips. Fat was better than sugar, at least at this hour. How did parents keep kids on healthy food anyway?

"I need to get you back to Trish's house and get this guy to bed," Fox said.

"Oh shit, the dogs!"

Fox looked at her.

"I've got prairie dogs I've got to put up."

"Then we better get going."

They were quiet on the way to Trish's house. By the time they pulled up, Fox turned and found Ricky conked out in the back seat.

"Thanks for the ride."

Fox turned off the engine. "Show me what to do. I'll help."

Faith started to object but Fox cut her off. "We've both had a long day. C'mon, let's get her done. He'll be fine back there." Fox gestured toward the back seat.

They worked for about forty-five minutes in the storage shed. Despite his big hands, Fox prided himself on quickly learning how to snag a prairie dog in the bottom of a kennel and transfer it to a larger kennel with food and water. He did drop one feisty male, but he and Faith were able to corner it fairly quickly.

Fox pulled off his leather gloves and brushed loose hay off his arms.

"How about a glass of water?" Faith asked.

They crossed the dirt driveway to the house. Fox peeked in the back seat. Ricky hadn't moved.

Faith turned on the light in the kitchen. Fox noticed that the large floor cage appeared empty. Apparently the prairie dog was tucked away inside a cloth pouch.

"So do you think this Hope thing is connected to Trish?" Faith asked.

He turned to see Faith watching him. "Could be just a one-night-stand gone bad. Or not. I just hope we didn't screw up too much evidence when we went in her place." Faith handed him a glass of water and he walked toward the living room. Faith's laptop and some books sat on the white tile surface of the coffee table.

"Have you written any more?"

"Not beyond what I've given you. Have you read it all?"

"No. Too much going on," Fox said with a smile. "I like what I've read, though. Especially how you portray Silas."

Faith sat on the couch.

"I don't know what I would have done if I were him. It's hard to take a stand against your own people."

Fox sat down at the other end of the couch. "Remember the My Lai Massacre?"

"Just the basics," Faith said.

"When I was in 'Nam, I met a guy once." He took a sip of water. "Told me about a chopper pilot named Hugh Thompson. He and his men saw the massacre happening from the air. Thompson landed his bird, and they stood between some of the rampaging soldiers and a bunch of civilians. They even flew some of the civilians out of there to save their lives. But did you ever hear of the guy?"

Faith shook her head.

"Most grunts considered the guy a pariah, a traitor. He ended up with Post Traumatic Stress Disorder. Drank too much, lost his marriage. He left the service and disappeared. Then the army decided to give him a medal. Only about thirty years too late. I hear he's got cancer."

Faith sighed. "People like Silas don't come along very often."

She retrieved a book from the table and opened it to a photo of men, some Indian, some white, posed in a room. Some of the Native Americans sat on chairs, as white and Indian men stood behind them. Two cavalrymen crouched in front of the Cheyenne and Arapahos. The description explained the photo was taken in Denver and identified the soldiers as Major Ned Wynkoop and Capt. Silas Soule. Wynkoop appeared jaunty, wearing his large dark cavalry hat and a cigarette between his lips. Soule, handsome as ever, held a light-colored hat with one hand and a cigarette between the gloved fingers of the other.

"He looks so, I don't know, sincere I guess," Faith said.

Fox laughed. "You sound like one of those Silas groupies I've heard of. You know, he wasn't the only soldier who opposed Chivington."

Faith stood up abruptly and walked to the kitchen. Fox followed her. She turned to face him.

"Silas stood up for what he believed in and in the end he paid the ultimate price. Hardly anyone in this country has ever heard of him. Does that seem fair?" Her voice was rough and shaking.

Fox looked down at her.

"Jesus, Faith, you sound like you're in love with him.

He's been dead for more than a hundred and thirty years. And he wasn't a saint."

Faith folded her arms and backed away to the kitchen sink.

"I'm tired," she said. "I think you should go home."

"Faith, maybe you think Silas was perfect, but—"

Faith stuck fingers in her ears. "La la la la la."

"Okay, okay. I'm leaving."

***

"Unsung Hero"
By Faith O'Neill
Chapter 25

Afternoon, Nov. 30, 1864
The Big Sandy, Colorado Territory

Jack Smith, half-breed son of Cavalry translator John Smith, had been taken prisoner the day of the attack on Nov. 29. Now, the afternoon following the attack, he sat in a cold Indian lodge in the decimated village, along with his father, four Indian children including a baby, and Private David Louderback.

Louderback was not a prisoner—he was there by choice. And the lodge was cold because Chivington's men had appropriated all the buffalo robes, blankets and food for the camp hospital, despite the protests of John Smith. Now and then John Smith and his son Jack exchanged a few words in Cheyenne, but Louderback had no idea what was said. The private was struck, however, by the fatalistic look on the faces of both men.

300

Private Louderback had cooked a meal for the prisoners the night before and breakfast this morning. After breakfast, a man had approached the lodge and said Louderback should be hung and shot, along with John Smith. Others had passed by the lodge, saying loudly that John Smith's son Jack was still alive, and wasn't it a shame. Still, Louderback had stayed with the group. But it was nearing four in the afternoon and none of them had eaten for hours. During the day they had been joined by a few squaws and the mulatto guide Jim Beckwith, who had been hired on by Chivington.

Louderback tried to stoke the fire in the middle of the lodge. Finally he could not bear watching the children shiver, so he took off his overcoat and wrapped it around the four of them.

Voices grew louder outside and Louderback pulled the skin back from the opening. Daylight was beginning to fade. The private watched as about fifteen soldiers approached, slapping each other on the back. They pushed him aside and crowded into the lodge. Louderback slipped in behind them.

One of the men stood looking down at Jack Smith.

"You half-breed son of a bitch. We should have shot you a long time ago." The soldier landed a blow with his foot to Jack Smith's thigh. The younger Smith did not move, but did look up at the soldier.

"If you want to kill me, shoot me and get it over with," Jack Smith said. "I don't give a damn."

Louderback exchanged a look with Beckwith. It occurred to the private that if shooting broke out, he might end up on the wrong end of a gun himself. The private got up and quickly left the lodge, making a beeline for Chivington's camp. He practically ran the sixty yards to the colonel and was just walking up to the man when he heard a shot.

"Halloo," Chivington said. "I wonder what that is."

Louderback walked up close to the big man.

"They've shot Jack Smith, is what, and it's a damned shame," Louderback said hotly. "There's been talk around the camp since last evening. You can't tell me you didn't know of it. No matter what a man has done, they ought to give him a show for his life and not shoot him down like a dog."

Chivington's beefy face turned a bright red. An officer near the colonel stepped forward.

"Look here, private, you better watch how you shoot off your mouth about killing Indians," the man said.

"I enlisted as a soldier, but I consider my tongue to be my own and not property of the United States government," Louderback said hotly.

Sergeant Lucien Palmer stepped forward and addressed the officer.

"I'll take care of this, sir, rest assured." With that, Palmer took Louderback's arm and led him away.

"Listen to me, Louderback. Get yourself back down to the company or you're gonna end up shot before you leave the village."

"They can shoot me in a few days," the unarmed private announced as he stalked off. "As soon as I get to the Fort and get myself something to shoot with."

32

Faith tossed and turned and finally gave up about 1 a.m. After Fox helped her put up the prairie dogs in the storage shed, Faith had decided to stay at Trish's house for the night instead of making the forty-five-minute drive home to Keyhole. She padded to the kitchen for a glass of water and carried it down the steps into Trish's cluttered basement. She stood there, glass in hand, trying to decide where to start. How would she ever find the energy to sort through all this stuff, much less decide what to do with whatever belonged to Trish?

The last time she'd been in this part of the house was nine years ago, when she'd helped Trish move into her dream house with her new and wonderful hubby. Since then, at least a couple stacks of boxes had been added to the chaos. She was tempted to turn right around and call Goodwill in the morning, have it all hauled away. Too bad if Tom hadn't taken all of his things when he decided to dump Trish. For that matter, maybe he had killed Trish to get his hands on all that jointly owned property that he could sell to support his habit. But then, why give Faith a chance to retrieve Trish's possessions?

Faith shrugged and took another sip. Off to the side was a small bookshelf. Instinctively she was drawn to the books. Trish had not been much of a reader. She was too busy saving the world. Curious, Faith crouched down and began scanning titles. There was a book that Faith recognized as the authority on prairie dog natural history, another on the plight of the black-footed ferret. She was about to stand upright when a title on the cover of a thin booklet caught her eye: "Phostoxin: Applications in Agricultural Settings." Faith pulled out the document to find it was a doctoral dissertation on agricultural engineering from sixteen years prior, by a doctoral candidate named Stanley F. Rodgers. Hmm. How many guys named Stan Rodgers could there be? Agricultural engineering seemed like an odd background for an open space manager, but Faith had heard of stranger things—like a wildlife biologist turned librarian. Nor was she particularly surprised that Rodgers was familiar with chemical extermination. Government types had been fond of poisoning prairie dogs until recent public pressure made them consider relocation instead. She flipped through the pages and her eyes glazed over at the chemical terminology. Why would Trish have a copy of this? Maybe Trish had argued with Rodgers about how nasty Phostoxin was and then Rodgers gave her his dissertation to read? Faith placed the book on top of the bookshelf and resolved to look at it later. She turned back toward the stacks of boxes and noticed a familiar patch of dark red nearly hidden behind them. She put her shoulder to the boxes and shoved them aside.

The old red trunk with the rounded lid had been in her

family forever. As little girls, she and Trish had pestered their mother to let them rummage in it, with their visions of parasols and petticoats tucked away inside. But their mother said she had lost the key and the girls had gone away disappointed.

Now Faith knelt in front of the old-fashioned lock attached to a cracked leather strap coming over the lid. She got up and within a few minutes found the items she was looking for. Faith wedged the end of the screwdriver behind the hasp of the lock, then picked up the hammer and began pounding the handle end of the Phillips. She fought with the lock for about five minutes, but finally it popped away from the trunk, bent and battered.

She put her hands on the lid and paused, preparing herself for the inevitable disappointment. Then she opened the trunk.

Ah, if only she had a Victorian parlor. Here were crocheted doilies and lace curtains and hand-embroidered tablecloths. Obviously, this had served as some young woman's—what did they call it, trousseau? A trunk full of dreams of elegant parties and the envy of friends.

Faith pulled out countless bundles of folded cloth, finally just piling them on the nearby boxes without opening them. She yawned. Maybe doctors should prescribe digging around in old trunks as a sedative. In any event, bed sounded more appealing than before. There seemed to be only one piece of material left on the bottom so she picked up a stack of linens to begin refilling the trunk. But then she realized the cloth didn't lay flat on the trunk bottom. Setting the linens aside, Faith lifted the last folded piece of material and found an old cigar box. She didn't know her antiques, but if she had to guess she'd estimate perhaps the late 1800s.

Finally excited, she opened the wooden box and found a smallish leather-bound bible, a couple yellowed newspaper clippings and an oddly shaped piece of rawhide.

One clipping, apparently from a New York newspaper, was an obituary for Charles Wesley Squier, who died a hero in a New York hospital on Dec. 9, 1869. Squier? The same man who murdered Silas?

Scanning the purple prose, Faith read that Squier had fought valiantly in the Civil War's Battle of Williamsburg, firing cannons at Confederate troops to cover his men during a forced retreat. And the obituary went on to laud Squier, an employee of the Erie Railroad, for apparently preventing a train derailment the previous Thanksgiving Day by jumping from the train to move a switch. In fact, he had died of injuries sustained in his heroic feat. The article noted that many dignitaries and generals attended his funeral. Not a word about Silas Soule.

The other clipping, fragile, about to fall apart in her hands, came from something called the Army Journal. This obituary referred to Squier heading west and in December 1864, joining a volunteer Colorado regiment that was fighting Indians. If he joined in December, he couldn't have been at Sand Creek in November, Faith thought. Again, no mention of Silas.

She sat, the clippings on her lap. If this was the man she believed he was, how could they have called him a hero? How could they have ignored what he did to Silas Soule? And why would these clippings be in an old trunk of her family's? She remembered her mother talking about an ancestor who was a famous Cavalry soldier, and when she first heard of Sand Creek she had fantasized she might actually be related to Silas Soule, even though he had no known offspring.

Faith put the clippings aside and reached for the bible, fingering the soft worn leather. On the page with family history, she saw that the first section listed a baby named Mary Louise Turner who was born July 15, 1870, in Ithaca, N.Y. to Agnes Margaret Turner. Nothing for the father's name. No reference to a marriage.

The next entry showed Mary L. Turner marrying William Benjamin O'Neill in May of 1901, with three offspring including a William Wesley O'Neill born in 1905. There were no entries after that.

Her great-grandfather had gone by his initials: W.W. O'Neill. This must be him. So who was the missing man who fathered Mary Louise Turner? Counting backwards for a normal pregnancy, Faith realized Mary Louise would have been conceived probably in October or November of 1869. Charles Squier had died in December of that year. And if he had had a girlfriend, some gullible thing who believed his promises of marriage, maybe someone named Agnes Margaret Turner?

As the implications sank in, Faith felt sick to her stomach. She thumbed through the bible, hoping to find something to counter her dread that Charles Squier might have been her great- great- great-grandfather. After all, anyone might have fathered Mary Louise. Frustrated, she was about to give up and return the bible to the cigar box when she spotted a faded inscription on the book's inside cover:

To Charles S.
With gratitude for his loyal service to God and country.
Just a token to remember the Battle of Sand Creek!
The Right Reverend John M. Chivington

***

"Unsung Hero"
By Faith O'Neill
Chapter 26

Morning, Dec. 31, 1864
The Big Sandy, Colorado Territory

"May ooooohld aquaintance be forgot and neeee'eeer brought to miiiiiind!" Silas slid sideways in the saddle and Delilah took a sidestep. "Whoooooa, Nelly!"

"Captain, are you alright?"

"Never been better. What more could a man want on New Year's Eve?"

Soule waved an arm across the area nearby, where maybe a dozen dogs pulled and tugged at corpses of people and ponies. Silas took a flask from his overcoat and offered it to Captain Booth—inspecting officer and chief of cavalry, district of the upper Arkansas.

"Soule, pull yourself together, man."

"A fine idea, yes, a fine idea."

Soule tucked the flask away, sat up straighter in the saddle and took Delilah off toward the creek, away from the group of about thirty soldiers sent back to investigate.

Two mongrels fought over the partially frozen and naked body of a young woman. Her scalp had been cut off.

Her ears and fingers had been cut off. Her breasts had been cut off. And there was a dark gash where her vagina had been.

Silas leaned over the side of his horse and vomited up a stream of whiskey, then quickly wiped his mouth. What a waste of good liquor.

He got off Delilah and continued leading the mare toward Sand Creek. Over the lip of the creek he came upon the body of a boy, perhaps eleven or twelve, partially dug into the sandy bank and slumped over a bow—one of the few souvenirs missed by the rampaging soldiers on November 29. Yes, here was one of the dangerous braves the army had ridden against. A man-child trying to stop the U.S. Cavalry, trying to defend his mother, sisters and brothers as they fled up the creek bed.

Silas walked toward the center of the dry creek and found one of the people he was looking for. At least, he thought he had found one.

The body barely looked human. The chest area was ragged and open. Apparently the dogs had followed the bullets in a bid for the internal organs.

In addition to the man being scalped and ears removed, his nose had been sliced off and several fingers were missing. Most of the man's leather clothing was gone—more souvenirs, Silas presumed. And the man's privates had been cut away. The voices he'd been trying to silence with the whiskey spoke in his mind. "That's it! That's what I'll make!" An image arose with the voice, a soldier joking with his companion, waving a shriveled bit of skin. "A tobacco pouch! Made out of an injun's balls! Bet I could sell it for a right fortune."

Rumors had abounded that one of the chiefs had run

into the creek bed, trying to stop the attacking troops. That he had stood there defenseless, singing his death song, before being gunned down and mutilated.

Soule walked around the corpse. Was it Black Kettle? He couldn't tell. He found himself praying it wasn't the chief to whom he had promised safety. And yet, what did it matter if it was Black Kettle, Left Hand, White Antelope or someone else?

Silas walked Delilah out of the creek bed and toward the lodges that had been burned to the ground at the hands of Cramer's men under orders from Chivington. Another voice in his head. "I checked every one myself," Joe had told Silas. "I made damned sure we didn't burn anyone alive."

Near one of the charred lodges, Soule found another corpse he was looking for. Jack Smith, the half-breed son of translator John Smith, lie a few feet away from the lodge. Soule recognized his beaded leather leggings. His body had not been mutilated and remained fairly recognizable, even though the dogs were still at him.

"Scat! Get away!" Silas charged the dogs, pulling Delilah alongside him. He drew his pistol, firing twice into the air. The mongrels scattered, but quickly returned. Silas pointed his gun at one of the dogs, ready to fire before remembering these animals had been companions to the slaughtered Indians. Now they struggled to survive by eating their former masters.

He holstered his pistol and knelt down by the remains of Jack Smith, wishing he'd known the man better. Private Louderback, who'd been in the village when Chivington's men attacked, had told him the young Smith had been steely and resolute until the end, unwilling to cower before the men determined to kill him. Another voice, then. "I was sittin' in the lodge with him when they called me out," the older Smith had said. "This soldier was walking me over to Chivington, near apologizing and saying they were going to kill my Jack. I said there was nothing I could do and the next instant I heard the shot."

What would Amasa have done? Would he have meekly allowed his son Silas to be gunned down in such a way, as John Smith appeared to do? But Smith still had an Indian wife and a young child. Perhaps he had figured his adult son Jack was beyond saving, and that his own death would only jeopardize those he might still have a chance to protect.

Silas sat down next to Jack Smith and pulled out his flask.

"Have a drink?" Silas cocked his head toward the voice coming from the corpse. "Don' mind if I do, thanks."

33

"She, or rather he, was born Timothy J. Cambert in Pittsburgh. The birthday you gave me was the same, so she's what, about 48?"

Fox held the phone to his ear with one hand and took notes with the other, fighting the cobwebs in his brain. Sam's phone call had drawn him out of bed, a good thing since he discovered that Ricky was already up and about with the critters. Poor kid was probably used to making breakfast for himself. Fox had a lot to learn about parenting, or whatever it was he was doing.

"Thanks Sam. I knew you'd figure it out."

"How's your nephew? You coming back to work soon?"

"I think so. Depends on whether we can wrangle a spot in a summer camp."

Fox got off the phone in time to persuade Ricky that tying a shoelace to Hissyfit's tail might be entertaining but also possibly dangerous, seeing as how she had never been de-clawed. Instead, he offered Ricky a trip with Abby to the pedestrian mall in downtown Green Mountain, where the boy could climb on giant frog sculptures and try to talk Fox into a foray to an expensive chocolate shop.

"But first, I need to make a quick stop."

Fox found a shady spot in front of Hope's house and parked the truck with the windows rolled down.

"You and dog. Stay here. Capiche?"

"Capiche."

It was his lucky day. The city cop standing guard at the door had been a classmate with Fox at the police academy. A batch of detectives had just left, the cop said.

Fox explained he was a friend of Hope's, that he had come to fetch a few of her things for her while she was in the hospital. Fending off the cop's look of indecision, Fox said breezily, "I'll be back out in five minutes" and opened the door. Not hearing the cop say anything behind him, Fox kept moving and took a quick look at his watch. He better be back with seconds to spare.

He headed straight for Hope's bedroom, partly to make sure he reappeared at the front door with pajamas, but also because people tended to keep their valuables there. Fox didn't know much about furniture, but he thought this bedroom stuff was expensive and some kind of Rodgers style, all white and girlie. The bed even had a white gauzy canopy over the top. A quick look in the closet revealed shoes in rows and clothing (women's) hung precisely. Fox closed the door and turned around. Avoiding the bloody patch on the carpet, he went to the dresser for the requisite sleepwear. He pulled out a lacy blue nightgown and some bikini briefs. Feeling the press of time, he shoved the drawer closed, only to have it jam.

"Shit," he muttered, struggling with the drawer and angry at himself at wasting precious seconds. Finally he gave up and jerked the drawer completely out of the dresser in order to reposition it. As he did, something fell onto the carpet. Fox picked up the smallish, leather-bound book and glanced inside. Jackpot. Shoving concerns about obstruction of justice to the side, he tucked the journal inside the bundle of lingerie and headed back to the front door.

Faith met Fox at the intensive care unit at noon, curious about his urgent phone call. Fortunately, she had been able to work the traps in the morning.

"Boy, have I got news for you," Fox said in a low voice, unwilling to pique Ricky's curiosity. Ricky was chatting with a friendly nurse.

Faith started to ask him what, but the doctor appeared.

"We haven't had any luck finding relatives," the doc said, pushing her half glasses up over her reddish brown hair. "The good news is she seems to have stabilized and we've upgraded her condition to serious. She's had a few moments of consciousness."

"Can we see her? She was good friends with my sister," Faith pleaded.

"Where's your sister?"

Faith squirmed. "She died recently."

"Oh. I'm sorry." The doctor paused. "I guess a few minutes wouldn't hurt. But no more than ten, understood?"

Fox conferred with the friendly nurse, who said she'd be happy to keep Ricky occupied. Entering the room, Faith thought Hope could give a good imitation of a mummy at a Halloween party. Her head was swathed in white bandages and her body in white sheets. A tube ran into her mouth and a respirator machine hummed next to the bed. Even if she were conscious, she would be unable to speak with the tube in her throat. But she might be able to gesture.

"Hope? Can you hear me?" Faith stood near Hope's head and watched for a reaction. Without makeup, the person in front of her had strong, masculine features and Faith felt like an idiot for not figuring everything out sooner.

Hope's eyelids twitched, but it might have been a spasm.

Faith looked over at Fox, who shrugged.

Fox spoke. "Hope, this is John Fox. I read your journal. I know about you and Trish."

"What?" Faith looked at Fox, who raised a warning palm. Faith took a breath and waited.

"I know you were upset about the photos—that Trish stalled when you asked for them."

Faith flashed on an image of Trish, laughing one night when the two of them had had too much to drink. "What I need is someone half man, half woman," she had quipped.

"Hope, I know you broke into my car," Fox said.

Faith thought she saw Hope twitch and worried about Fox accusing her while she was in this condition. Again Faith tried to interrupt, and again Fox held up his hand.

"How'd you find out about the film?" Fox asked. "Wait a minute. The kid at the drugstore. He looks like you. Is he a relative? Did he say something about photos and you thought I had the nude poses?"

Hope remained unresponsive.

The friendly nurse appeared at the doorway. "Sorry folks. Time to go. And the little guy says he's getting hungry."

As if on cue, Ricky appeared at the nurse's side.

"Can we go to the Ben and Jerry's Ice Cream place, Uncle Johnny?"

They sat on a bench at the Green Mountain Mall, watching Ricky climb on top of the giant metal frog that he had begged to return to.

Faith sighed. "So were they a couple?"

"Hard to say. The passages in the journal are vague. But Hope apparently fell in love and when Trish said the feeling wasn't mutual, Hope hung on. Sounds like Trish referred to the photos and Hope took it as a threat."

Faith looked down at her hands. "Trish was always so good with animals. And she tried to be—she was a good person. But sometimes she just didn't know how to relate to people."

"Might be a motive for murder," Fox said. "First being jilted, and then feeling threatened with proof that you have two sexes going at the same time. Weird thing is that Hope went on working for her, maybe hoping Trish would change her mind. A few days before Trish died, there was this."

Fox pulled a black leather journal out of his jeans pocket and began reading.

"*'TO and I got in big fight today over how she treated Maryann.'*" Fox paused and looked up at Faith. "Who's Maryann?"

Faith frowned. "She might have been one of Trish's volunteers. I never met her."

Fox looked back down at Hope's handwriting.

"'*TO yelled, 'Don't you tell me what to do, you freak! Remember I've got the photos to prove it!' She apologized later, said she was stressed about Tom leaving. But I can't believe I fell in love with her. It's making me crazy and I still dream about her. And what am I going to do without the money? I can't stop now. I won't stop now.'*"

Fox stopped and showed Faith the entry. "See how she underlined that last sentence?"

"That's all?"

"That's the last day she wrote in the book. Nothing after that. So she knew Trish had photos of her, they just weren't on the film you found. Who knows where they are."

"What does she mean about the money thing?"

Fox flipped back some fifteen pages and began reading again.

"'*Thank the Goddess, I think Trish is going to help me out. I'm so lucky to have found someone like her. She said she'd go down to Trinidad with me and help me get everything set up.*'"

Fox stopped again and looked up.

"So you think Trish promised to pay for an operation so Hope could finish her sex change?" Faith looked at Fox, then turned toward the frog when she heard Ricky holler. He and another boy were playing chase around the giant amphibian.

"Sounds like it."

"It's a strange world," Faith said.

"You said it."

"So who attacked Hope? And why?"

Fox shook his head.

"Beats me."

***

"Unsung Hero"
By Faith O'Neill
Chapter 27

Morning, Jan. 14, 1865
Fort Lyon, Colorado Territory

"Jesus, Ned, thank God you're back and that sonuvabitch Anthony is removed."

Silas was shaking Wynkoop's hand and slapping him on the shoulder, first in line at the coach ahead of Cramer and other troops. "We're trying to determine how to protect our women and children. We fear an attack at any time."

Ned shook hands all around before addressing the men.

"Gentlemen, I want you to know officially that I have been ordered to resume command of this post and to make a thorough investigation of Sand Creek. My first order of business is to make sure our women and children are safe. We will fortify the commissary at Bent's New Fort, and we will begin today."

Wynkoop, Soule and the other officers conferred and agreed to build breastworks on the north and east sides of the building, as well as to mount cannons on the northeast and northwest sides.

"I fear the building could be cut off from water," Wynkoop added. "I want the men to build a stone wall along the road to the river. I want every man on this except the officer of the day and the guard."

Soule, Cannon, Cramer and other officers organized the men. Within an hour the fort was a bustle of troops gathering shovels, picks and other gear.

Wynkoop and Soule removed their uniform jackets, grabbed shovels and soon were at the commissary, working alongside the men.

"Did you get our letters?" Soule asked between swings of his pick.

"I couldn't believe it, to tell you true," Ned said, stopping to roll up the sleeves of his shirt. "What you and Joe told me. Then when I did believe it, I wanted to find the first horse and ride back here as soon as I could. I tell you, I was livid."

Wynkoop thrust his shovel into the hard frozen soil and planted his boot on the metal to make it go deeper. "When we have made a good start here, I plan to pull aside Smith, Cannon and some of the others, take testimony."

"Make sure you talk to Louderback," Soule said. "From where he was in the camp, he saw many things. Horrible things. He said finally he couldn't bear it after a time and stopped watching."

"I wrote letters up the chain of command as soon as I heard, and word has already reached Washington." Wynkoop paused to remove his bandana from his neck and tie it around his forehead. "The U.S. Congress has already decided to investigate, and Tappan has told me he plans to convene an army commission on the matter. I'll be damned if I know what they can do to Chivington, though."

Silas nodded. After the massacre, word had circulated that Chivington's military commission had expired on

September 23, more than two months before the attack.

"Perhaps nothing officially, although the man should be strung up for his crimes." Soule paused to make sure his men were keeping up a good pace in the deep January cold. At least they had a full sun overhead. "Of course, I hear up in Denver they are talking of doing the same thing to me for being a mutineer."

"Are you willing to testify before Tappan's commission?"

Silas took a deep breath. "Of course. But I've been trying to puzzle it out. I could be court-martialed for disobeying orders to attack the village. Still, I'll go to my grave happy that neither I nor my men killed a single Indian. Before we set off from the post, I told them I didn't want to see a single man open fire unless they heard the order from me. They held, Ned, to a man. Even when we saw squaws and children running past."

Wynkoop rested a hand on the top of his shovel, and put the other hand on Silas's shoulder.

"I'll talk to Tappan. I think you have nothing to fear. You can honestly say you took your men down the creek to get them out of the line of the crossfire. Just don't volunteer any information you are not asked."

Soule nodded again.

Wynkoop smiled. "You are an officer and a gentleman, and I am proud to have served with you."

"We feel the same of you, to a man."

34

Ricky got the hang of the traps in no time.

Faith stopped to watch the boy propping open the doors and sprinkling extra Sweet Feed where needed. He already moved as fast as she did and with practice, he'd be even faster. She'd been hesitant when Fox suggested Ricky accompany her. Fox said he needed to spend a few hours catching up on email and phone calls. Faith wondered if he saw her as a baby sitter, then decided it didn't matter. Today was Friday and time was running out. The quicker the traps were set, the more dogs she was likely to catch. Besides, she liked the kid.

Apparently the hardest part of the arrangement was getting Ricky out of bed at "oh-dark-thirty" to get to the airport by dawn. Fox did pull her aside to let her know Ricky had asthma.

"He's got his inhaler with him, so it shouldn't be a problem. Just keep an eye on him, okay?"

"Sure." They had piled in the car and were driving down the street when Faith slapped her forehead. Asthma. Inhalers. Where was Trish's inhaler? It hadn't been with her things at the sheriff's office. There was no way Trish would be without the medicine. She had lived with asthma since she was a kid, and the inhaler was like a part of her clothing.

All the way to the airport, Faith had chewed on the question. Now, a couple hours later she had more questions than answers. Had Trish somehow lost the inhaler? Had someone taken it? But if so, why?

She and Ricky finished opening the traps just as the sun was popping up over the eastern horizon. They returned to the car and she drove to the road overlooking the airport. As a special treat, Fox had bought the boy a small computer game to keep him entertained during the long stretches of waiting. "I told him he only gets to play it at certain times," Fox said, apparently noticing her disapproval. She had to admit the game kept the boy busy on the seat beside her.

Faith glassed the traps, but it was early. Since she had started trapping she had taken in fifty-three animals, but she figured there were at least another hundred-fifty on the site. Of course, she only had permission to relocate a hundred total. How many times had Trish pushed the envelope on those numbers? She put the binoculars down and pulled her backpack up from the rear seat.

She opened the black leather bible she had found in the trunk and again looked at the inscription on the inside cover. Why would Chivington give Squier a bible, and how had it ended up with Agnes Margaret Turner? Popular belief was that Chivington or his supporters had hired Squier to murder Silas. Then Squier had escaped from jail, apparently to return back east and lead a normal life. Had he fallen in love with Agnes?

Frustrated, she put the bible back in her pack and noticed

the slim booklet on Phostoxin by Stanley Rodgers. Deciding to take another stab at the work, she scanned the pages. Rodgers seemed to really know this particular world of pesticides, and Faith wondered if he had grown up on a ranch or farm, where tradition dictated that the only good prairie dog was a dead one. However, she did not find the dissertation scintillating reading and her eyelids drooped.

Faith turned the page and sat upright, suddenly awake. She was looking at a section title: "Delivery Methods," illustrated with graphics of metal capsules. One line in particular jumped out at her:

Manufacture and transfer of Phostoxin into delivery containers requires special care to prevent contamination and/or accidental inhalation of the gas, which may lead to severe lung injury or death...

Her brain was whirling but she couldn't quite get the pieces to come together.

"Faith? I think I see five dogs in traps." Ricky had the binoculars to his eyes.

"Okay. Time for a trap run." Faith drove them back down to the airstrip. When they got out of the car, Rodgers's dissertation fell off her lap and onto the ground. Focused on getting the dogs out of the traps, Faith jammed a hat on her head and rolled up the booklet to stash in her back pocket.

Late in the day with his routine work out of the way, Fox sat in his home office and started running background checks on everyone close to Trish. Despite the indications, he was not convinced that Hope had killed her former lover.

He started with Faith. And was relieved when he only came up with a couple speeding tickets. Sam had already told him that Hope (aka Timothy Cambert) was clean. Fox ran Tom Baker and couldn't even find a traffic ticket. He wanted to talk to Faith about that one. If Baker was making and selling meth, he needed to be stopped. Borsich turned out to be a fellow Vietnam vet who was busted on a marijuana charge in the mid 70s, but seemed to be clean since.

Fox pushed Bodhi off his lap and headed for the kitchen for a glass of water. The house was oddly quiet without an eight-year-old to liven things up. Glass in hand, he noticed Rajul jumping up on the dining room table again. Fox hollered "No!" Sighing, he got the bottle of bleach from under the sink and wiped down the plastic table cloth. The bottle was getting low. Fox stuck the container in his open backpack as a visual reminder to stop at the store. On the side table near the front door, he noticed the orange plastic bag with the day's newspaper. He'd left it there when he sent Ricky off with Faith for prairie dog duty. He paused and decided to take a look.

Native Americans Plan March to Protest Street Name, said one headline. Another said, *Developer's Wife Slams Plan to Kill Prairie Dogs.* Now that got his attention. The adjacent photo showed an attractive, thirty-something blonde holding a protest sign outside the Keyhole City Hall. The sign said, "They were here first!" The photo caption identified the woman as Liz Borsich, who was also featured in the news story.

The wife of local developer John Borsich protested in

324

front of Keyhole City Hall Thursday along with local residents angry about a city decision to expand the extermination of prairie dogs because of a plague outbreak.

"It was bad enough when they said they were going to do the south end of town, but now to do this everywhere—even at the airport where a relocation effort is underway—is absolutely absurd," Liz Borsich said. "All they have to do is keep the areas off limits until the disease runs its course."

Borsich said she and others would rally at the airport at 7 p.m. Friday to protest the city's emergency ruling issued early Thursday.

Developer John Borsich has been the subject of pressure by residents demanding that he relocate prairie dogs from a planned development site. Asked what her husband thought of her plans, Liz Borsich said, "I have not discussed my plans with him. I love him, but I'm an individual and I have my own moral compass."

City officials said they would allow the protest as long as protesters stayed beyond the airport fence and did not hinder airport operations. Open space director Stan Rodgers, who is overseeing the relocation of prairie dogs from the airport, said the effort is wrapping up and any remaining animals will be destroyed.

My, my, Fox thought. Interesting. Borsich had himself quite a woman.

Fox put the paper back down and returned to the computer, staring at the screen. On a whim, he typed in Rodgers's name along with commands to scan the man's past. Nothing. Clean as a whistle.

Except.

His name was flagged for a juvenile court case, closed to public scrutiny but available to a law enforcement officer. Fox quickly typed the information that allowed him to see Rodgers's juvenile record.

Fox read for awhile, then stood up so fast that Bodhi hissed as she was flung off his lap. He called Abby, grabbed his backpack and charged out the front door.

***

"Unsung Hero"
By Faith O'Neill
Chapter 28

Afternoon, Feb. 15, 1865
Headquarters District of Colorado, City of Denver

"Do you swear to tell the truth, the whole truth and nothing but the truth, so help you God?" Lt. Col. Sam Tappan held the bible upon which Soule's left hand rested.

"I do."

As the first witness in the inquiry, Silas sat at the wooden table provided, facing the three commission officers: Tappan—who was known to loathe Chivington; Captain Ed Jacobs; and Captain George Stilwell, all of the veteran battalion first Colorado cavalry.

At a table to the side of Soule's sat Chivington himself, with his legal counsel. However, as the commission had already made clear, this was no court of law, only an investigation of the facts. Chivington, no longer in the military, was dressed in a fine gray linen suit.

"Your full name, age and rank in the army?" Tappan asked. Stilwell, as the junior member of the commission, sat with pen in hand to take notes.

"Silas S. Soule, twenty-six years of age, captain Company D, veteran battalion first Colorado cavalry, and assistant provost marshal general, district of Colorado."

Had a nice ring to it, Soule thought, 'assistant provost marshal general.' Tappan had seen to his transfer to Denver as the military equivalent of a deputy sheriff.

"How long have you been an officer in the first regiment Colorado volunteers?"

"Since December 11, 1861."

"Did you accompany Major Wynkoop's command to an Indian camp on the Smoky Hill in September 1864?"

"I did."

And so the questions went, with Soule describing the council between Black Kettle and Wynkoop's men, how they had brought the chiefs to Denver, and then directed the chiefs to bring their people near Fort Lyon where the Indians stayed until Anthony's appearance some two weeks later. How Wynkoop had sent a messenger to Gen. Curtis immediately upon the group's return to Fort Lyon from Denver, to get a response to the Indian's request to surrender.

"What was the understanding with the Indians while in and about Fort Lyon?" Tappan asked.

Silas felt Chivington's glare but looked at Tappan.

"That they were to be protected by the troops there

327

until the messenger returned from General Curtis."

"Did a messenger arrive at the fort from General Curtis prior to the first of December, 1864?"

"There was not."

Responding to Tappan's inquiries, Soule described how he had accidentally come upon Chivington's force of nearly 1,000 "one hundred-days men" as it approached on Nov. 28, and how he had been asked about Indians at the fort.

"I said that there were some Indians camped near the fort, below the fort, but they were not dangerous, that they were waiting to hear from General Curtis. They were considered as prisoners. Someone made answer that they wouldn't be prisoners after they got there."

Silas heard a light tapping sound coming from Chivington's table. From the corner of his eye, Silas could see that the older man was tapping a ring on his finger on the wooden surface. Soule recalled his time as the man's assistant, how he would often tap that ring just so when he was dressing down one of his junior officers.

After a couple more questions, the commission adjourned until 9:30 a.m. the next day. Soule gathered his hat and walked into the cold gray Denver afternoon.

A couple of rough-looking types leaned against a railing outside the door. Silas nodded briefly to them and headed down the boardwalk.

"Better watch your back, you fuckin' Indian lover." The voice was low and menacing.

Silas kept walking. He was pondering which restaurant's wait staff was least likely to spit in his soup when he saw her walking straight toward him.

"My God. Hersa, how are you?"

He had not sought her out in the week he'd been in the town. It seemed pointless.

"Captain—Provost Marshal? Yes, I'm fine and you?" Silas saw her cheeks were red. From the cold?

The pleasantries over, Silas steeled himself to walk on. But the man's voice he had just heard outside the hearing room echoed in his mind. And a vision of the corpses at Sand Creek floated in front of him.

"Hersa, will you dine with me this evening?" The words spilled out before he could censor them.

She became very still. "Yes. Yes, I will."

The next morning Tappan again wasted no time in asking Soule to describe the events on the previous November 28 and 29. Soule recounted how by the time he returned to the fort on the 28th, Chivington had assigned a guard at the post to prevent anyone from leaving. He described the all-night march to Sand Creek and the arrival before sunrise on the 29th.

"Major Anthony then moved our battalion to within about one hundred yards of the lodges and ordered us to open fire," Soule said. He paused, reminding himself to choose his words carefully. "Some firing done, when the battery came up in our rear."

And practically blasted us off the face of the earth, Soule thought.

"Major Anthony ordered my company, which was directly in the line of fire of the battery, to move down into the creek, with orders to move up the creek and for the purpose of killing Indians which were under the banks. Before I got into the creek there were troops upon both sides firing across."

Men with bloodlust and no discipline, taking shots at Indians dug into both banks. God knew how many of the idiots were shot by their own friends with poor aim firing from the other side of the creek.

Soule described how he moved his troops along the creek, adding the shooting went on until about 2 in the afternoon. He did not say that his company participated in the shooting. Nor did he say specifically that they did not.

"Did any of the Indians advance toward Colonel Chivington's command, making signs that they were friends?"

"I saw them advance towards the line, some of them holding their hands up."

"Were the women and children shot while attempting to escape by Colonel Chivington's command?"

"They were."

"Were the women and children followed while attempting to escape, shot down and scalped, and otherwise mutilated, by any of Colonel Chivington's command?"

"They were."

And in his memory, he saw dogs growling and fighting over the disfigured remains of a tiny naked child, shot in the back and sprawled in the sand.

35

The airport runways sat quiet and baking in the late day heat. Blue-black thunderheads in the shape of anvils were building in the west, teasing her with the promise of shade and moisture.

Faith figured most folks had gotten where they wanted to go and were settling into a good meal before the July 4 fireworks. Near her, Ricky used a stick to knock the raised doors of the traps, releasing the locking mechanisms and allowing them to close.

For the last time. It was too late to pick them up. She figured Stan Rodgers wouldn't care as long as she collected the traps tomorrow. Faith hoped she wouldn't have to watch the poison crew dropping pellets into the burrows.

"Take your time," she called to the boy. "We want to make sure they're all closed."

The kid was a trooper. They'd made one run with a load of 13 dogs before a brief food break, then trapped and transferred another group of 16 in the afternoon. It was a good day's haul. All day a mantra had run through her brain: "The last train is leaving the station. The last train is leaving

331

the station. All aboard." Now, listening to the traps clanking shut, she remembered one of the reasons she had left the wildlife biz. She, like her sister, found it hard to let go of the animals she couldn't help.

Faith would have stayed into the night, but she had promised Fox she'd bring Ricky home before dark so they could watch the pyrotechnics over at the county fairgrounds. In her head she apologized to the one or two animals she might have caught in the three hours of daylight left.

She turned and stopped in her tracks.

Toward the far end of the runway, she saw two men wearing masks, one carrying a shovel, the other dropping something into a burrow. The man with the shovel stuffed some paper in the ground and then began digging at the burrow. Sealing the entrance with soil, she knew.

Faith felt sick.

She heard shouts and turned toward the road beyond the airport fence. Where had those people come from? There were maybe a dozen, carrying signs and raising their fists.

"Murderers!" one woman yelled.

"Pick on someone your own size!" A man's voice this time.

Faith glanced back at the two men on the opposite end of the runway, but either they didn't hear the protesters or were ignoring them.

Standing there, Faith began to hear other voices in the distance. Some kind of chant. And then over a rise, she saw people walking in a group down one lane of the road, also carrying signs, approaching the airport and moving with purpose. She watched transfixed, only vaguely aware that Ricky had moved to her side.

The line of people marching down the street kept getting longer as more and more people came over the rise. And now she could begin to make out the chant.

Let's get Chivington out of Keyhole! Let's get Chivington out of Keyhole!

Many of the marchers appeared to be Native American, with long black braids and sunglasses, fists pumping the air, faces hard and angry. The marchers began passing the protesters at the fence, and some of the marchers wandered over to talk to the animal rights folks.

"Faith, you need to get out of here."

Faith jumped. Rodgers stood next to her and she hadn't even seen him come up behind her.

"Our security guards are getting prepared and the police are on their way. It could be a real mess," Rodgers added. "I'm worried about you and your young helper."

Faith looked up at the open space director, who seemed genuinely concerned about their welfare. She thought of his dissertation on Phostoxin, and Trish's missing inhaler. Surely what she was considering couldn't be right. Besides, why would he want to hurt Trish?

"We're just finishing up," she said. "We have to get the traps closed."

"Faith, there are rumors some of the Indian marchers are armed. They're supposed to just go past the airport, but with the other kooks at the fence, who knows what could happen. You have to leave now!"

Faith took Ricky's hand.

"You're right," she said, and began walking.

She heard something falling in the dirt behind her and stopped. When she turned, Rodgers was picking up the roll of paper that had fallen from her pocket.

His own doctoral dissertation.

Faith felt hairs stand up on the back of her neck.

***

"Unsung Hero"
By Faith O'Neill
Chapter 29

Evening, April 23, 1865
The Soule Residence, City of Denver

"Will ya be havin' a cuppa tea after such a fine dinner, Mrs. Soule?"

Hersa knew the grin was on his face even though she couldn't see him, since Silas stood behind her, removing the shawl from her shoulders.

"I still think I married an Irishman in disguise."

Hersa turned and found herself in a tight embrace.

"Now then, would it matter to ya?" Soule nuzzled her neck, tickling her with his mustache as she wriggled.

"I suppose not." She laughed. "Stop that this instant."

"Sure an' begorah, what a feisty lass you are Mrs. Soule."

"Too feisty for a provost marshal?"

"True, tis a brave law man to take you as his bride."

The wedding on April 1 had been a simple and small affair. Hersa's mother had refused to attend, but her sister had been there as maid of honor. And Silas had been full of jokes about being an "April Fool."

"What a nice dinner the Prices had for us."

"And now I'm looking forward to dessert," Soule said,

dropping the accent and fingering the buttons of her blouse.

"You are incorrigible!"

"Why, thank you, madam."

He had two buttons undone when the sound of gunfire stopped his hands.

Immediately he moved away from her, grabbing his hat off the kitchen table and heading toward the door. Silas was already armed with the derringer he kept with him at all times.

"Siley!" She had tried to remain silent. After all, it was probably just another drunk firing rounds into the sky.

He turned and smiled.

"I know. Be careful."

Then he was gone.

36

"I'm flattered by your choice of reading material,"
Rodgers said in a neutral tone.

Faith wanted to confront him, demand the truth. Then
she remembered the child at her side.

"I was doing some research and came across it. Very
impressive." She tightened her grip on Ricky's hand.

He seemed to reach some decision and his face softened.
"Definitely flattering," he said, holding the manual out. As
she reached, a scrap of paper fell from the booklet. Faith
picked it up, saw Trish's handwriting:

> *Stan, stop pestering me. If you don't, I'll let your wife
> and your precious congregation know how you chase
> married women. Just stick to our agreement and we'll
> be fine.*

And underneath, a few printed words:

> *Please, please reconsider. I NEED you.*

Faith looked up from the note in her hand.

She vaguely heard shouts nearby, but the only thing she was taking in was the look in Stan Rodgers's eyes. Definitely not neutral.

"Like you said, Stan, we need to get going."

"Faith, look!" Ricky was trying to pull away from her as he pointed toward the people starting to climb over the airport fence.

Thunder rumbled in the distance. Things were heating up.

Fox noticed the yellow Volkswagen Beetle parked outside the airport fence before he turned his truck into the airport grounds. Borsich? More likely his wife, the prairie dog protector. Now he saw people climbing the airport fence, an odd mix of WASPs and Indians in Native American regalia.

Shit.

He sped through the hangar area, unable to see the runways and praying someone wouldn't come around a corner. Past the hangars he took his foot off the gas, trying to assess the scene. To his left, the odd mix of protesters ran westward along the runway. To his right, at the opposite end of the runway, two men in white Tyvek suits stood frozen, watching the crowd run in their direction. And in the middle, several hundred feet away, he saw two adults and one small boy. Fox yanked the wheel in that direction. As he watched, the man in that small group put his hand on the shoulder of the boy. Oh God.

Fox mashed the accelerator, driving across the runway to

reach the little group of three while simultaneously stretching over to the glove box. Now Fox saw the knife blade at Ricky's throat, and the little group slowly moving in the direction of the old beat-up van, Faith's vehicle.

Some ten feet away he slammed on the brakes and jumped from the truck. He pointed the Glock at Rodgers's chest and yelled "Stop!"

Rodgers paused, but kept the knife to the quiet boy at his side.

"Forget it, Fox. I'll kill him before you fire a shot."

At that moment something dark flew past Fox and landed on top of Rodgers, knocking him to the ground. Abby's teeth were locked on the man's arm and Fox heard the man scream. Then Abby yelped and slumped, but Ricky broke free and ran.

"Get in the truck!" Fox yelled at the boy. He heard the passenger door open. Before Fox could get a clean shot, Rodgers jumped to his feet and grabbed Faith, holding her in front of him with the now bloody knife. Abby's blood.

"Drop the gun," Rodgers demanded.

Fox let the Glock fall to the dirt.

"You can drive our little party. We're gonna take a trip."

Fox met Faith's eyes. Vaguely he heard people yelling somewhere behind him.

"C'mon, Stan, whatever happened I'm sure you had good reasons. Don't make things worse." Fox realized with a sinking heart that Ricky had gotten back out of the truck and now stood at his side. Keeping his focus on Rodgers, Fox tried to push the boy behind him.

"Just do it!" Rodgers said, keeping the knife at Faith's carotid artery.

"Okay, okay," Fox said, trying to remember what he had learned about hostage situations. The only thing that came to mind was "keep 'em talking."

Rodgers laughed. "Actually, I don't need your help. Your precious Sam has too much to lose to let me go to jail."

Fox's brain locked. The only Sam he knew was confined to a wheelchair. And worked for the Division of Wildlife. Sam Gary, a man of integrity.

"That's right," Rodgers said, watching Fox connect the dots. "Kickbacks and deals aimed to keep Keyhole on the development road. No black-footed ferrets allowed. Sam thought that human freak show in white gave you some fake proof about the ferret, so he sent me to find it and… Shit, I'm talking too much. Start walking."

"Stan, I know you loved Trish," Faith said. Fox saw Faith shift her eyes to some point behind him, where the yells were getting closer. He gave a tiny nod without taking his gaze off Rodgers. Knowing that Rodgers had been the one who savagely beat Hope made Fox even more vigilant, if that was possible.

"I know she lied about the black-footed ferret thing," Faith continued. "To manipulate you and the city. She made you mad. Things happen in the heat of the moment. People will understand."

Then the protesters were running by on both sides of them, heading for the poison crew. Thunder boomed. Fox lunged for the gun on the ground and with his peripheral vision, saw Ricky run past with a white plastic bottle. The boy flung liquid into Rodgers's face.

Stan screamed and dropped the knife. He clutched his

eyes and began running and stumbling toward the middle of the dog town between the runways. His foot caught in a burrow and he fell to the ground, still yelling.

A puzzled Fox looked down at Ricky, who held a cap-less bleach bottle in the air like a trophy. Then Ricky cried out and ran to the bloody dog.

Fox turned toward the blinded man, still writhing but now pinned to the ground by two people sitting on his back. One was a beautiful blonde woman in jeans who looked like Borsich's wife, the other a smiling Henry Grayfeather in buckskin.

"You looked like you were in trouble, my friend," Grayfeather said.

The sky opened, dumping a torrent of rain on the earth.

37

"Are you going to finish it?"

"I don't know. I can't seem to see anything beyond Silas running out the door of his house. I can't visualize that last confrontation, the gunman shooting him down."

They were sitting on Fox's tiny backyard deck.

"How'd you know it was Stan?" Faith asked, stroking Polly's fur. The little prairie dog slept soundly in the crook of her arm.

"I didn't until about fifteen minutes before I got there." Fox looked out into the back yard, where Ricky sat in the grass.

"Rodgers was busted as a juvenile for poisoning a neighbor's cat. He was asthmatic as a kid and hated cats. Apparently he found an unused cartridge of Phostoxin and somehow figured out how to transfer the gas into the inhaler. He lured the cat over and then squirted the gas right in its face. He didn't think anyone was around, but another neighbor was watching from an upstairs window, saw the cat collapse."

"How do you think he did it?"

Fox knew exactly what she was talking about.

"Maybe he showed up that night while Trish was trying to rescue prairie dogs. Maybe he figured he could get her agitated enough that she'd have an attack and use the inhaler he rigged. Or maybe he just got close to her and sprayed the thing in her face."

"But then why didn't he put another inhaler in her vehicle? Afterward, I mean. He had to figure someone like me might notice it was missing, at least at some point."

Fox shrugged. "Maybe something scared him off." He remembered the reported lion he had decided didn't exist.

"But why kill her?"

"Maybe she threatened to go public about his scams, ruin his marriage, his career. To get him to force the city into relocating the dogs at the airport. Maybe he didn't mean to kill her, just make her sick. And of course, there was the photo of the black-footed ferret."

Faith paused. "Do you think it's real? The photo?"

Fox looked at her. "Your guess is as good as mine. I'll keep an eye out at the development site, but I wouldn't hold my breath."

Faith studied her hands. "They won't be able to prove he killed Trish, will they. I mean, we can tell them what we think, but it doesn't mean anything." It was a statement, not a question.

"He'll face charges of assault and attempted kidnapping for the airport thing. And has Hope decided if she's going to prosecute?"

Faith took a sip of iced tea. "She's still thinking about it. I think she'd rather focus on the future. She's already scheduling her last transgender surgery in Trinidad."

John Fox turned toward her. "Really? How did she get the money?"

Faith smiled. "I just happen to know a good lawyer with some extra cash, one who would prefer not to be disbarred for drug use. And who has promised to go straight."

Fox laughed.

But Faith turned serious again. "So what about Trish? Stan just gets away with murder?"

Fox met her gaze. "I'll talk to a local prosecutor friend of mine, see if there's enough proof to take him to trial for murder. Meanwhile, Pierce says it looks like Rodgers will go blind from the bleach. He'll lose his job, maybe his family. I don't think he's a threat to us now."

"Yeah, the bleach. How did Ricky think of that?"

Fox paused, looking at the child in the grass.

"I wondered too. He told me his mom was being beaten by some guy. Ricky had been told not to mess with the chemicals around the house, that they would hurt him. Probably stuff used for meth production. To save his mom, he grabbed a bottle of something and threw the liquid at the guy. The man screamed and ran off, and Ricky remembered."

Faith shook her head, apparently at the insanity of the world.

"What about the mayor?" she asked. "I don't think that airplane thing was an accident, do you?"

"Who knows. But if we can't prove much against Rodgers, we have even less against her."

They sat in silence, contemplating conspiracies. Fox thought about the possible conspiracies surrounding the death of Faith's hero, Silas Soule.

"You could talk about that guy, Cannon." Fox could tell Faith was struggling to make the transition from the events at the airport to his sudden reference to her book. "You know, the guy who went to New Mexico to bring back the man who killed Silas. Squier. Cannon brings Squier back, then Squier escapes from jail in Denver about the time Cannon is found dead in his hotel room. Poisoned. Or maybe just an overdose of booze and drugs. They found morphine in his room, I read somewhere."

"Cannon ended up involved in the massacre," Faith said. "He bragged about taking souvenirs like buffalo robes from the site."

"Okay, so he wasn't a saint. But he testified against Chivington like Silas did. And when Silas was murdered, Cannon was the one who rode hundreds of miles to find Squier, catch him and bring him back. That probably didn't make him popular with the anti-Silas crowd. Maybe it got him killed."

Fox saw Faith look down, worry written on her face.

"What's wrong?"

She paused. Then she reached in her daypack and handed him a small bible with cracked leather.

"Look at the inscription."

Fox looked. "Whoa."

"Yeah. Chivington gave him the bible."

Faith reached over and flipped pages to the family history section, pointing out the missing father and the lineage that led to her. Fox paused to digest the idea that Faith's great-great-great-grandfather might have been the man who killed Silas Soule. Holy crap.

"Does it matter? We're all a mix of good and bad. Even

Silas—"

Faith raised a palm. He stopped. They watched Ricky plucking dandelion heads.

Faith sighed. "Okay. Go ahead."

Fox looked at her but she wouldn't make eye contact.

"You already know he was quite the ladies man," Fox said, watching Faith nod in agreement. "Well, there are accounts that many years after Silas died, a woman showed up, said she and Silas got married before he supposedly married Hersa. The woman tried to claim widow's benefits from the government."

Faith turned to look at him. "Why didn't I find that?"

"Maybe you didn't want to. Didn't you notice he and Hersa got married on April First? April Fools'? Laura Roper, the teenage girl that the Indians kidnapped? She said 'Capt. Soule and wife' were with the troops that brought the rescued prisoners to Denver. That was in September, months before he married Hersa. Or maybe married Hersa."

Faith groaned.

"Look, who knows if he had another wife. But even if he did, so what?" Fox took Faith's hand, squeezed and let go. "He stood up for his principles. He disobeyed orders to shoot. He heard the threats and he testified against Chivington anyway. That takes guts."

Faith looked down and sighed. Then she turned to him. "What are you going to do about your friend Sam?" Now it was Fox's turn to look away.

"I've got an appointment with the director on Monday."

"What if he doesn't believe you? Isn't he close to Sam?"

Fox rubbed his eyes. "I can't control that. I can only do what I can do. Besides, I was looking for a job when I found

345

this one. And maybe I'd have some free time to do that memorial run from Sand Creek to Denver."

"Why does life have to be so messy?" Faith asked. "Those women and kids butchered at Sand Creek. Trish with all her good intentions and bad relationships. Me idealizing a guy who might have been a bigamist, who might have been shot by a relative of mine. So many unhappy endings."

Fox laughed again. "Ah, come on Faith. Stay in the moment. The sun is shining and we're fine. Life is good."

Without looking her way, he reached out and took her hand. She did not pull away. They went quiet again, watching the child in the grass. Ricky stood, assisting the bandaged German shepherd as she stumbled to her feet. Fox watched Abby lick the boy's face. The dog would be okay. But what about the boy?

"He needs time. And love," Faith said, appearing to read his thoughts.

He's not the only one, Fox thought.

"Does ice cream help?"

"Couldn't hurt," she said.

Fall 2005
Riverside Cemetery
Denver, Colorado

She crouched before the neat tombstone of gray granite, *precisely inscribed in military fashion. The stone couldn't be more than 20 or 30 years old. She was impressed the army still replaced tombstones for soldiers so long dead and so forgotten in an old cemetery surrounded by industrial wasteland. And yet, not completely forgotten. Someone had placed a handful of plastic flowers at the grave, and a small bouquet of daisies now wilted.*

A car drove down the road nearby and she was reminded that if she wasn't careful, she'd get caught in Denver's "pre-rush" rush hour.

"I met someone, Silas. I think you'd like him. And I finished the book."

She spoke to his bones, but who knew if he was even there. Years after Silas died, the city of Denver moved his grave and hundreds more from what became a downtown park. The grave digger hadn't worried much about which body was which. Maybe Silas was buried here. Maybe not. Cramer's grave was in another state. No one seemed to know where Cannon was buried.

A bird chirped in a nearby tree. She got to her feet, brushing off some dry grass. She placed her bouquet of red roses next to the plastic flowers and turned toward her car.

347

So many stones, so many fallible men of flesh and blood.

Two rows down, her eye caught on words etched on another monument. She walked back to Silas' grave, pulled out one of the roses.

And left it at the stone for Unknown.

Author's Note

Regarding the Sand Creek Massacre, to the extent possible I have tried to stick to the historical record. My primary source was *The Sand Creek Massacre: A Documentary History*, first published as a report of the Joint Committee on the Conduct of the War, Massacre of the Cheyenne Indians, 38th Congress, Second Session, Washington, 1865, and report of the Secretary of War, 39th Congress, Second Session, Senate Executive Document No. 26, Washington, 1867. Other sources include: *The Sand Creek Massacre,* by Stan Hoig; *Silas Soule: A Short Eventful Life of Moral Courage,* by Tom Bensing; and *Song of Sorrow: Massacre at Sand Creek,* by Patrick Mendoza. I am also extremely grateful to Silas Soule's relatives Byron Strom and his father Malcolm Strom for their kindness and assistance.

My eternal thanks go to my writer friends: authors Sandy Bolton, Steve Anderson and John Johnson. I also thank John Davidson and Richard Fox for providing additional input, and Jeannie Pomeroy who proof-read an earlier version. I'm very grateful to author Steven Havill, for his generosity in conducting free novel-writing workshops, which taught me vital techniques. Thanks to Kimberly Fraser at the National Black Footed Ferret Conservation Center of the U.S. Fish and Wildlife Service near Wellington, CO for reviewing pertinent information. (Sorry—I took artistic license regarding parking lot security!) My friend, writer David Kohn, graciously shared agent contacts with me early in the game. Most especially I thank my partner Al Frydryk for his love, support, and thoughtful feedback on this book.

Finally, this work has been a long time in the oven and I thank anyone whose help I've overlooked. Any mistakes are my own.